★

"When Grigory Malmudov leapt from a bouncing twin-engined C-46 on a spring night in 1946, he did not know that he was living through the critical moment of his existence, one he could not regain or reconsider. Until the instant of his leap he had retained a degree of mastery over the course his life would follow. But after that instant it was beyond his power to return. He had no chance to reconsider. He could only regret it for the rest of his life.

He often thought of the details of that night in the C-46, silently wishing he had not jumped, or that having jumped, he had not let his parachute open."

DZERZHINSKY SQUARE

JAMES O. JACKSON

DZERZHINSKY SQUARE

A GOLD EAGLE BOOK FROM

W🌐RLDWIDE

TORONTO • NEW YORK • LONDON • PARIS
AMSTERDAM • STOCKHOLM • HAMBURG
ATHENS • MILAN • TOKYO • SYDNEY

DZERZHINSKY SQUARE

A Gold Eagle Book/September 1987

First published by St. Martin's Press, Incorporated

Copyright © 1986 by James O. Jackson

ISBN 0-373-62108-6

Printed in Canada

For Mary Chase

1.

Before opening the box, John Cabot paused to study the elegant, fine-lined painting on the lid. It measured about six by eleven inches, and it depicted the Princess Yaroslavna standing upon a Russian fortress wall, a diamondlike tear on her cheek. She wept for the return of her husband, Prince Igor, taken captive in a long-ago war. At the bottom of the box lid, written in gold with a fine, one-hair brush, was the word "Kholui." Kholui was one of the north Russian towns that specializes in the painting of fairy-tale pictures on lacquered boxes. It was a rare example of the Kholui painters' art, done with a glowing red background instead of the more usual black. It struck Cabot as strange that a troubled Russian woman would have used such a valuable container—no doubt a keepsake—to transmit a bundle of documents to him.

He gently lifted the lid and began removing the contents. They were an odd assortment of docu-

ments: a birth certificate with old cruciform Cyrillic
letters, papers folded in the distinctive triangle of Soviet wartime mail, faded telegrams bearing the impri-
matur of SOVTELEGRAF, graduation certificates, a
marriage certificate—all the odds and ends of documents that people collect in a lifetime, especially people in the Soviet Union.

At the bottom of the box Cabot found a thick sheaf
of papers, folded in thirds and bound with a black
ribbon. He brought it out last, carefully set the box
aside, and arranged the documents on the soft suede
cover of his desk.

As he unfolded the brittle old pieces of paper he
began to remember: a serious young Ukrainian, two
front upper teeth missing, brighter than most of the
others, more determined to do what the OSS was
making possible for him. Here was a birth certificate:
Malmudov, Grigory Nikolayevich, born March 10,
1922, Stepanovka, Krivoi Rog, the Ukraine; a formal
letter from an orphanage superintendent notifying
Malmudov of acceptance in a factory work program;
a marriage certificate binding Malmudov to a Sonya
Vinogradova; a 1941 draft notice summoning Malmudov to war; a military letter conferring upon Malmudov a medal for heroism; a letter from Mrs.
Malmudova marked undeliverable; a telegram informing Mrs. Malmudova that Malmudov was missing; a letter dated January 3, 1946, informing her that
Malmudov was presumed dead.

Clipped together were three newer pieces of paper:
two 1973 TASS reports on the trial of Malmudov on

charges of treason, espionage, and wrecking, and the warden's report from Butyrka Prison describing the death of Malmudov before an army firing squad.

Cabot read the warden's report with interest. It intrigued him to learn, for the first time in detail, how the Soviet state disposed of its traitors: firing squad, blindfold, and a coup de grace from a revolver. Cabot smiled. He had thought that a Soviet execution would be more exotic, but it was not. Just a prosaic firing squad.

There was the one final document, the sheaf of papers folded in thirds, which Cabot now untied and opened. There were more than thirty pages of tissue-like Russian stationery, covered on both sides with a flawless and elegant handwriting that was the same as that on the letter from Mrs. Malmudova.

It was addressed "To my loving daughter," and Cabot began to read, slowly, because his Russian had lain long in disuse.

This is to tell you the truth of your father so that you may know and love his memory not as it was presented by the authorities, but as it was known to me. I loved your father in his youth, when we conceived you, our beloved child; and I loved him also in his absence, not knowing if he lived or died; and I loved him in his sudden, painful return to our lives as a prisoner, accused of treason to the Motherland. I loved him because in that time he did not change; the world around him changed, and the world used him—

used his love for me and for you—to make his life
a misery.

I wish you to know your father, and now I will
tell you of him...

Cabot set the paper aside and pressed a button on
his intercom.

"Please get Bob Evans for me, Marian."

A moment later the telephone buzzed.

"Bob, Jack here," he said. "Bob, I have this box
the woman took into the Moscow embassy and I'd like
to be briefed on how it got there. Is that courier still
around?... Good, please send him right up."

Cabot returned to reading the letter, and a few
minutes later the door opened. His secretary announced a Mr. Kellog.

A tall young man stepped uncertainly into the office. He paused, took a breath, and strode across the
deep carpeting to the desk. Cabot rose, reached across
to shake the young man's hand, and motioned him to
take a seat on a divan.

"So you brought this handsome box to me, did you,
Kellog?" Cabot said, taking a seat in an easy chair
opposite him.

"Yes, sir," Kellog said, adding uneasily, "we didn't
think it was very important, but I was making the
regular run, so I brought it along. She said it would
mean something to you."

"She?"

"Yes, sir, the woman who brought it. She said you would know what it meant. She didn't seem to know you were the director of the CIA."

"I see," Cabot said, his brow wrinkling in slight puzzlement. "Can you tell me anything about her?"

"Not a lot, really," Kellog said. "She was an unusually good-looking woman in a Russian way: rather a full figure, straight-backed, dark hair, and dark eyes that were very striking. In fact, she got past the militiaman at the embassy gate by glaring at him with those black eyes. The Marine on duty said the man made a move toward her but she gave him a look that stopped him dead. Before he knew what was happening, she was at the Marine desk, demanding to see you."

"Me?"

"Yes, sir. She seemed to think you'd be there."

"Then what happened?"

"Well, I went down and took her into an interview room and she gave me the box," Kellog said, nodding toward the Kholui box on Cabot's desk. "She said it was for you, so you'd know—" he paused "—so you'd know what you did to her father. That's what she said, anyway." Kellog shifted uneasily.

"Yes. Anything more?"

"That was about it. I told her I'd get it to the right people, and she left."

"What happened outside?"

"What always happens," Kellog said. "The goons were there. As soon as she walked out, they grabbed her. Damn near knocked her head off."

"How do you mean?"

"Well," Kellog said, "she was a dignified, stiff-backed lady, like I said, and I guess she didn't intend to take any shit . . . er, that is, she stood up to them. When they shoved her into the car, she wouldn't drop her head, and they banged it against the door frame. Pretty hard, too. She was wearing a black beret and it went flying into the street and she looked like she was going to pass out. But she pulled herself up and they took off."

"Hear anything more?"

"Well, we did a check with some people, and they say she was put into the Palinsky Institute."

Cabot frowned. "The psychiatric place?"

"Yes, sir. The one they use for dissidents and so forth. Not a good place to be."

"I see. Anything else?"

"Sorry, sir, that's it. I . . ." Kellog paused. "We didn't attach much importance to it, sir. I didn't know you'd need more info on it, so . . ."

"No, no problem, it really isn't very important," Cabot said, smiling to reassure the young man. "I'll tell you the story about this woman and her father if you have time."

"Oh, I have plenty of time," Kellog replied, regretting instantly having said so. Bright young CIA agents aren't supposed to have plenty of time. But Cabot took no notice. He stretched his legs in front of him and began his story.

"This fellow, Malmudov was his name, was one of those people they call 'the victims of Yalta.' You re-

member the Soviet citizens who were sent back to Stalin after the war. It was one of the least edifying
chapters of Allied performance during that conflict.
Churchill must have been tired of arguing, or squiffed
on his brandy, but he agreed to repatriate all the Soviet citizens in the Western zones.

"A lot of them didn't want to go, of course. They
figured they'd be shot or sent to the camps, and they
were right. Oh, some were probably collaborators or
real war criminals and they had it coming. But most
of them were just poor mopes who wound up in the
West: prisoners of war, refugees, slave laborers, people like that.

"Malmudov was one of them, but he was a victim
of Yalta with a difference. We recruited him for espionage, trained him, sent him into the USSR, and
then dropped him cold."

Kellog looked puzzled. "Dropped him?"

"Yes, dropped him," Cabot said, pressing the tips
of his fingers together and staring through them.
"Him and about two hundred and fifty others.

"It was a thing we called 'Operation Early Word,'
and we took advantage of Churchill's promise to Stalin. We offered a chosen few the chance to return to
their homelands without going to the camps or the
firing squad. But there was a catch: They had to work
for us.

"It was nothing fancy, really, and as it turned out,
it wasn't even necessary. We gave them false identity
papers and a radio and dropped them into the USSR;

usually into the Ukraine. They were supposed to warn us of any impending Soviet advance to the West.

"In those days, right after the war, we were afraid the Russians would try to take all of Germany and Austria and maybe more. The war had left everything in a shambles and we had no way of watching Soviet movements, no early warning. So we decided to take a bunch of these POWs and make them our eyes and ears. As I said, about two hundred and fifty of them. But by around 1948 it was obvious that the Russians were too beat up by the war to make any move, not for many years, anyway. And we were getting better intelligence by other means. So we terminated these guys, told them they were on their own and Uncle thanks you."

"What happened to them?" Kellog asked.

Cabot shook his head. "Some got caught and shot. We knew of thirty or forty who were taken when they landed, and another couple dozen who were caught when somebody saw them with a radio.

"But surprisingly enough, a lot of them did what we told them to do. Most, in fact. They set up their radios, checked in, and spent three years telling us that nothing was happening. Then we sent them instructions to destroy the radio and make no effort to communicate with us. And they did. And we don't know what happened to them."

"God," Kellog whispered. "You mean they're still there?"

"Some of them. Maybe quite a few. We only know of one or two cases where they tried to communicate with their families. Most are still there, living under false identifications, afraid to contact their relatives.''

''But why?''

''Why?'' Cabot asked, raising an eyebrow. ''Because they loved their families so much that they wouldn't go to them and compromise them. The wife or mother or father of a traitor is not held in high regard in the USSR, not then and not now.''

''So,'' Kellog said, nodding toward the box. ''That's how it was with that guy?''

''Apparently,'' Cabot replied. ''He was caught, tried, and shot in 1973. I haven't read it all, but there is a letter there from the mother to the daughter, explaining things. The daughter must have wanted me to know, as you said, what I did to her father.

''I remember the fellow,'' Cabot continued. ''He was one of the best we recruited. Good kid, missing teeth. I remember the missing teeth, because he was a handsome young man and the gap hurt his looks. I got an army dentist to make him a bridge, a really nice one.

''He pointed out to me that the bridge would give him away. If they looked into his mouth and found such beautiful bridgework, they'd know he was a spy.

''But I said, 'Hey, Kuznetsov'—that was his new name, and we used it in training—'hey, Kuznetsov, if they get far enough to look into your mouth, it means they've already looked at your papers, and if they take a good look at those papers, they'll already know you're an American spy.'''

"You mean the papers weren't good?" Kellog asked.

"They were good," Cabot said. "As good as we could get. We used the files the Germans took from captured Soviet factories. The Germans kept everything, filed everything. They were good papers. But they wouldn't stand up to a real check. They would get a guy a job and a place to live and let him travel around. But if any cop started doing a close check, those papers would fall apart.

"But I guess they must have been pretty good. This fellow Malmudov," he said, motioning toward the box as if Malmudov himself were inside, "this fellow actually got to be the chief engineer of a big plant in Moscow on those papers. That's what his job was when they caught him."

"My God, sir," Kellog said. "I wouldn't mind finding out where some of those people are now. They'd be around sixty, wouldn't they? I'll bet some are in positions to do us some good. Maybe we could do some checking." The young CIA officer warmed to the idea. "We could run the names through the computers and see if they match up anywhere."

Cabot put his fingertips together and thought a moment. "No, I don't think so," he said. "I doubt we'd find anybody of much use to us. Anyway, that was a long time ago. Better leave it alone."

He rose from his chair, signaling the end of the conversation. Kellog stood to go.

"Thanks for the box," Cabot said. "It's a Kholui, you know, and a nice one."

"No trouble," Kellog said, shaking the director's hand. "My pleasure."

The agent left the office and Cabot returned to the desk. He looked again at the box with its glowing depiction of Yaroslavna weeping upon the wall for her missing warrior.

He remembered the words from the story:

"ОНА МНАКАНА НА СТЕНЕ."

"She wept upon the wall."

Cabot studied the medieval Russian princess, mourning endlessly and faithfully through all the years that Prince Igor was held captive.

He picked up the letter from mother to daughter and held it a moment. He pressed the intercom. "Marian, hold all calls, please," he said. "I have some reading to do."

TOP SECRET
OFFICE OF STRATEGIC SERVICES
UNITED STATES OF AMERICA
EUROPEAN THEATER OF OPERATIONS

April 24, 1946

From: CO, ETO Field Operations
To: CO, OSS Washington, D.C.
Subj: Operative, Deployment of
Encl: Briefing Folder (Inventory attached)

1) Successful deployment of operative Malmudov, G. N., has been confirmed with receipt of On Station check message in Region IV(A), EastEuro OpArea, on this date.

2) Subject operative is functioning under documentation identifying him as Kuznetsov, Alexander Nikolayevich. Documentation was derived from captured files of German SS Fourth Region Command. SS files identify Kuznetsov as Corporal, Red Army, captured 28 Jan 43, executed 14 Jun 44 following successful escape from POW camp. Files indicate Kuznetsov's recapture and execution remained unknown to other Sov POWs, but documentation is evaluated as unreliable for any other than routine examination and subject operative has been advised of the low reliability of his documentation.

3) Pending study of his future performance, subject operative should be judged unreliable and subject to possible early arrest because of strong motivation to contact his family in Leningrad. As expounded more fully in enclosed Briefing Folder, the decision was made to deploy subject operative because of command judgment that, once he had successfully entered upon his assignment, he would judge contact with family to be beyond feasibility.

4) In view of questionable prospects of subject operative, Euro Operations has commenced training an additional operative for Region IV(A), with deployment anticipated by August.

Lt. Col. John Cabot
Commanding

TOP SECRET

Some of the pivotal events of our lives pass obscurely, their importance unrecognized until the future lends them significance. The success or failure of an entire life can be determined by the most forgettable of trivialities. An event, seemingly minor, can launch an irreversible chain of events. Only later, with hindsight, can we measure the meaning of that moment and know that it determined our happiness, or our misery.

So it was when Grigory Malmudov leapt from a bouncing, twin-engined C-46 on a spring night in 1946. He did not know that he was living through the critical moment of his existence, one he could not regain or reconsider. Until the instant of his leap he had retained a degree of mastery over the course his life would follow. But after that instant, it was beyond his power to return. He had no chance to reconsider it. He could only regret it for the rest of his life.

He often thought of the details of that night in the C-46, silently wishing he had not jumped, or that, having jumped, he had not let his parachute open.

2.

The crew chief of the C-46 was a silent, hard-eyed Slovak. He drove to the barracks an hour before dark in a mud-splattered Citroën, picked up Kuznetsov, and drove him to the airfield east of Munich. The Slovak said only what he considered necessary as he readied the unmarked aircraft for flight, and he did not bother to introduce the two Poles who came to fly the airplane. Kuznetsov—he used the name on his documents, not the one his father gave him—made an attempt at conversation, but they spoke little Russian.

The airplane took off an hour before midnight, he and the Slovak sitting opposite each other on canvas sling seats, silent in the overpowering roar of the engines. The C-46 lurched and bounced as it flew low over the darkened countryside. At twenty-one minutes past midnight, the Slovak leaned across and spoke into Kuznetsov's ear.

"End of the road," he said in German.

"Eh?" Kuznetsov did not understand.

"The end. Finish. Out," the Slovak said, speaking a harsh and heavily accented Russian.

Kuznetsov nodded in understanding and smiled nervously at the Slovak. The man looked down with his hard eyes, but he said nothing.

Kuznetsov was ready for the jump. He stood, adjusted the straps of his parachute, and hefted the greasy old rucksack secured at his belly. He attached the static line to the overhead cable. He went to the open door and paused, looking out into the black night and holding on to the frame to keep his balance. The copilot turned, gave a thumbs-up sign and waved. The Slovak nodded and laid a hand on Kuznetsov's shoulder.

"Hey," he shouted, his voice nearly carried away by the roar of the engines and the rush of the wind. "Hey, good luck, brother," he shouted in Russian. "Don't take no wooden kopecks, huh?"

Kuznetsov looked at the Slovak and saw that he had forced a thin smile.

"Thanks for the ride, brother," Kuznetsov shouted. He smiled, turned, and leapt head-first into the black void.

That was it. When the blast of the slipstream hit Kuznetsov's ears, it was already too late. His moment of personal history was past. But he was not thinking of that. He was thinking about where he would come down and what he would do if somebody saw him. He was thinking about how he would find the road to

Kiev, about the questions he might be asked and the answers he might give. His heart hammered, and he was aware of it even through the roar of the wind in his ears.

Abruptly, the nylon lines snatched him upright and the roar stopped. There was silence, except for the vanishing drone of the C-46 engines, and his mind steadied. He peered down, seeking the earth, holding his body loose for the landing. There was a moon, and looming below in its dim light was a broad field and something that appeared to be a roadway not far off. If he was lucky he would land near the road and find it without difficulty. He felt the cold in the places where the parachute straps cut into his groin.

The earth came to meet him with a rush. He hit, rolled, and stood upright easily, his hands groping for the lines. There was no wind, and he quickly hauled the collapsed nylon into his arms. He ran awkwardly, the parachute folds dragging under his feet, until he reached a hedgerow. He unslung the rucksack from his belly and unhooked the parachute harness. He gouged out a shallow hole in the loam and buried the parachute with its harness, making sure none of the olive-drab folds showed on the surface. Then he adjusted the straps of the battered old rucksack and slung it on his back. He stood up and looked around in the gloom. Picking a direction where he thought the road should be, he set off at a fast walk.

About two hours before sunup he found the road, crossed it, and made his way into a woods beyond. Birch trees and scrub oak sheltered him from the road, and he made a place for himself in the scrub. He was numb from exhaustion, and fell asleep quickly, without eating.

Twice before sunrise Kuznetsov jerked awake amidst confused dreams, his heart thudding. He stared into the silent darkness for several seconds without knowing where he was. Remembering, he put his head down on the rucksack, listened to the night sounds, and dropped back into an uneasy slumber.

When, finally, the sun rose, it dried the early dew and spread a blanket of warmth over Kuznetsov's body. He slept more soundly then, but his hand twitched and his eyelids quivered as he dreamed vivid dreams, scenes from his childhood in the Ukraine. He dreamed he was a boy again, sitting on the back of a cart. Nearby, a man and a woman tossed fodder into the air with wooden pitchforks, chatting amiably while they worked. The fodder rustled as it flew aloft on the pitchforks, and the chattering peasant voices grew louder.

The dry sound of flying fodder increased, and the woman laughed.

"Ho!" she cried, her voice high and cracking. "I told her, I really did, she has no right, I says, no right, and I told her she's a slut, too, I said . . ."

The man laughed, and the dry fodder crashed.

Kuznetsov's eyes flew open. Through the scrub oak he caught sight of a woman's kerchief. The kerchief bobbed up and down with the woman's voice, shrill and piercing.

"Old man Shevchenko has his eye on her, too. Ha ha ha! He's a goat, that one. He don't know what time to eat!"

Kuznetsov pressed his forehead against the loamy earth as the voices trailed off in the distance. He carefully pulled himself to his hands and knees and through the scrub he saw a man and a woman in rough country peasants' clothing making their way to the road. They jumped into the ditch and climbed up the other side to the dirt roadbed, setting off along it in the direction of Mukachevo.

"My God, that was close," Kuznetsov whispered. He rose to his knees, trembling, and he saw that he had been sleeping within a dozen feet of a footpath. Scrub-oak branches stuck into the path far enough to brush against the legs of the peasants, and that was the rustling sound Kuznetsov had heard in the dream.

He looked around. Got to get the hell out of here, he thought. His instructions were to travel only at night, lying low and sleeping during the day, but he was in danger where he was. His papers had been prepared on the assumption he would not have to show them until he reached Ivano-Frankovsk. He could not take a chance on being found here.

The sun had risen well into the sky, and Kuznetsov estimated the time to be around eight o'clock. The peasant couple was probably coming from a village, so he must not use the path. There would be others going to work in the fields below. He watched until the man and woman disappeared. He picked up his ruck-sack and, crouching low, set off through the woods.

After half an hour he came to a rugged place where a small stream flowed through a stand of birch trees. Among the trees he found a cool grotto formed of tree roots and limestone outcroppings. He set the rucksack against a tree and pulled a sausage and a loaf of black bread from it. He cut generous portions of each, leaned against the rucksack, and chewed hungrily at his breakfast.

When he had finished eating, he took a tin cup from the rucksack, dipped it into the stream, and drank. He filled it and drank twice more. He put away the cup and leaned against the rucksack, picking up a handful of leaves to wipe the grease from his hands. He felt comfortable and drowsy and safe in the grotto. Crossing one muddy boot over the other, he closed his eyes.

Lying there, Kuznetsov looked like any of a million Soviet war veterans on the move in 1946: calf-length, army-issue pigskin boots many times resoled and deeply creased at ankles and toes; patched black civilian trousers tucked into the boots; a greasy cotton army tunic with a high collar; a scarred leather belt around his waist; an ordinary Russian workingman's cap set squarely on his head.

From beneath the cap jutted a shock of coarse brown hair, the unruly end of a cowlick that dominated his forehead. His face was like the cowlick, simple and countrified, the face of a young man who grew up on a farm: nose wide and lumpy at the end; face broad and Slavic; a somber full-lipped mouth surrounded by a stubble of beard. A plain face, direct and honest, without a hint of guile.

The old rucksack was equally plain. It contained the ordinary paraphernalia of a single worker on the move: woolen army greatcoat with the insignia gone; another tunic even greasier than the one he was wearing; an extra pair of footcloths; bread and sausage; a sack of tobacco; a canteen, spoon, and tin cup.

But in the bottom there lay a black case, cushioned by the folds of the greatcoat. The case held a piece of equipment quite different from the usual possessions of a young worker on the move. A fleeting memory of the case came to Kuznetsov and made him stir uneasily. But soon he dropped off to sleep, breathing regularly and deeply.

When he awoke the day was nearly gone. The sun already had descended to the horizon and he felt the onset of a damp early evening chill. He listened for new sounds, and hearing none, knelt beside the rivulet to splash water on his face. He pulled the sausage and bread from the rucksack and sat chewing at it while darkness set in around him.

He waited until it grew nearly dark, and then rose and walked back in the direction from which he had come. It was slower going in the dark, and it took an hour for him to find his way back to the road. He stood briefly on the roadway, watching and listening, then climbed down into the ditch and set off walking toward Mukachevo.

The trip proved easier than he had imagined. He had memorized scores of maps in his training and they turned out to be accurate. Twice he came to bridges where the road crossed small rivers, exactly where his memorized maps said they should be. The bridges were manned by armed sentries, asleep on duty in both cases, and he made wide circles around them, wading carefully through the creeks. He dealt the same with villages, leaving the road more than a half a mile before he reached each settlement and skirting the darkened houses. Once, a dog at one of the houses set up a racket, but Kuznetsov crouched in silence until the dog stopped barking.

He made some thirty kilometers that night, and toward morning he again found a sleeping place, this time a spot nearly at the top of a wooded rise that overlooked the Mukachevo road and its valley, a place where nobody was likely to go. He ate the last of the bread and sausage and slept peacefully through the day while the peasants toiled in the fields below.

During the following night's trek Kuznetsov reached Mukachevo, and the railroad line that ran from Mukachevo to Ivano-Frankovsk. It was about midnight when he reached the tracks, and less than an hour later he found his way to a long uphill curve where the tracks worked their way through some of the low hills outside Mukachevo. He hid among bushes close to the roadbed and waited, listening for the train. Finally, at about three o'clock, he caught the sound of a steam engine. He pulled on his rucksack and crouched at the edge of the bushes.

Ten minutes later the headlight of a locomotive appeared, laboring up the long grade. It cast a dim light on the track and roadbed in front of Kuznetsov, and he pulled back so it would not shine on him. The engine labored past, and looking up, he saw a man's silhouette in the door of the engineer's cab. The coal car passed, and Kuznetsov peered down the grade. He watched until a flatbed car, cumbered by a tarpaulin-covered load, came even with him. He sprang from the bushes and leapt to the car, swinging aboard on a cargo rope.

He worked his way to the front end of the flatcar and found a place where the canvas was loose enough for him to shove the rucksack under it. Kuznetsov squeezed under the canvas and sought a comfortable place among the metal surfaces of the machinery cargo. He stretched out with his head near the loose place where he had entered, and raised the canvas and watched the dark shapes of rocks and telegraph poles move by.

He checked off landmarks of the memorized map: a water tower with three small buildings behind it; a village of twelve houses with a crossing over the tracks and no station; a produce warehouse and a loading platform; an overhead power line.

The first pink light of dawn showed in the eastern sky as Kuznetsov caught the odor of petroleum. He peered as far up the track as he could see. In the distance, black against the dim light of the morning sky, he recognized the square outlines of oil storage tanks. He hurriedly clambered out from under the canvas, pulling the rucksack behind him. He looked quickly up and down the train and then leapt.

The train was moving faster than he realized, and Kuznetsov's feet shot from under him when he hit the gravel. He tumbled headlong down the steep embankment, landing in a heap at the bottom.

He lay flat against the embankment until the train passed, and then retrieved the rucksack and set off across the tracks and into the field on the other side, heading in the direction of Ivano-Frankovsk. His memorized map ended beyond Stanislav, but he knew the streets, houses, machine shops, and petroleum depots of the town as they had appeared on the German ordnance maps he'd studied so carefully in Munich. He entered the outskirts as the full light of dawn broke, and he suddenly realized how terribly hungry and thirsty he was. He walked through back streets, his stomach growling and his mouth parched, until he came to a well. He drew up a bucket of water and took a long drink, splashing some of it onto his face and pouring the rest over his head. The icy water revived him, and he headed toward the center of town to find food and get a ticket for the train to Kiev.

He found the main street and approached a shop bearing a sign that read: PRODUCE STORE NO. 1. It was closed. He peered through the window and saw a shelf with a few cans on it, but neither bread nor sausage. He felt savagely hungry and stood wondering where he might find food when an old lady appeared. She had a bag thrown over her shoulder, and she gazed intently at him as she approached.

"Good day, granny," he said politely.

"Good day yourself, sonny," the old woman said, stopping to look him over.

"Waiting for the train," he said. "Know where I can find a bite of breakfast?"

"No use standing in front of this place," the woman said, breaking into a cackle. "No breakfast in there, unless you want rotten fish for breakfast. Got any tobacco, sonny?"

"I have some money. I could pay for a little bread. Hey, what's in the sack for a hungry man?"

"Hee hee, it's hay, sonny," she crowed. "Money's no good these days. Hard times. Tobacco is money. Hee hee. Tobacco is money. Got any?" She eyed him carefully.

Kuznetsov swung his rucksack down from his back and the crone cackled, unslinging her sack.

"Well, now," she said as she watched Kuznetsov pull a small pouch of tobacco from inside the rucksack. "Is that real tobacco or your army tree-leaf shag, boy?"

"It's good tobacco, grandma," Kuznetsov said, taking out a tiny pinch and letting the old lady sniff it. "I'll give you some for a bit of that 'hay' in the sack, huh?"

The old lady plunged her scrawny arm into the sack and came up with a kilogram of black bread. She shoved it toward Kuznetsov without a word and grabbed for the tobacco sack with her other hand.

"Hey, hold on a minute," he said, yanking the tobacco pouch out of her reach. "A kilo of bread ain't worth all this good tobacco, granny. A kilo will get you enough for one smoke, no more.''

"Ah, c'mon, sonny," she wheedled. "I'll give you two kilos.''

"Nothing doing," Kuznetsov said. His mouth watered at the sight of the rich black bread clenched in the old lady's grimy hand.

"Look," he said. "I'll give you enough for four smokes if you'll give me two kilos.''

She eyed him slyly, gauging the size of the pouch in Kuznetsov's hand. "I have some lard," she said. "I'll give you some lard and two kilos for the tobacco, all of it.''

"How much lard?" he asked.

"Two hundred grams.''

He considered that for a moment. "Make it a half-kilo and it's yours," he said.

"Owwr, a half-kilo, the bandit says. A half-kilo! They raise children for robbers these days." She paused, her squinty little black eyes on the tobacco sack. "All right, a half-kilo, robber," she muttered. Her hand shot into the sack, and Kuznetsov saw several onions.

"And two onions," he said.

"Oh, sweet blood of Jesus, listen to him!" she wailed. "Let a robber have a little milk and he wants the whole cow!''

"Come on, granny," Kuznetsov said, his stomach rumbling. "Onions aren't diamonds.''

"And tobacco ain't gold," she muttered. "Ah, all right. Done.''

She handed over the two loaves of bread and the onions, and then cut off a lump of lard. It looked short of a half-kilo, but Kuznetsov was too hungry to haggle any longer. She wrapped the lard in a piece of newspaper and gave it to him. He gave her the tobacco. She heaved the sack onto her shoulder and hobbled off, muttering and grumbling.

Kuznetsov immediately sliced off two big pieces of bread, smeared them with thick layers of lard, and ate greedily. He cut one of the onions in half and ate it with the bread.

The breakfast left him feeling much better, and he was pleased that he had been able to get enough food to last him to Kiev.

But the prospect of taking a passenger train to Kiev banished thoughts of food. Buying the ticket would be the first test of the documents they'd provided for him in Munich; he had no idea if they would stand up to scrutiny. He carefully wrapped the remainder of the food in the newspaper with the lard, and stuffed it into the rucksack. Then he set off across the street toward the train station, doing a mental inventory of the official papers he carried in a cloth wallet of his trouser pocket. He took a breath and pushed open the station door.

Kuznetsov saw nobody inside, so he approached the ticket window and looked in. A man in a railway tunic sat writing at a desk, his back to the ticket window.

"Good morning, comrade," Kuznetsov said.

The man continued writing, and without turning around said, "Yes?"

"Ticket to Kiev, please," Kuznetsov said.

The head turned and a flat face with rimless glasses stared at him. "Kiev?"

"Right, comrade. Kiev."

"What you wanna go to Kiev for?"

The railway worker stared impassively through the rimless glasses. He made no move to write a ticket.

"I have a travel voucher," Kuznetsov murmured.

"So you have a travel voucher."

"Yes." Kuznetsov felt sweat prickling at his back beneath the rucksack.

"Well then? Let's have your travel voucher."

Kuznetsov pulled the cloth wallet from his pocket and untied it. He took out a folded piece of paper. It was covered with printed words and blanks filled in with ink by a crude hand. It bore two pink stamps and an ornate signature at the bottom.

The face with the rimless glasses rose, floated to the window, and stared at the voucher.

"The Dobrov Works, huh? Why do they want you to go to Kiev?"

"Because they do," Kuznetsov snapped, annoyed. "Read the God-damned thing; it says everything."

"No need to be uncivil," the rimless glasses said. He took the voucher and carried it to the desk. He sat down, took up his pen, and commenced writing.

For several more minutes the railway official continued working: opening ledgers, folding papers, pounding rubber stamps.

Finally, he rose and returned to the window.

"Passport?"

Kuznetsov unfolded the wallet. What the hell does he want the passport for? he thought, bringing out an olive-drab booklet with the hammer-and-sickle emblem embossed on its cover. The railway official took it and returned to his desk. He began writing again, copying numbers from the passport. He paused and reached for a telephone. Kuznetsov's stomach grew uneasy. He grasped the narrow countertop.

The official turned a crank and gave a number.

"Vasily Matveich? Good morning, Ivanov here. A voucher. Yes. Kiev. Yes. Ah, yes, name's Kuznetsov, Alexander Nikolayevich. No. Lathe operator. Dobrov Works. Official transfer to the Kaganovich Machine-Tool Plant. Yes. Yes, of course...."

Kuznetsov felt panicky for the first time since before the jump from the C-46. For a dizzy moment he thought of running for the door, making a break while he had the chance.

Through the dizziness he heard the railway agent's voice: "What's your service card say?"

Kuznetsov stared a moment, then replied in a voice too high, too nervous: "Third category, comrade."

"Third category, Vasily Matveich," the railway official said to the telephone.

"Yes. Yes, of course ... right ..."

The official replaced the receiver and sat writing for another five minutes.

"Why don't you sit down?" he said finally. "I can't stand your breathing."

Kuznetsov moved away from the window, but he could not sit. He stood looking through a dirty pane of glass, and he wondered if he should clear out and leave his papers behind. He wondered why the man didn't simply give him a ticket. Whom had he called on the telephone?

He turned abruptly and glared at the railway official's impassive back.

"Hey, comrade, where the hell's my ticket?" he demanded.

The back did not move. "Your ticket will be ready when it's ready," he said. "Don't bother me."

Ten minutes passed. A freight train came into the station and rumbled through slowly, without stopping. A man in peasant clothes came in to ask the time of the Mukachevo train. The official told him and the peasant left. Kuznetsov continued standing, staring through the dirty window at the tracks.

Suddenly the door opened and Kuznetsov turned. A man in the green cap and epaulettes of a senior lieutenant of the NKVD came through the door. He was tall, with green eyes the same color of his cap and epaulettes. He carried a pistol in a holster at his waist.

"Kuznetsov?" the officer asked, looking directly at him.

"Yes, me," Kuznetsov replied. He was the only person in the station.

"Let's have your passport."

Kuznetsov opened his mouth to say that the railway official had it, but at that instant the rimless glasses appeared at the ticket window. "Here it is, Vasily Matveich," he said.

The NKVD lieutenant took the booklet and the travel voucher and studied them carefully, looking up and staring with his harsh green eyes at Kuznetsov.

"Service card?" he barked.

Kuznetsov brought out the cloth wallet and started to pull the service card from it. The NKVD officer glanced sharply at the wallet.

"Let's see what we have here," he said, snatching the wallet away. He flipped through the documents and began pulling them out, one by one, inspecting each in turn. Kuznetsov felt ill. The bread, lard, and onion lay in a ball in his stomach. He was afraid he would vomit.

"You're from the Dobrov Works?" the officer asked.

"Yes, Dobrov."

"How did you get here?"

"Truck, Comrade Lieutenant. They gave me a ride on the truck, last night."

"What truck?"

Kuznetsov's mouth and throat had gone dry. The need to vomit arose again.

"They sent a truck last night. To Kolomyya. They gave me a lift."

The lieutenant raised his eyes from the documents. He looked intently at Kuznetsov, holding the passport in his right hand. He tapped the wallet with it. His eyes fell to the rucksack.

"What's in there?"

"Just my stuff," Kuznetsov replied.

"Let's have a look." The NKVD officer cast his green eyes on Kuznetsov.

Kuznetsov's gorge rose; he would surely vomit. He pulled the rucksack toward him and opened it. His fingers trembled on the straps.

The NKVD lieutenant peered into the rucksack; he knelt beside it. With his right hand, he rummaged through the clothes on top, pushing more and more deeply, nearer and nearer the black case at the bottom. Kuznetsov held his breath.

Suddenly the officer jerked his hand from the rucksack.

"God damn!" he snarled. "Shit!" His fingers were smeared with lard. He scowled at Kuznetsov and wiped his hand on the rucksack. "Why didn't you tell me you had that shit in there, jackass?" he said.

"I . . . I'm sorry, Comrade Lieutenant," Kuznetsov stammered. "I forgot that . . ."

"Ah, shut up!" the NKVD officer snapped. He straightened, pondered the rucksack and the cloth wallet, and with a sudden movement tossed the wallet on the floor and barked at the railway official: "All right. Give it to him!"

He spun on his heel and strode out, slamming the door.

The slamming door echoed through the empty station. Kuznetsov closed the rucksack, put his papers in order, and a few minutes later the railway official handed him a ticket to Kiev.

"Have a nice trip," the official said. The rimless glasses bore no expression. Kuznetsov did not reply.

At ten-thirty the train arrived, a freight with two
creaking passenger cars coupled on behind. Kuznetsov handed his ticket to the train guard, found a place
on a bench near the rear of the second car, and collapsed.

He remembered little of the ride to Kiev. He had
fallen into the rhythm of sleeping during the day, and
slept soundly despite the discomfort of the hard bench
and the bumpy, jerking ride of the old rail car. He
awoke once or twice as the train stopped in stations on
the way. At one of the stops he got off to buy a glass
of kvass from a vendor, and ate some bread and lard
with it. Then he went back to sleep on his bench.
When he awoke they were nearing Kiev and he saw a
pink sunset reflected in the waters of the Dneiper.

As the train lumbered into the Kiev station, Kuznetsov prepared himself for another inspection. He
had been warned that they examined documents in all
the major cities, and when he clambered off the train
he saw a team of NKVD men on the platform. Kuznetsov walked to the checkpoint with the same feeling
of nausea and panic that he had experienced in Ivano-
Frankovsk.

He waited several minutes in the crowds of passengers before an NKVD sergeant motioned him forward.

"Papers?" the sergeant asked.

Kuznetsov pulled his passport and travel voucher
from the wallet and handed them to the sergeant. The
NKVD man took them, looking at them, then at Kuznetsov.

He handed the papers back.

"Next!" the sergeant shouted, motioning him past.

Relieved, Kuznetsov moved with the crowd through the station toward its front entrance.

It was already dark, and outside the station he turned into a gloomy street lined with bombed-out buildings. He did not pause, but walked six blocks straight ahead and then turned right.

He walked three more blocks until he reached a low bridge crossing a canal that led to the Dneiper. He stopped in the shadow of a smashed wall, studying the bridge and the bomb-ravaged buildings. Then he clambered down the embankment toward the canal and walked along a narrow concrete ledge that led beneath the bridge. The clearance at the bridge was too low for him to stand upright, so he pulled off the rucksack and dragged it in behind him on hands and knees. He felt the underside of the structure until he found the series of metal conduits for the electrical cables crossing the bridge.

It was as he expected, and it was here that he would use his black case until he found something better.

He propped the rucksack against a pillar and rummaged in the dark. He found matches and a short wax candle. He paused, listened, and lit the candle, which he put on the flange of a beam. The light revealed a junction box, and using a ten-kopeck coin, Kuznetsov unscrewed the metal cover.

As he peered into the box he heard the distant sound of an automobile engine. He blew out the candle and waited as the sound grew louder. The engine hum rose to a roar and rubber tires hammered on the planks directly over his head. The vehicle passed to the end of the bridge and the noise died away.

When it was again quiet, Kuznetsov lit the candle and looked again into the junction box. He loosened two more screws and turned back to the rucksack. In the dim light of the candle he removed the clothes and then the black case. He opened it and pulled from it a coil of wire which he attached to the loosened screws in the junction box. He tightened the screws and replaced the cover so that the coil of wire hung out beneath it.

He carefully placed the black case on the flange of the beam, and using a roll of cord from the rucksack, he secured the case to it. Opening the door on the front of the case, he attached the wires that hung from the junction box to screws on the front of the case. He pulled a third wire from the case and worked his way along the ledge, stretching it to a length of several meters, and tying the end to a bridge support before returning to the box.

Kuznetsov turned a knob. There was a click, and a dim light went on in the box. After a few seconds came a hissing sound, barely audible, then a tiny beeping. Kuznetsov listened without moving. Finally he stirred, turned another switch, and reached into a small pigeonhole in the case. His wrist moved quickly, and a louder beeping sound came from the box. It was in code, and it said:

NCD DE OXR.

A pause. Then, again.

NCD DE OXR.

The call was repeated five times, with a pause between each.

Kuznetsov waited thirty seconds and his wrist vibrated again.

NCD DE OXR. ON STATION. REPEAT. ON STATION. OUT.

Kuznetsov pulled his hand from the pigeonhole, snapped the switch, and replaced the cover. He put the clothes back into the rucksack, blew out the candle, climbed up the embankment, and walked briskly toward the railroad station.

TOP SECRET
UNITED STATES OF AMERICA
CENTRAL INTELLIGENCE AGENCY

Aug. 1, 1948

From: Director
To: Chief of Operations, Europe
Re: Operative, termination of
Ref: Your ltr dtd 5 Jun, 1948

1) You are directed to terminate without prejudice operative designated HEARTFELT, Region IV(A), EastEuro.

2) Operative to be instructed by coded message to destroy radio and codes and to avoid any future effort to contact Euro Control, or any agency of the United States Government, by any means.

3) In response to your ltr of 5 Jun, all files and documents relating to subject operative are to be forwarded by courier to Central Control for disposition.

4) Euro Control is authorized to include in termination message a sentiment of gratitude from "People of Europe." Under no circumstances is reference to be made to United States of America.

ss/ Benedict Wilde III
For the Director

3.

Alexander Nikolayevich Kuznetsov left his office at the Red Banner Generator Factory at two minutes before five o'clock, having first arranged his papers in an orderly stack on the left-hand corner of his desk. He pulled on a dark gray suit jacket, concealing sweat stains in the armpits of his shirt, and he joined the other factory office workers headed toward the exit at the end of the corridor. As he left the office, a thin young man passing by in the corridor made an awkward, walking bow in his direction.

"Good day, Alexander Nikolayevich," the young man said.

Kuznetsov smiled. "Hello, Sasha. Have a nice weekend."

The young man repeated the awkward bow and hurried away down the corridor. Other eyes glanced sidelong at Kuznetsov, making him feel uncomfortable and lonely. When he was appointed chief engineer less than a year ago, his coworkers' attitudes toward him changed abruptly from familiarity to formality. People who had used the intimacy of "thou" and called him by the nickname "Sasha" now opted for the formal "you" and "Alexander Nikolayevich." Some even called him "Comrade Kuznetsov."

As he approached the exit at the end of the corridor, a voice called from an office doorway.

"Hey, Sasha, what's doing on the weekend?"

Kuznetsov shuddered. There was still one man who addressed him familiarly. He turned to the open doorway and forced a smile for the handsome, dark-haired man inside.

"Same as the other tired bachelors," Kuznetsov said. "Sit in the park and look at the girls and sweat. And you, Genya?"

"Oh, party conference tomorrow," the dark-haired man replied. "Busy days coming."

Kuznetsov paused uncertainly at the door. Above it was a black sign with gold letters reading "Directorate of Personnel," and in smaller letters below, "E. Repin."

Personnel Director Evgeny Repin smiled, but his cold gray eyes robbed the smile of warmth.

"We personnel workers have a thankless job, Sasha, a thankless job. We look out for people's souls and their minds, both the one and the other."

"Yes, well," Kuznetsov said. "Well, uh, I guess my lathes and rotors don't give me any trouble about souls and minds." He wished he could say something sensible to this cold-eyed man, but he always felt awkward and stupid in his presence.

"Right you are, Sasha boy, right you are," Repin said, still smiling. "You know, you're never too old to join the Party. Have you reconsidered?"

Kuznetsov sighed inwardly. Repin was always at him to apply for candidate membership in the Communist Party, something that was out of the question for him. Applicants underwent detailed security checks; his fabricated past would not stand up to it.

"No, I think not," he said. "As I always say, I'm not the Party-activist type."

"Yes, but you're a senior executive of a major industrial concern," Repin said. "You're lucky you got that far without joining. You'll never get the directorship...."

"Oh well, I don't have any ambitions for that," Kuznetsov said, waving the suggestion away.

Repin regarded him soberly with his gray eyes, making Kuznetsov uncomfortable. Finally the personnel director sighed and smiled genially.

"Well, have a nice time for yourself this weekend, hey, Sasha? We have to take it while we can. Hey?"

"Yes, right, Genya. Well, eh, I'm off. See you Monday." Kuznetsov retreated from Repin's chilly smile and fled out the main door. The man upset him not because of what he said but because of who he was: Soviet personnel directors did more than process job applications. They also served as the eyes and ears of the Committee for State Security, the KGB.

What does he mean, "Take it while you can?"
Kuznetsov thought. He can't know. He can't even
suspect!

Preoccupied with thoughts of Repin, Kuznetsov
joined the flow of homebound working people at the
gate as it merged with a dark mass of Russian humanity moving toward the Metro station a block away.

In that stream of Muscovites, Kuznetsov was unre-
markable: a man of middle age, with a middle-aged
thickness at the waist and a middle-aged drabness of
dress and demeanor. He wore a gray suit, white shirt
beginning to fray at the collar, scuffed brown shoes
and pale blue nylon socks showing between shoetops
and cuffs.

He was the sort of man who was loved by cats and
ignored by dogs, although he himself disliked cats and
loved dogs. A cat, seeing Kuznetsov from a distance,
would rush to him and rub against his leg. Dogs
looked at him askance and crossed to the other side of
the street.

The stream of pedestrians eddied at the entrance to
the Metro station, and Kuznetsov was swept along
with it down the steps and into the Metro's dark bowels. The flow swirled into a rank of polished turnstiles
which popped people onto the platform like cookies
in a bakery.

Kuznetsov pushed forward until he reached a turnstile and inserted his five-kopeck coin in the slot. He
felt a kick from behind. His preoccupation with Repin vanished, and he glared over his shoulder at a

squat old woman who pressed behind him, stepping on his heels with her pigskin boots.

"Take it easy, granny," he snapped. "What's the rush?"

The crone cackled and shoved past him, jamming an elbow into his ribs. "Get a move on, sonny," she screeched. "This ain't no restaurant."

The old lady plunged into the mass at the train door and fought her way inside with a practiced use of elbows and boots. Kuznetsov muttered to himself and did the same, shoving and bumping until he managed to get inside and take the last empty seat.

He sat down and caught a glimpse of his reflection in the window across the aisle. He saw a face that was pale and pasty and fifty years old. There were bags beneath eyes that lacked the merry wrinkles that come from the habit of laughter. The skin at the cheeks sagged, pulling the mouth into a sour line. He felt the thickness of his stomach, straining shirt buttons and pushing over his belt. His own body odor in the hot Metro car rose to his nose, a whiff of sour sweat and urine. He wondered if others in the car could smell it.

Should've washed underwear yesterday, he thought.

A woman in a seat opposite arranged a shopping bag in her lap, and in it Kuznetsov saw the neck of a yogurt jar. He forgot underwear and thought of supper. He decided to get off at the Arbat and buy something for the evening meal, maybe some yogurt and a nice bit of sausage. He'd need some fresh bread, too.

As he planned the meal, the train stopped at the Kirov station and the car quickly filled with another shoving rush of Muscovites. A large, heavy-breasted woman gave Kuznetsov a poke with her forefinger.

"Hey," she said. "Get up."

"Huh?" Kuznetsov looked up in surprise. "What for?"

The forefinger jabbed at a decal on the window. "Can't you read?" the woman snapped.

The decal said: RESERVED FOR INVALIDS AND PREGNANT WOMEN.

"You don't look like no invalid to me, comrade," Kuznetsov said, looking away.

The thick finger jabbed him again. "I'm pregnant, dolt."

Kuznetsov stared. It was possible that somewhere within the bulk of womanhood before him were the beginnings of another Russian. He stood up.

"So," he said. "Sit."

The woman dropped heavily into the seat without speaking and Kuznetsov squeezed into the standing space she had left. He gripped the chrome bar overhead and cursed softly to himself. He hated crowds, and no amount of living in Moscow or riding on the Metro could accustom himself to the shoving rudeness of the city.

"They're asses, these Muscovites," Kuznetsov thought. "Peasants in lace-up shoes. You can send a jackass to Paris and he'll still come back home with a brown hide and long ears."

Each lurch of the crowded train pressed him closer to the pregnant woman. His knee bumped hers, and he glanced down to see her angry black eyes glaring at him. He tried to move his knee so it would not touch hers; somebody behind pushed and the knees touched again. She glared again.

"Oof. God," he muttered. He strained to keep from touching her, and a rivulet of sweat trickled down his back. The arm on the chrome bar trembled. He tried to shift his other hand to the bar but the train lurched and he lost his grip entirely. He fell forward over the pregnant woman, catching the edge of the window just in time to keep from dropping straight into her lap. He came face to face with her, three inches from the angry black eyes.

"What're you trying to do?" she snarled. "I'll call a conductor."

"Sorry, sorry," Kuznetsov said. He pushed himself upright and saw with relief that the train was stopping at the Arbat station. He shoved his way to the door and stumbled onto the platform.

Outside the Metro tunnel in the bright Moscow afternoon he took a deep breath and paused to wipe the sweat from his face. He joined the pack of Muscovites pushing out the Metro entrance in the direction of Kalinin Prospekt.

Kuznetsov walked briskly, enjoying the broad Kalinin Prospekt with its rows of tall modern buildings and spacious stores. After twenty years of living in a dreary communal apartment he could appreciate their clean lines and open space even if, as a bachelor, he could not apply for one of the new apartments. It was pleasing simply to know they were there.

He often bought his bread and sausage in the stores on the prospekt rather than in the dank shops near his apartment. It was the same bread and the same sausage and it sold for the same price, but he preferred to get it here all the same.

He went first to the bakery by the Oktyabrsky Cinema and joined the row of women at the bread bins. He elbowed his way to the black bread, the staple of his diet. He picked up a stainless-steel fork and pressed the loaves with the flat of the tines. He selected the softest one, speared it with the fork, and dropped it into a fishnet bag he pulled from his pocket.

Next, he pushed among the women to the last bins on the row. He chose two sugared buns for his breakfast, added them to the black bread in the fishnet bag, and joined the queue at the checkout counter.

At the checkout a bored woman in a white coat and knitted pink beret totaled his purchases on an abacus and took his twenty-kopeck coin, shoving back a pair of one-kopeck coins in change.

"Got any two-kopeck pieces, comrade?" Kuznetsov asked.

"Nope," the woman snapped, turning to the next customer and clicking the beads on her abacus. Kuznetsov did not move.

"Need it for the phone," he said. His voice took the wheedling tone used with Moscow store clerks.

"Doesn't everybody," she said, click-click-clicking her abacus. "Go ask the Communications Ministry. I ain't got any."

Kuznetsov sighed and left the store. He had no need to make a telephone call, but he liked to get his hands on two-kopeck coins when he could. The telephones took only two-kopeck coins; therefore there was a shortage.

From the bakery, Kuznetsov went to the big supermarket on the opposite side of Kalinin Prospekt, where he picked up a bottle of yogurt and a box of Red October candies. He decided to walk home instead of taking the trolley, so he crossed the prospekt at the underpass, strolled to the corner, crossed Tchaikovsky Street at the light, and turned right toward Mayakovsky Square.

He had gone less than a block when he caught sight of a garish American flag and a militiaman; he realized he was about to walk directly past the United States Embassy. A cold sensation swept over him. He thought of turning back, but the militiaman at the south entrance turned and looked directly at him. Everybody feels guilty in the presence of a policeman, but Kuznetsov more so; and more so especially at that place.

It was a public sidewalk, and thousands of Muscovites walked along it every day. He knew that. But he always made it a point to avoid that particular stretch of sidewalk, and he should have made it a special point today after what Repin had said about "taking it while you can." He should have been more careful.

"Take yourself in hand," he said to himself. But the icy feeling in his bowels would not go away. The hair on his neck prickled. The militiaman continued to look at him.

He passed the embassy's south entrance without looking back; ahead was the north entrance, with another Soviet militiaman standing guard. The officer glanced at Kuznetsov as he approached, but at that moment two women emerged from the embassy doorway and they distracted the officer's attention. The women headed across the wide sidewalk to a lime-green American car parked on Tchaikovsky Street.

Kuznetsov stopped, struck by the sudden rush of color as the two women passed in front of him. Their clothes in the brassy sunshine were so bright they nearly hurt his eyes; the colors were rich, appetizing, and fragrant, like a bowl of fresh fruit.

The first woman wore a yellow dress of a clinging material that just reached her knees and outlined her hips and thighs. The dress was open at the neck, and Kuznetsov caught a glimpse of her collarbone and of small freckles in the depression above her breasts.

The second woman was tall, with hair brown and shiny, long and straight and flowing. She wore slacks of a brazen red, and took five long-legged mannish strides to the car door. She spoke in a laughing English voice to a man sitting in the driver's seat of the car. The man reached across the seat and opened the door, speaking in English to the woman in red.

The women got inside the car and he saw the faces of all three. They were smiling. The tall woman's lips, red, full, with gleaming white teeth, moved rapidly as she spoke. The man laughed. The lime-green American car sped away.

"Hey, citizen! You looking for something?"

Kuznetsov leapt at the sound of the militiaman's voice. He realized that he was standing stock-still on the sidewalk in front of the United States Embassy.

"Waiting for somebody?" The militiaman's eyes took on a hard, unblinking policeman's stare.

"Er, I...eh..." Kuznetsov stammered. He grinned foolishly. "Looking at the foreign car, comrade," he said, moving off with sidewise steps.

The militiaman sauntered in Kuznetsov's direction, and Kuznetsov turned and fled at a quick walk along Tchaikovsky Street, sweat popping from his forehead and soaking the shirt beneath his jacket.

"What devil made me go near that place?" he asked himself, cursing his carelessness. "What if they tell Repin I was loitering around there? What if they follow me?"

He glanced back at the embassy. The officer stood at his post, looking the other way. Kuznetsov breathed a sigh of relief and continued walking. He glanced back once more and saw that a man in a gray jacket and an open-necked white shirt had fallen in behind him. The man looked away.

Kuznetsov turned and hurried along Tchaikovsky Street, sweating profusely. He yanked a handkerchief from his pocket and mopped his face and neck. He turned at the corner and stood waiting for the light to change. Looking furtively to his right, he saw the man in the gray jacket stop and look in the window of a shoe store. Kuznetsov wiped his face again as the light changed; he stepped into the crosswalk.

As he reached the opposite curb he glanced back and his heart leapt: The man in the gray jacket was crossing behind him, stepping along briskly.

A tail! he thought. They're watching me.

A dull, aching pain came to his chest and he took deep breaths to ease it. He walked as quickly as he dared along Tchaikovsky Street until he came to an electrical appliance store. He stopped as if to look in the window. He stole a glance, and saw the gray-jacketed figure standing in front of a store window twenty yards behind him. Another man in a gray jacket emerged from the store and began strolling along Tchaikovsky Street in Kuznetsov's direction.

"Jesus," he thought. "Half the men in Moscow wear gray jackets."

He walked toward Mayakovsky Square, and each time he glanced back he saw a gray-jacketed figure behind him, but he could no longer be sure it was the same man. The sweat was soaking through his coat, making a dark streak down the back and large dark circles under the arms. The pain in his chest sharpened.

He hurried past Tchaikovsky Theater, but instead of going straight for the three blocks to his apartment, he abruptly turned into Gorky Street. If he had a tail, he did not want it to follow him to his apartment in Oruzheiny Lane.

Kuznetsov made a sudden decision. He turned and ran into the Metro station at the corner, diving down the steps. He fished a five-kopek coin from his pocket, jammed it into the turnstile and leapt to the escalator, taking the steps two at a time. He heard a train coming, and it stopped as he clambered to the bottom of the escalator. He jumped aboard, squeezed against the packed bodies, and turned to look back. He was panting heavily and sweat ran in a stream down his back and face.

The other passengers eyed him with sullen curiosity as the car stood in the station, doors open. A compressor motor beneath the train switched on, humming in the fetid silence. Two more passengers got aboard, pushing Kuznetsov farther into the car. He fidgeted and blinked.

Close the doors! Close the doors!

The muscles in his jaw twitched. He tried to hold his breath to silence the heavy breathing. He blew it out. The doors stood open and the compressor motor hummed.

Please! Close the doors!

Four more passengers pressed into the car and the doors began to close. Then they stopped halfway. They opened again.

No! No! Close the doors!

The doors started to close again, but at that moment the gray-jacketed man jumped from the escalator and ran across the platform to the doors at the other end of the car. He threw a shoulder between the closing doors and squeezed through. The train groaned and began to move. Kuznetsov peered down the car. He saw the gray-jacketed man looking back at

him. Kuznetsov quickly looked away, then back again.
The gray-jacketed man was staring fixedly at him.
Kuznetsov looked away, and he saw his reflection in
the window: eyes wide, face gleaming with sweat. He
struggled to control his breathing.

The train stopped next at Sverdlov Square and passengers shoved and grunted as some tried to get off
and others struggled toward vacated seats. The man in
the gray jacket pushed into the car toward Kuznetsov
and their eyes met once more. The man looked at
Kuznetsov with a blank expression, then looked away.

The outward flow of passengers stopped and those
on the platform began pushing their way inside. Kuznetsov decided to get off. He shoved against the stream
of boarding passengers, fending off elbows and brief-
cases. He looked back once and saw the gray jacket
working its way toward him. The doors began to close,
and Kuznetsov plunged, knocking a woman to one
side. Grabbing the rubber edges of the doors, he
squeezed through and dived across the platform into
the crowd. The doors slammed shut behind him and
with a groan the train began to move. He looked back
once more. The train was moving. He could no longer
see the man in the gray jacket.

Kuznetsov hurried down a crowded passageway to
a point where the walkway divided, right to the Green
Line trains and left to Revolution Square. He turned
right, ducked behind a pillar, and paused. Head down,
he moved away from the pillar to the left, across the
flow of pedestrian traffic, and joined the stream
heading into the left-hand passageway. At the end, he

took another turn, ran up the escalator two steps at a time, and burst out into Karl Marx Prospekt. A bus was pulling up to the stop and he went for it at a dead run, jumping aboard just as the doors closed. He found a seat and fell into it, gasping. Between him and the window sat a slim young woman in a cotton dress. She pulled away from him and frowned with disgust.

Kuznetsov was soaked with sweat and radiating heat and odor like a stove. His damp coat sleeve touched her bare forearm. She pulled still farther away, but Kuznetsov did not notice her.

"Lost him," he said to himself. "Thank God, lost him."

The bus turned into Gorky Street, and he stayed aboard until it turned again at Pushkin Square. He got off there and walked the six blocks to his apartment in Oruzheiny Lane.

At the entrance, Kuznetsov pushed open a brown, dingy door and dragged himself up two flights of dark stairwell. He opened another door with a key and entered an L-shaped hallway that smelled of stale grease and damp mops. With a second key he opened another door at the angle of the L and entered a small room. He stood a moment in the center of the room, between a green divan and a wardrobe. He pulled off his jacket. It was wet through with his sweat, and he hung it on a hook inside the wardrobe door. He unbuttoned his shirt, peeled it away from the damp skin, and tossed it on the floor.

He stood shirtless in the middle of the room and licked his lips. He spoke softly to himself:

"When can I stop it? When will it end?"

He went to the divan and sagged down on it. Only then did he realize he had lost his fishnet bag with the bread, sausage, yogurt, and Red October candies, though he could not remember where.

Kuznetsov sighed heavily. He lay down on the divan and closed his eyes.

NKVD
CERTIFICATE OF BIRTH
NO. _4643_

THE BIRTH OF

Malmudov, Grigory Nikolayevich

HAS BEEN DULY REGISTERED BY THE
REPRESENTATIVE OF THE PEOPLE'S
COMMISSARIAT FOR INTERNAL AFFAIRS IN THE
LOCALITY OF _Stepanovka_, KRIVOI
ROG DISTRICT, UKRAINIAN SSR, IN
ACCORDANCE WITH UKASE NO. K2.3382 OF
THE UKRAINIAN COUNCIL OF WORKERS' AND
PEASANTS' DEPUTIES.

DATE OF BIRTH _March 10, 1922_
PLACE OF BIRTH _Stepanovka_
NAME OF FATHER _Nikolai Leontievich_
FATHER'S CLASS ORIGIN _Peasant_
NAME OF MOTHER _Klavdya Ivanovna_
MOTHER'S CLASS ORIGIN _Peasant_

CERTIFIED: _Stepan Mstislavovich Venko_

REGISTERED
March 13, 1922

4.

Grigory Nikolayevich Malmudov remembered his childhood as a rich blend of sights, sounds, and smells, the whole of it bound together by a ramshackle slat fence surrounding the house in Stepanovka where he was born. That house stood third from the last on the village's only street. It was not the largest house in the village. Neither was it the smallest.

It had three rooms, a low roof, small windows, and a shed with no windows. Like all the other houses on the street, its walls were not level and its angles were not square. It had been built squarely, but over the years it had settled and sagged, adapting itself to the uneven earth beneath it.

Through the long winters of the Ukrainian steppe it took warmth from a massive earthen stove that filled one whole wall of the main room. As in all such peasant stoves, there was a nook on one side that was per-

petually cozy and warm. In this nook the children—
the boy and his toddler sister—slept during the cold
months of the year.

The other two rooms led off this main room. The
boy's mother and father slept in the larger of them.
His Uncle Fyodor slept in the other room, first with a
small, shrill woman, his Auntie Lyuda, then alone
because Auntie Lyuda had gone away.

Of these people the boy had memories connected
more with odors, sounds, and colors than with spe-
cific events.

The house bore a sour, vinegary scent that arose
from the bucket used to collect pig slop. The bucket
stood just outside the door, filled through the day with
soured milk, stale bread, potato peelings, cabbage
leaves, and the poor scraps that members of the family left on their plates at mealtimes. It was a rank,
bacterial smell, one that, in later years, made him
homesick.

The memory of his father had no face connected
with it. It had a beard: a great, black, greasy beard
that hung in glistening curls down his father's shirt
front and which sprouted over his face, starting just
below two sharp black eyes set close together over a
pugged nose. A pungent aroma arose from the beard
in an invisible cloud, one concocted of onions, black
bread, and cabbage. Sometimes the hot odor of vodka
joined the others and he would show a grinning line of
long, brownish, crooked teeth. At those times he sang
peasant songs in a hoarse voice and slapped his mother's broad buttocks.

When the vodka smell was in the air the father teased the boy, tousling his unruly blond hair and singing children's songs:

> *Little Grisha,*
> *Mama's boy,*
> *Won't eat his kasha,*
> *Won't get his toy.*
>
> *Little Grisha*
> *Makes a face,*
> *But smiling Grisha*
> *Wins the race.*

The teasing made the boy pout with anger, but his black-bearded father only laughed.

"Ho! Look! Grishenka's mad. Gonna pick a fight with his old man! Grishka's mad! Ho!"

They called him Grisha, Grishka, Grishenka, or Golubchik, all pet names, and they loved him.

The boy's mother was a large woman, with immense hips and arms so heavy that the flesh swung back and forth as she kneaded dough on the big wooden table in the center of the main room. She was fair and blond, with hair luxuriant and long, streaming in rich tresses all the way to her hips when she brushed it at night. In the daytime she wore her hair in tight braids wrapped and knotted in a bun, concealing its nighttime glory.

His mother talked incessantly in a high-pitched chortle that resounded through the house and carried into the yard. Every day, neighbor women stamped in and out of the rough wooden door of the house, adding their gossip to that of his mother's. She had wide gaps in her teeth, and one upper front tooth was so snaggled that it overlapped its neighbor and jutted out far enough to touch her lower lip when she closed her mouth. The tooth often got in the way of her words, making tiny droplets of spittle explode between it and the lower lip.

She had a sweetish, sweaty smell about her, a warm and rich animal smell that surrounded her as she stooped to wipe the boy's nose or tie the earflaps on his shapka or, when he fell ill, to cover his forehead with a vinegar-soaked rag.

Grisha's Uncle Fyodor was a morose man, skinny and pale, with gray, sunken cheeks instead of a beard. He breathed the vodka smell more often than the boy's father, and when Auntie Lyuda lived there, they quarreled constantly. One night, he chased her around the room, pounding her with his fists until she bled from the ears, then yanked her by the hair as she screamed and howled. It was after that night that Auntie Lyuda went away.

Uncle Fyodor stayed on for a year, but he, too, left the house in Stepanovka during the last winter there, the winter of 1930.

The boy played in the yard among goats and sheep, and in the evenings he often sat on an upturned bucket in the shed to watch his mother milk their cow, her big, plump hands tugging the teats, bringing milk in short squirts into the foamy bucket.

During the last winter in Stepanovka, Grigory's father made him a sled. With a neighbor boy named

Misha he coasted on the sled down the bank of the ravine behind the village. During that winter his sister fell ill, and one afternoon the boys came home from the coasting hill to find neighbors crowding into Grigory's house and his mother slumped on a bench, red-eyed and moaning. His sister lay under a blanket on the table. He understood that she was dead. It was the first time he had known death and it struck terror in him. For many nights afterward he lay awake trembling in fear of death, and he prayed to the icon in the corner of the room that he would not have to die.

That was the only time in his life that Grisha could remember praying. He had no recollection of attending masses in the village church, which was closed and padlocked from as early as he could remember. The Malmudovs were devout, however, and they kept an icon in the corner of the room with a candle always burning. They crossed themselves before it each morning after they arose and each evening before they went to bed.

Stepanovka had no school, but one year a woman came and taught letters and figures to the village children in one of the houses. She did not remain there the whole year, and the school was canceled. Grisha did not learn reading or writing at home, for neither his father nor his mother possessed those skills.

If Grigory Nikolayevich's memory of his earliest childhood was limited, his memory of his last night in the house in Stepanovka was not. He remembered the night in its every detail.

It was near the end of that final winter of 1930, when his sister died and when Uncle Fyodor went away. There had been thaws that melted the snow from the sled run, but it turned bitterly cold again.

For several days there was unusual activity in the village. The neighbor women tramped in and out of the house as always, but their chatter was subdued, with much whispering and clucking. A banner appeared over the front of one of the houses, red with white letters, and the village men gathered in small knots around it. They smoked and talked in excited, quarrelsome voices.

In their conversation the boy picked out incomprehensible words and phrases: "District Revoluntionary Council." "Regional Soviet." "Collectivization." "Hoarder." "Kulak."

Sometimes the words were muttered; sometimes they were shouted; sometimes some of the men fell out punching each other. The boy smelled vodka on the breaths of many of the men, and he smelled it in the black beard of his father when he came home.

On the second night after they put up the banner at the house in the village, Grisha's father returned home in a sullen and irritable mood. But after sitting for a time at the big table, he suddenly turned to the boy and chuckled. He took a handful of Grisha's hair in his hard, blackened fist.

"Hey, Comrade Grisha," he bellowed. "We're comrades now, sonny. You can tell your old man to go to hell and he can't lift a little finger to shut your trap, hey?"

He put derisive emphasis on the word "comrade."

"Nowadays any son of a bitch can tell a man what to do and where to go," he said, laughing through his yellowed teeth. "Well, Comrade Golubchik, we'll see about that, hey?"

His father let go of the boy's hair and gave him a playful cuff on the ear. He shouted to his wife that there would be a meeting in the village, and he left the house.

The boy's father did not come home before his bedtime, and Grisha remembered waking up and seeing his mother blow out the kerosene lamp on the table. He watched her make her way through the darkness to bed, and soon fell back asleep in the stove nook. It seemed a long time had passed when he awoke to the sounds of angry shouting.

"No, the hell with it, I don't have to go along."

It was his father, and he was just outside the door of the house. The boy did not recognize the voice that answered his father.

"Well, you sure as hell will go along," the voice cried. "The Russian working class didn't make no revolution so you God-damned jug-headed kulaks could get rich on our sweat! You don't have no choice about it, and if you're smart, you'll—"

"If you're smart, you'll take your ass out of here," Grisha's father shouted. "I wouldn't mind thrashing you."

The stranger's voice grew louder.

"You fucking kulak, your days are numbered," he shouted. "We know how to handle fucking kulak robbers, you snake. We'll kick you out in the—"

"Get the hell out of here," his father shouted. There was a heavy thud as a body hit the door; boots stamped in the yard; men grunted and cursed.

In the darkness, the boy's mother flew through the room and flung the door open.

"Get away, you trash," she screamed.

More scuffling, a thud, and a splash.

"Agh! Agh! Pig slop! Pah, the bitch threw pig slop on me! I'll get your—" A sudden thump stopped the stranger's voice. He made a coughing, gagging sound.

"I'll split your head open, you four-eyed horse!" his father bellowed, enraged. "Go on, get the hell out of here!"

"That's all right, kulak; that's all right. We have ways to take care of you shits," the stranger's voice shouted from farther out in the yard. He spat and coughed between curses.

"You'll be sorry, kulaks, snakes, turds!" he cried. "By God, you wait. You'll get it!"

Peering out from the stove nook, the boy could see his father's silhouette against the moonlit doorway. He held an axe in one hand; his chest heaved with his breathing.

"God save us, God save us, what's with that scum, Kolya, what does he want?" the mother wailed. She scurried inside and lit the kerosene lamp on the table. She was wearing her gray woolen nightdress and on her legs a pair of thick woolen stockings.

"They want to take our little plot, the crocodiles, they said they'll kick us out. Well, we'll see; we'll see about that!"

Grisha crouched in the shadowy niche, watching his parents with wide, terrified eyes. He did not speak and they did not notice him in their fear, anger, and confusion.

His father took down a tin cup from a shelf, and a bottle. He splashed vodka into the cup and took a deep swallow. The liquid dribbled onto his beard and he wiped it away with his sleeve.

"These bastards from the regional Soviet, they say it's supposed to be collectivization now. We kick out one czar, and we get a whole committee in his place! The snakes want to make us serfs again. They want to take our land away from us. Well, the hell with that!"

He took another swallow from the cup. His wife held her head in her hands and moaned.

"These bastards get a bit of red rag on their arms and they think they're God Almighty," he said.

Grisha's father talked in angry, incoherent outbursts. He talked of the meetings in the village, the speeches, the voting, the shouting, and the fights.

His wife moaned and rocked back and forth on the bench. "Ay, Kolya," she wailed. "They say they shot three kulaks in Krivoi Rog, and..."

"So what the hell does that have to do with me?" he raged, turning his angry, bloodshot eyes on his wife. "I ain't no kulak. Do I look rich?" He spread his arms and looked around the room. "Is this the Winter Palace? I work for my bread and my kasha." He held up his two gnarled fists.

"A kulak is a kulak. I ain't one."

"Please, please, Kolya," his wife wailed. "Please don't provoke them; they have guns...."

The boy's father paused, staring into his cup. He poured some more from the bottle.

"Well, so what?" he growled. "They can't just go around and shoot anybody they please. Even before '17 they didn't go around like that, shooting whoever looked cockeyed. I talked to Stephan Leontievich, and he agrees. We'll go to the authorities and complain; they'll take these bastards in hand...."

Suddenly the sounds of tramping boots and men's voices sounded outside. The father leapt to his feet, sending the tin cup to the floor with a clatter.

The boy's heart pounded. He looked toward the door, where the stamping of boots rose to a thunder.

The door burst open, so hard that it tore away from the top hinge. It smashed against the wall and sagged over crookedly. At the sound of the crash the boy's heart rose to his throat and he squeezed back into the dark stove niche.

His mother screamed.

A tall man strode across the room, followed by more strange men. A band of red streaked the tall man's arm, and in his hand the boy saw a black revolver. A bench crashed to the floor; his mother's scream filled the room.

"All right, kulak, now we'll see..." It was the voice of the man who had fought with his father outside.

The space around the table became a jumble of red armbands and brown leather jackets. Grisha's father spoke in a choked, frightened voice: "Agh, get way, you devils... you'd better... aach... let go... damn you..."

The boy pressed his body against the back of the stone wall. His heart hammered beneath his cotton nightshirt. He saw the back of his mother's head, her blond hair flowing.

He heard her scream.

The figures parted for a second and the boy saw his father's face. It was contorted with fear and rage, the black eyes rolling, the mouth gaping. A fist, the fist of the tall man, shot out. It grabbed the curls of the father's beard, entangling itself in them.

The tall man gave a jerk, and Grisha saw his father's head come down, the fist in the beard showing white against the glistening curls. His father's body lurched forward and the boy saw boots dragging across the earthen floor. They bounced as they clattered over the threshold. His father's voice, strangled, cried out: "Let go, you shits, you worms... aach... turd..."

Suddenly the room was empty, the kerosene lamp sending shadows dancing on the walls. The door, with its hanging, broken hinge, framed the blackness of the night.

From outside came the prolonged sound of his mother's scream, and beneath it came a sharp slap: a pistol shot. A brief silence, and the scream again, higher, louder.

A second shot.

Silence.

As the crack of the second shot echoed away, the boy sucked in his breath and held it. He heard only the wild thudding of his heart.

He heard another shot in the yard. Another. Voices. Footsteps. The gate squeaked.

Silence.

The boy crouched in the niche, pressed against the stone wall, his eyes fixed unblinking on the open space where the door hung on its one hinge. The kerosene lamp sputtered and went out; a chill crept in. But the boy neither moved nor shivered. He stayed there for a long time. He could not tell how long it was or what time it was until a gray light began to show in the sky. He did not take his eyes from the doorway.

He moved slightly, paused, and then crept to the edge of the stove niche and dropped silently to the icy floor. He found his felt boots, his trousers, and his sheepskin coat. He put them on.

He crept to the broken door and looked into the yard. In the dim light he saw a formless shape, halfway from the door to the gate. It was black, with a pale slash across it. He stood a long while in the doorway, barely breathing. Then he walked slowly into the yard.

He approached the black shape, and it began to take form.

His father lay face down, nose against the frozen earth. The back of his head glistened with dark blood, small streams that had trickled around his ears and merged into a hard, frozen puddle beneath the black beard.

The boy's mother sprawled face down over her husband's body, her large belly across the small of his back. On the woolen nightdress, midway between the shoulders, was a dark spot the size of a pancake. The gown was twisted and its hem was pulled halfway up the thighs. Stark white flesh showed there, lumpy and veined behind the knees. The toes turned inward in the woolen stockings.

His mother's blond hair lay upon the earth around her head, rich and luxurious. Only the hair seemed to have life remaining.

Tears formed in Grisha's eyes, but he made no sound. He stood, looking at the cold white flesh and the soft blond hair, for a very long time.

5.

Moscow is a northern city of short summer nights. When Kuznetsov awoke late Friday evening, the sky still shed a pale glow through the window. He lay for several minutes on the lumpy divan blinking at the plastic-shaded wall lamp above, deciding whether he should try to go back to sleep or reach up and turn on the light. At length, he raised himself on one elbow and snapped on the light. The sudden glare made him squint, and it drove away the soft ivory luminescence at the window.

He groaned heavily, dropped his legs to the floor, and sat up on the edge of the divan. He was sore from the unaccustomed exertion of running from the man in the gray jacket. His trousers still were damp from the sweat. Kuznetsov felt cold. He looked at his watch. It was almost ten o'clock in the evening, a good time to take a bath and wash underwear. Kuznetsov lived in an apartment that had belonged to a well-to-do merchant until the Revolution, when it was taken over by the state and divided so four families could live in it. It was the same with most of the old Moscow apartments, but the government was on a building program that promised to put all Moscow families in private apartments within ten years. Kuznetsov did not care about that. As a bachelor he had last priority for private apartments and he was content that it should be so. He had lived ten years in the room on Oruzheiny Lane and was accustomed to it. He needed nothing more.

In his apartment nine persons shared a single bathroom and they all cooked their meals on the four-burner gas range in a small kitchen. Two years before, they had pooled money to buy a ZIL refrigerator.

The space inside the refrigerator was divided among them. Kuznetsov shared the bottom shelf with Alexandra Ivanovna Fomina, a kindly, heavy-breasted pediatrician from the Botkinsky Hospital. Dr. Fomina was the single occupant of a spacious room near the entrance, once the parlor of the merchant's household. She had lived in it since before the war, longer than any other tenant of the building.

She was a widow.

The middle shelf of the ZIL refrigerator belonged to the Gemiches: big, hearty Vasily Gemich and his wife and their two children. Vasily Efimovich Gemich was the chairman of the house committee that administered the twelve communal apartments in the four-story building, a jovial and likable man, a can-

didate member of the Communist Party. He hoped
and expected soon to become a full member.

The top shelf of the ZIL belonged to the old Velidze
couple, who lived in a former bedroom and pantry of
the apartment with their grown son, Volodya Velidze.
The Velidzes, parents and son, were secretive, swarthy
people who provoked frequent disputes over the use of
the bathroom and kitchen. They had moved into the
apartment six years before, later than any of the others, and Gemich's house committee had adjudicated
more than a dozen quarrels involving them. The most
recent difficulties had arisen because the Velidzes ob-
jected to the length of time spent in the bathroom by
Gemich's fourteen-year-old daughter, Valya. The
matter came to a head when Volodya Velidze angrily
kicked open the locked door one morning and ordered Valya out. The girl's father, seething with rage,
called a house committee meeting to issue a formal
warning to Volodya that he would be expelled from the
house if such incidents continued.

That was how Kuznetsov and his neighbors divided
their refrigerator, their apartment, and their lives.

On this night Kuznetsov found both the bathroom
and the kitchen blessedly empty. In his section of the
refrigerator was a piece of black bread, butter, and a
can of fish. He ate it gratefully, but wished that he had
not lost the bag with the yogurt. He felt hungry for
yogurt, and after he finished his meal he wished for
the candies he had bought for dessert and which had
gone the way of the yogurt.

After his supper he went to the bathroom and washed five suits of underwear in the sink. Then he undressed and squatted in the tub for a thorough washing with the hand shower. He soaped and scrubbed his hair, murmuring with concern as a half dozen strands, some black and some gray, washed down the drain with the rinse water.

He dried himself, put on a pair of clean pajamas, and went back to his room with his pile of wet laundry. He stretched a cotton cord from the corner of the wardrobe to the door frame and draped the wet underwear and socks over it. He made up the divan with a coarse cotton sheet and a light blanket and went to bed. He snapped off the wall lamp and closed his eyes, smelling the freshness of the clean pajamas. His legs ached from fatigue, and thinking of the ache his mind turned to the panic of the afternoon in the Metro. He opened his eyes to stare into the darkness. He closed them again, and after a time he slept.

It did not stay dark for long. The northern sun rises a little after two-thirty at that time of year, and it already was high in a flawless blue sky Saturday morning when Kuznetsov rolled out of bed. He smelled the beauty of the day and went to the window to let it in. He unlatched the double-framed window and threw it wide open, taking a deep breath of fresh air that rippled in on a light breeze.

Because it was a weekend, there was not much traffic noise from outside. On the sidewalk below he could see people in shirt-sleeves and light dresses. A sense of well-being rose in him and it made him smile.

He decided to do what he'd so evasively told Repin he planned to do: go to the park, and sweat, and look at the girls.

He hung the pajamas on their hook and pulled on a clean pair of underwear from among those hanging from the cotton cord. He started to take down his suit and tie from the wardrobe, but he changed his mind and put on a pair of light brown cotton trousers, a soft knitted shirt, and a pair of sandals over thin nylon socks. He buttoned the shirt to the top button, smiled at his prim reflection in the mirror, and unbuttoned the top button. He examined himself in the mirror, smiled again, and left the room.

Kuznetsov locked the door behind him and was opening the communal apartment's outer door when he heard Dr. Fomina's door click behind him.

"Well, well, the proper Engineer Kuznetsov is loosening his collar today?" Dr. Fomina clucked cheerfully and winked. Kuznetsov turned to smile a greeting for his refrigerator shelf-mate.

"Ah, even proper engineers can't resist a day like today, Doctor," he said. She looked nice today, Kuznetsov thought. She wore a flowered dress and white shoes. Her hair had been brushed out and was allowed to hang free with only a clasp at the back, in contrast to the stern professional bun she normally wore. Her dress was belted at the waist and Kuznetsov noticed that her figure was more attractively full and feminine than it appeared when she was wearing her usual dark suit.

"And I don't suppose this is the uniform of a baby doctor, eh?" Kuznetsov said, smiling.

Dr. Fomina smoothed the dress self-consciously. "Not on this day," she said, laughing. "No squalling kids today—I'm going outside."

An oddly boyish feeling of exhilaration came over Kuznetsov. He bowed awkwardly and held the door open for her.

"In that case," he said, "perhaps Madame Doctor would accept the company of an honorable engineer...." He paused. "Er, that is, unless you have plans..."

"I'd be delighted," she said. "I'm not meeting anybody, that's for sure. We can chaperone each other. I'll keep the young girls away from you, and you keep the young men away from me."

They went out into the sunshine, laughing. On the street Kuznetsov offered her his arm.

They strolled leisurely across Mayakovsky Square and along Gorky Street, passing the Metro entrance where Kuznetsov had bolted down the stairs the day before. The recollection of fear and panic started to come back to him, but Dr. Fomina grasped his arm and pointed across the street.

"Hey, engineer," she said, "let's get a picnic lunch at Yeliseyev's!"

They crossed the street and walked past Pushkin Square to the elegant facade of a food store that bore the name in gold letters: GASTRONOM NO. 1. That was its official name, but to every Muscovite it was Yeliseyev's, the name of the rich merchant family that had owned it before the government took over food retailing and replaced the prerevolutionary names with assigned numbers. It was a tribute to Yeliseyev's prominence that it was given No. 1, and over the years the ministry had taken care to preserve the nineteenth-century elegance: hand-carved hardwood fittings, cut-glass windows, chandeliers, and marble countertops. Burnished wooden shelves carried the best foodstuffs available on the open market. It was said that the manager kept even better foodstuffs on hand in the stock rooms for special customers—who made themselves special by paying bribes. The goods, arranged in attractive display pyramids, were sold by red-capped girls chosen for good looks and manners. It was the best store in Moscow.

"What would you like for lunch today, Shura?" Kuznetsov asked as they pushed through the store's crowded aisles. He used her nickname self-consciously, but she showed no sign of embarrassment. He always had called her Alexandra Ivanovna, and she always had called him Alexander Nikolayevich; never once had they adopted the intimacy of nicknames or the familiar "thou" form of speech during the entire ten years that Kuznetsov had lived in the house on Oruzheiny Lane.

Dr. Fomina put two fingers to her cheek and surveyed the shelves. "I think, for a starter, red caviar, eh?" she said. "On black bread. And for the main course a sausage, with some little onions; how does that sound?"

"A feast," he said. "They've got salted sturgeon, too; we can get some sour cream to go with it."

They divided, Dr. Fomina joining the queues for the sausage and sour cream, Kuznetsov lining up for the sturgeon and a jar of red caviar. They made their purchases and Kuznetsov guided her to the wine counter.

"White or red, madame?" he asked.

"Oh, how wickedly elegant." She laughed. "On a day like this, I think a robust red, don't you?"

"Red it is," Kuznetsov said, joining the queue at the counter. He bought a bottle of rich Georgian Khvanchkara—it was said to be Stalin's favorite—and then stopped at the confectionery counter for a box of Red October candies.

"Dessert," he said. "I've had my mouth set for these candies for the past two days."

They stuffed their purchases into a net bag that Dr. Fomina pulled from her handbag. At a bakery nearby they stopped for a half loaf of fresh black bread and added it to the bulging net bag.

"What a kitchen we have here, Shura!" He laughed. "This would have fed my whole platoon for a week during the war."

"You were a soldier in the war?" she asked. "Where?"

Kuznetsov hesitated. It was a general rule of his life that he did not talk about the past. It was for that reason he had never remarried, never made close friends, and never took ladies to the park.

He glanced at Dr. Fomina. "The Leningrad front," he said. He volunteered nothing else and neither of them spoke for a moment. Dr. Fomina finally broke the awkward silence.

"You never say anything about your war experiences, do you, Sasha?" she said.

Kuznetsov felt a quiver of pleasure at the use of his nickname. His apprehension eased. "They weren't very pleasant, Shura," he said. "I prefer to forget them. And I don't believe you talk of the war either, do you?"

Dr. Fomina smiled gently as they crossed Tverskoy Boulevard and entered the shaded park dividing the two lanes of traffic.

"I spent the war here in Moscow," she said. "It was not so bad, of course, but it was here that I...that I last saw my Alyosha."

"Your husband?" Kuznetsov made the question a statement.

She smiled and cast a glance at Kuznetsov. "Well, he got a three-day leave in August, before the Germans got close to Moscow. It was beautiful weather that year, the sun shining every day but not too hot. Like today." She paused and laughed in a girlish way that pleased Kuznetsov. He looked at her and saw she was blushing.

"It was lovely weather, Sasha, but I have to tell you we didn't even go outside for the whole three days. We spent day and night in my big room on Oruzheiny Lane."

Her blush turned crimson, and he was surprised at how young and pretty she looked. He imagined her in the room with its wide bed, she and her Alyosha in it, clinging to each other. And he thought of his own big carved bed in Leningrad, where he and his Sonya had lain clutching each other during their short, happy married life in 1941, and of the fine weather that summer. They, too, almost never went outside.

"And Alyosha?" he asked.

The smile faded. So did the blush. "Stalingrad in '43," she said. "His division was surrounded by the Germans and God knows what happened. I spent a lot of time sending letters to the Ministry of Defense and contacting soldiers who fought at Stalingrad, but never found out anything. A lot of the men were killed, but he was not listed as dead. He was listed as missing. Maybe he was taken prisoner, but you know how that was," she continued.

"Yes," Kuznetsov murmured. "Yes, I know how that was."

Dr. Fomina took Kuznetsov's arm and they walked in silence along the boulevard.

"Lots of our prisoners died in the German camps," she said. "I think they may have been the lucky ones. The ones who came back went to our own camps in the east and they died there. I think it would be better to die at the hands of the enemy than in the bosom of an ungrateful motherland...." She broke off and looked away.

Kuznetsov felt cold and heavy. They passed a bench where two old men sat studying a chessboard. He wanted to say something, but the only appropriate thing to say would be too close to the truth of his life.

"We..." he began, and stopped. He was silent a moment, and then continued. "We have some things in common, Shura," he said. She turned and looked at him and he saw that her eyes shone with the beginnings of tears. "I had a wife, and our time together we spent in, well...what the hell, in bed." A blush rose to his own cheeks.

"Not really, Sasha, not the proper engineer!" She laughed.

"Not so proper then," he retorted. "I was just a peasant boy, fresh from the fields, working in Leningrad..." He stopped. He was saying too much.

"Was she pretty, Sasha?" she asked.

"Yes," he said after a pause. "Very pretty. She was a student of engineering at the university; very smart, she was. Smart and hardworking. A Komsomol leader. And a real Russian beauty."

He chuckled. "We married just before the war. Including the few days we had after the war began, I guess we probably spent all of six weeks together as man and wife."

Kuznetsov and Dr. Fomina crossed the street and walked in silence past the Union of Journalists. Kuznetsov did not speak. Dr. Fomina glanced at him and asked softly, "What became of her, Sasha?"

"As I say, we have a lot in common," he replied. He stuffed his hands in his pockets. He felt an intense discomfort at the need to lie. "I don't know. I had a letter saying she was pregnant; that was just before the Germans cut the roads to Leningrad. It was the last I heard. I got back to Leningrad after the blockade and the apartment where we...not just the apartment, but the whole building. It was all gone. Not a wall left standing. Most of the people were evacuated or they were dead...."

"And you don't know whether she..."

Kuznetsov looked down at the sidewalk and frowned. He was saying far too much.

"No." The word was abrupt. He looked up and grimaced. "Hey, look, why are we so gloomy on such a day? Let's leave the past behind and go to Luzhniki Park."

He strode ahead so quickly that Dr. Fomina had to take skipping steps to keep up with him. They crossed Kalinin Prospekt at the underpass and took the Metro at the Arbat station. The train was crowded with Muscovites dressed for pleasure and laden with sausages and wine. All the seats were taken, so Kuznetsov and Dr. Fomina had to stand.

"My goodness, Sasha," she said. "It looks like all of Moscow is going to the park today."

The crowd pushed into the car and it started off with a jolt that caught Dr. Fomina by surprise. She stumbled backward and Kuznetsov put out his hand to steady her, feeling the soft smooth curve midway between hip and waist. He held her a moment before he realized she had regained her balance and had grasped the chrome bar overhead. He pulled his hand away in embarrassment; they both reddened. Dr. Fomina laughed, and Kuznetsov experienced a pleasant tingling in his stomach.

They rode in silence to the Luzhniki stop and by the time they reached the grassy park Kuznetsov had forgotten the unease that had troubled him earlier. They found a spot on an open, grassy area with a view of the Moscow River and of Lenin Hills beyond, where the government kept plush guest houses for important visitors. Dr. Fomina arranged her handbag and the picnic lunch on an unfolded copy of *Izvestia*, and they sat for a few minutes admiring the bright day.

Dr. Fomina shifted restlessly and declared, ''Well, no need to waste this sun.'' She loosened the sash of her dress and began to unbutton it. Kuznetsov looked away, embarrassed, but from the corner of his eye he could see the movements of her arms as she pulled the dress over her head and he glimpsed the shiny pink of her rayon brassiere and panties. He never would get used to the custom of Moscow women, normally prim to the point of intolerance, of stripping to their underwear in public parks. He waited until Dr. Fomina lay back on the grass and then he unbuttoned his shirt and pulled it over his head.

He caught sight of the double roll of fat at his waist and pulled in his stomach. He struggled to hold it in as he folded his shirt and lay down on his back. He put the folded shirt under his head and cast a glance at Dr. Fomina. Her eyes were closed and Kuznetsov could see the rising and falling of her generous breasts and belly. He was surprised at the smoothness of her skin, at the full and graceful lines of her figure, which were so much more womanly now than when hidden beneath the severe blue suit of a middle-aged baby doctor. Ev-

idently it was not her first time in the sun this summer. She was tanned a light brown, with a whiteness
between her breasts where the sun had not reached.

"This is very nice," she said, suddenly opening her
eyes and glancing at Kuznetsov. He jerked his eyes
away and stared at the sky, embarrassed. She chuckled softly.

A little after noon they ate their lunch, drinking the
heady Khvanchkara wine directly from the bottle,
passing it back and forth. They spread the red caviar
on bread and munched the onions with slices of sausage or strips of pink sturgeon. Soon they felt full and
drowsy and they dozed quietly on the grass. Once,
when Kuznetsov stirred, he felt the warmth of Dr.
Fomina's shoulder against his. He moved his fingers
and they touched hers; as he drifted into sleep her
hand slipped gently into his.

He awoke later, and with a start he realized that
their fingers were closely twined. He lay for several
minutes listening to her breath, light and shallow, and
feeling their fingers together. He glanced at her and
saw that her eyes, too, were open. As his head moved,
she turned to look at him and their eyes met. They
held the eye contact for a moment, and he felt her
hand lightly squeeze his own. He returned the pressure and both of them smiled slightly. They did not
speak then, or later, when Dr. Fomina sat up and began putting on her dress.

They wrapped the remains of the picnic in newspaper and were walking along the footpath of the river
embankment before Dr. Fomina spoke. "It was a

lovely picnic, Sasha," she said. "Thank you very much."

Kuznetsov smiled, and inside he felt a quiver of excitement and anticipation, something he had not experienced since his days of courting Sonya in Leningrad before the war. He took Dr. Fomina's hand in his, and at his touch she grasped his fingers firmly. They walked like that, hand in hand like a pair of school children, all the way to the Metro.

They took the train to Mayakovsky Square, saying little and holding hands all the way to the house on Oruzheiny Lane. Kuznetsov pushed open the old brown door and they climbed the stairs. He opened the apartment door with his key and they stepped inside the dim hallway. Kuznetsov shuffled awkwardly as if to move toward his room, but he stopped and looked at Dr. Fomina. She was gazing directly at him with a steady, womanly smile.

"Will you have some tea with me, Comrade Engineer?" she asked.

"Of...of course, I would be delighted," Kuznetsov said, standing stiffly. He thought of the big bed, and again his heart pounded and that fine tingling sensation came again to his stomach. He followed her into her apartment and sat at an old dining table while she went to the kitchen to fill the electric samovar. The bed lay in front of him, covered with a rich Central Asian spread. He looked at it until she returned with the samovar and plugged it in.

They talked of work and weather and food prices as the samovar boiled for tea, and they continued talk-

ing and drinking tea as the afternoon sun fell behind
the buildings on the opposite side of the street, envel-
oping the room in subdued light. Then they sat for a
long while in silence, looking at each other across the
width of the old dining table.

Keeping her eyes on his, Dr. Fomina slowly rose.
Kuznetsov also stood. She walked to the bed and sat
on the edge of the Central Asian cover; after a moment he followed her, and sat beside her. He took her
hand and held it, and they turned their heads to each
other and they kissed, lightly and long. She gently
slipped her hand from his, took her lips away and
rested her forehead against his. He could sense the
movement of her hands on the sash and on the buttons of her dress; then she moved, stood, and her
clothes fell to the floor, leaving her naked before him.
She began folding back the cover and Kuznetsov stood
and watched her large breasts swing heavy and comfortable beneath her, nippled and smooth. He began
removing his shirt, unbuckling his belt, all the while
watching Shura, the muscles of her thigh, the bend-
ing knee as she climbed into the bed, turning, a triangle of dark hair that vanished as she slipped beneath
the sheet, her face and her round eyes looking at him,
a soft woman's smile.

His trousers dropped to the floor and he fumbled
awkwardly to pull down his underdrawers and take off
his sandals and socks. He sat at the edge of the bed
and felt the weight of her body near him. She reached
up and pulled gently at his shoulder and he slipped

easily beneath the sheet; both her arms went around him, her thigh over his thigh, firm and heavy.

"Love me, Sasha," she whispered; she kissed his ear. Her breath was heavy and warm and rich with the scent of onions and he liked it; he moved his face to her neck and shoulder, smelling the strong and natural scent of womanly skin. It was familiar. Too familiar. He opened his eyes.

The image of his mother burst before him, her smell, her big arms, her wide hips, her round belly in the small of his father's back and the white flesh of her thighs beneath the twisted hem of her gown; her lush blond hair. Kuznetsov drew back. Shura sensed the change and her voluptuous, rhythmic movements stopped; her breath came more slowly, more shallowly. There was a long silence.

"Sasha," she murmured. "What is it?"

He could not answer.

"Sasha," she whispered. "I ... Sasha, please, it's been a long time, Sasha, I'd like ..."

Kuznetsov sighed heavily. "Please forgive me, Shura," he mumbled. "It was a mistake for me to...I shouldn't have."

She forced a laugh. "Please don't worry, Sasha, I'll make no demands. I ask little." They were silent another moment. "You and I, Sasha," she said in a soft, serious voice, "we're two lonely people. Don't think I'll trick you, or trap you. I know I'm...well, I'm old and fat...."

"No, Shura, don't say that!" Kuznetsov said. He sat on the edge of the bed, awkward in his nakedness.

"You are a very kind woman, and a pretty woman, too. But, you see, I'm an old dog; it's much too late for me to be a . . . well, a companion, a companion of the soul, so to speak. . . ."

She lay quietly and did not answer him.

"I've been alone for such a long time, and I'm afraid I would not . . . from long habit I'd keep secret thoughts to myself, and, you see, these thoughts would become like a poison for us. I'm afraid you'd be very unhappy: you'd regret . . ."

"How could I be more unhappy?" Her voice quavered, and Kuznetsov realized with a sinking feeling that she was going to cry.

"We . . ." Her voice broke. "We, Sasha, we could share our thoughts, I know we could . . ." She stopped and swallowed.

Kuznetsov rose and commenced dressing.

"Perhaps it would be better to share with somebody," Shura said, tears and desperation in her voice. "It would be easier." She wiped at her eyes with the pillowcase and she sat up in the bed, pulling up the sheet to cover her naked breasts. Kuznetsov buckled his belt and pulled on his shirt.

"I'm sorry, Shura," he said. "My secrets are not easily shared, even with you." He started slowly toward the door and paused to look back at her. She sat on the bed with her knees pulled up to her breasts, gripping the sheet at her shoulders. Her eyes glistened and tears shone on her cheeks.

"Please forgive me, Shura," he murmured, and he left.

Kuznetsov closed the door softly behind him and went down the dark corridor to his own apartment. He opened the door and went inside. It was hot and stuffy in the gloomy room and he started to open the windows.

He stopped short and stared incredulously at the windows. His head spun and he felt the pain in his chest, just as he had the day before.

The windows! They're closed! They're closed tight and the curtains are drawn. I left the windows open. I left them open. Somebody was here!

Kuznetsov searched his memory. Could he have closed them and forgotten? No. He remembered the brightness of the room as he left it for the gloomy darkness of the hallway. The windows had been open. So had the curtains. He peered around the room and his eye caught the dry underwear, still hanging on the cotton cord he had stretched from the wardrobe to the door frame. One undershirt bore a distinct crease, made by the cord where it had hung. But the crease was two inches below the cord. The undershirt had been taken off the cord, or it had fallen off and it had been replaced differently.

Frantically, Kuznetsov examined the room. He opened drawers and tried to remember if they were as he had left them. He pulled open the wardrobe; the clothes seemed to be in order. At the bottom of the wardrobe lay a suitcase he used for keeping his papers and his winter clothing; he dragged it out, put it on the divan and snapped it open. On one side was a stack of folded woolen clothing; on the other, papers and en-

velopes. He felt through the papers and pulled out the
old cloth wallet, the one he had brought with him in
'46 and which contained all the papers, the ones they
gave him in Munich. He unfolded the wallet and took
out the yellowed documents.

They were all there. The passport; the travel vouch-
ers; the discharge papers; all of them. He checked,
then rechecked. They seemed to be in order. He sat
heavily on the divan, holding the wallet in his hands
and staring at it.

Had he been followed from the embassy? Did Repin have a suspicion? He stood and paced the room.
He went to the window and pulled back the curtain:
The window latches were firmly in place. He looked
down at the street, at the few pedestrians walking in
the fading twilight.

And he thought of Dr. Fomina.

With a sick feeling he went over the events of the
day. She had come out of her room just after he left
his. She'd managed to keep him out the whole day, in
the park and then in her room.

*My God! Were they using her to keep me away? And
those questions! She got me talking about things I've
never mentioned to a soul.*

Kuznetsov pressed his hands to his eyes and re-
called all he had told Shura about himself: a wife,
army service on the Leningrad front, all things that his
papers would not support. He paced the room, running a hand through his hair.

He smashed a fist into his hand, cursing himself and
her. He'd told her that he had secrets he could share

with nobody. But he had; he had shared them with her, and perhaps she would share the secrets with *them*.

He felt choked and confined. He needed air. He opened the door and stepped into the hallway. Dr. Fomina's door clicked open. He looked toward the sound.

Her eyes were red and ugly, and her hair hung down in unruly tangles. He saw puffy blotched folds of skin on her face; her body stood bulky and lumpy in a tattered brown robe. He felt a surge of revulsion and he glared at her.

"Sasha?" she said. "What have I..."

He spun away and rushed out, slamming the door behind him.

NKVD

PEOPLE'S MILITIA DIVISION

April 16, 1932

From: Youth Services Section, People's Militia, Tver
To: Superintendent, Dzerzhinsky Children's Home,
         Leningrad
Subject: Child Malmudov, Grigory Nikolayevich

Comrade Superintendent:

The subject child Malmudov, G.N., of upper-middle peasant class origin, is transferred to your custody and responsibility in accordance with directives of the NKVD regarding the Communist rehabilitation and education of orphaned children.

The subject child was taken into Militia custody while engaged in the theft of bread from Bakery No. 8, Stalin District, Tver. Investigation revealed subject child is of upper-middle kulak parents who were subjected to state discipline for class crimes, and are deceased.

The People's Procurator has suspended prosecution of subject child on condition of acceptable behavior in the Dzerzhinsky Home for Children.

You are hereby directed to report to the office of the procurator monthly on the political and educational deportment of subject child.

V. Petrov
Major, PM

6.

The killings of his mother and father brought terrible and incomprehensible misery to the small life of Grisha Malmudov, a misery that did not abate until Leningrad.

Leningrad: enormous, bustling, healthy, happy city; tram lines and electric lights; spires, ships, smoke-stacks, pavement, steam heat, canned food. It was paradise, and Grisha always felt a deep, human love for the city, its River Neva and its European sheen.

Leningrad relieved his sufferings; it gave him home, warmth, food, dignity; it gave him his first love.

By most standards, even those of the Soviet Union in the 1930s, Grisha Malmudov did not live well in Leningrad. But he never complained and could not tolerate those who did.

"What have you got to grumble about?" he once scolded a tablemate who disparaged the cabbage soup. "Not too long ago I was eating rat, and without cooking it," he said. "There's real honest-to-God beef meat in this soup, comrade; you're lucky to have it."

Despite his sufferings in the collectivization campaign, Grisha knew he could have been much worse off. He was often cold, but did not freeze to death. He was often hungry, but survived. And he never had to eat human flesh.

AFTER NEIGHBORS CAME and took away the stiffened corpses of his mother and father, there was more death and much hunger. He lived for a few weeks with the family of his friend Misha, but one day some people came to the house and Misha's parents, frightened, told Grisha he had to leave because he was of the kulak class. He slept two nights in the open before his Uncle Fyodor came and fetched him. Uncle Fyodor was drunk when he arrived, and the cursing, red-eyed little man smashed him in the ear because he couldn't walk fast enough on the road to the nearby village of Davidenko.

In some ways it was worse with Uncle Fyodor than it had been when he was sleeping in the open. There never was enough to eat, and his Uncle Fyodor and Aunt Lyuda resented his presence and his hunger. Fyodor frequently lashed him with a harness strap and called him a hog; his aunt also beat him, but it was worse when she heaped abuse upon him in her shrill, nasal voice.

"He's a human tapeworm," she wailed. "He eats like a pig, eat, eat, eat; why, oh why did God give me this little hog? Times are so bad the flies are dying, and God sent me this piglet to fatten.''

Despite her complaints, Grisha had little to eat and he was constantly hungry. Later, when they moved from Dadidenko to Krylo, things became really hard. Uncle Fyodor finally died there. He had been sick and he grew so thin that after the people came and stripped his body for burial, all his bones showed through the gray skin.

Auntie Lyuda always had been thin, but she did not seem to get any thinner during the Collectivization famine. She kept her strength.

Only once in Krylo did Grisha eat his fill, and that time he ate so much he became ill. The peasants in the town heard that the state expropriation squads were coming to take a proportion of their animals. In defiance, they themselves slaughtered all their cattle, pigs, goats, and chickens; they ate what they could but left most of the dead animals in the fields. When the state squad came, all they found were stinking carcasses, swollen and swarming with flies, and uncommonly well-fed villagers.

The state squad leader was enraged, and he had two village men taken into a field beside the road. There they were shot as a warning to the others. Many of the peasants fled the village, both out of fear of further retaliation and because the slaughter meant there would be nothing to eat there. Among those who fled was Auntie Lyuda, who had killed her goat and chickens.

Grisha had a clear memory of the stink of dead livestock as he and Auntie Lyuda walked along the road from the village. They passed by the two dead men, who had been left unburied in the field. They lay face down with their hands tied at their backs. A black, shiny gore oozed from the backs of their heads and their bodies were bloated like the carcasses of the dead livestock.

After the slaughter, the hard times worsened to real famine. With the coming of winter, his Auntie Lyuda abandoned Grisha in a dismal Russian town called Gryaznaya Voda, which meant "dirty water." They had gone to sleep in a cowshed and when he awoke she was gone, leaving him his clothes and a few crusts of bread.

After that, Grisha lived by his wits, and during that bitter winter he ate rats and witnessed cannibalism. He killed the rats by hitting them with stones. He skinned them and cooked them when he could. When he could get no fire, he ate them uncooked. He ate all, even cracking the larger bones for the marrow. He ate the intestines after sliding two fingers down their slippery length to rid them of their contents. Sometimes he lived briefly among groups of men or older boys, foraging through the countryside stealing and poaching. But life among the packs of starved, desperate youths was treacherous. Grisha preferred to be on his own.

During that winter he saw human flesh cooked and eaten. He had hidden near a bridge where three men were cooking meat, waiting for them to finish their meal so he could search for leftovers. When they finally went away, he scurried under the bridge and found bones with warm meat still on them. He grabbed one and tore off a strip of meat, but as he was about to shove it into his mouth he saw charred human fingers at the end of the bone. He stared in horror at the hand, and then he saw a head, the head of a woman, lying in the frozen dirt. He threw down the bone and fled.

Near the end of the winter, when the thaw had turned much of Russia to mud, Grisha had the good fortune to be caught breaking into a bread store in Tver. The local Party Committee chairwoman, an old-style Communist who still saw her duty as serving the needs of the downtrodden, intervened to put him in an orphanage instead of a jail. The district procurator sent him to an orphans' home in Leningrad, a bright, airy place overlooking the Neva River and the needle spire of the Peter and Paul Fortress.

The orphanage was one of many to be named in honor of Felix Dzerzhinsky—described in the official literature as "a great revolutionary, who organized the Cheka to protect the security of the young workers and peasants' state from its enemies yet still had time to look after the welfare of orphans."

To Grisha Malmudov, Dzerzhinsky was something like a personal guardian angel.

"Comrade Dzerzhinsky was a follower and close friend of our Lenin and of our beloved Comrade Stalin," the orphanage history teacher said. "They saw that the class enemies would stop at nothing to destroy the victory of the Soviet working class, and they asked Comrade Dzerzhinsky to find a way to parry the attacks of the capitalist-monarchist classes and the wolves in sheep's clothing who plotted all sorts of ways to destroy the unity of our dear Party.''

Dzerzhinsky, the teacher explained, organized the Extraordinary Committee for the Combating of Counterrevolution and Sabotage, shortened to the acronym Cheka. The Chekists, he said, smashed the class enemies—the Trotskyites, the Left Opposition, the Right Opposition, the Social Revolutionaries and the kulaks.

Grisha absorbed the story of his benefactor with rapt attention, just as he absorbed the food and warmth that came with it. Although he was behind his classmates at the beginning, he caught up and passed them within a few months. He quickly learned to read the thin clothbound textbooks with their abbreviated, childlike biographies of Lenin and Stalin, histories of czarist tyranny, and descriptions of the October Revolution.

He excelled in arithmetic. The wild complexities of Russian grammar sometimes baffled him, but he won the class prize in mathematics when he completed elementary school at the orphanage in 1939. The arithmetical tables, like the Dzerzhinsky orphanage, offered him the comfort and security of predictability.

Before matriculation, the school director gave Grisha a chance to take the tests for advancement into upper school, but he politely declined the offer. He said he wanted to be a worker, and he asked the direc-

tor to find him a place in a factory apprentice school.
She promised to do so, and in a rush of emotion she
kissed him and sent him on his way, confused and
blushing with embarrassed pleasure.

Of all the teachers at the orphanage school Grisha
best remembered a teacher of trigonometry who
taught briefly in 1936, the year of the trial of the Anti-
Soviet Bloc of Rights and Trotskyites. The teacher was
at the slateboard explaining a theorem when three men
entered the room at the rear. The teacher stopped
talking and turned a ghostly pale as they advanced up
the narrow aisles between the children's desks, but
before they reached him, he spoke in a firm voice:

"If you please, comrades, kindly wait until I have
finished the lesson."

The men stopped and glanced at the one who
seemed to be in charge. He hesitated, then nodded.
They went to the back of the room and stood while the
teacher finished his explanation of the theorem in a
voice that trembled and broke with emotion. When the
explanation was done, the teacher put the chalk in its
tray, erased the board, and dismissed the class.

The children went into the schoolyard and watched
the doors. In a few minutes the men came out of the
school, two of them holding the teacher's arms and the
third walking behind him. The teacher walked erectly,
eyes straight ahead and jaw set in a firm line, but he
was quite pale. The four of them got into a black car
and drove away.

The next day the director summoned the children to
the assembly hall to read a statement charging that the

teacher was an "enemy of the people." Reading in a subdued voice, head down, she said:

"The Enemy of the People Galanov came from the petty bourgeois class, and in accordance with his class interests he has tried to turn back the gains of the Great Proletarian Revolution. He was exposed before the Party Aktiv as a follower of the traitor Trotsky, and it was shown that he actively opposed the correct decisions of the Party leadership regarding the teaching of mathematics, injecting anti-socialist, anti-people, and anti-Leninist notions into his teaching."

Later two more teachers, including the one assigned to replace the arrested Enemy of the People Galanov, also disappeared. Rumors flew among the children, but the teachers would not discuss the cases, and there was no assembly called to read an indictment against them.

The disappearances of the teachers darkened Grisha's life at the orphanage but did not destroy the security he found there. When it came time to leave the orphanage for the factory apprentice school, he became profoundly homesick.

The Proletarian Victory Diesel Engine Factory, when he reached it, did little at first to relieve his homesickness for the Dzerzhinsky orphanage. The factory was only half finished, and Grisha lived in a severely crowded barracks with a hundred other young apprentices. The boys were the charter class of the apprentice school, but at the beginning of their apprenticeship they learned nothing about factory crafts—they learned about heavy loads. They were assigned to work as ordinary laborers, carrying bricks, digging ditches, and manhandling wheelbarrows over the rough grounds of the a-building factory.

But after the first few weeks of loneliness and homesickness, Grisha began to enjoy his new life: the rough-and-tumble camaraderie of the boys' barracks, the new freedom, the new responsibility. He was well liked and he soon became a leader, joining the factory Komsomol, or Communist Youth League, and rising quickly to membership in the Guidance Committee of the Komsomol. That position made him one of the four or five most important leaders among the new apprentices, and it gave him a working day of twelve to fourteen hours. After work, he put in long hours on Komsomol chores, making posters, leading political discussion groups, and helping oversee the organization of apprentice teams.

Through the winter of 1939-40, the apprentices worked on construction of the plant, and it was nearly summer before the machinery began arriving for installation in the completed structure. For this phase of the work, Grisha was formally designated an apprentice lathe operator. Because he was a Komsomol official, he was appointed team leader of all the apprentices in the lathe shop.

It was because of these new duties that he met Sonya.

Sofia Arkadievna Vinogradova was a student-member of the chief engineer's staff and was doing a responsible engineering job even though she was only halfway through the Leningrad Engineering Institute.

Her studies were temporarily held in abeyance because there was such a severe shortage of engineers to complete the Third Five-Year plan that the most promising students of the institute were drafted to help get the factories started.

Grisha noticed her as soon as he arrived at the lathe shop to get instructions from the chief engineer, Nikolai Ivanovich Chudov. Chudov, a tall man with leonine gray hair and a distinguished manner, climbed to a packing case and addressed the apprentices. As he spoke, a girl stood beside the packing case with a stack of papers held to her bosom. Grisha could see only her shoulders and head, but that was enough.

She had jet-black hair, parted in the middle and pulled back in a bun at the nape of her neck. Her eyes were the kind that Russian artists idealized when they painted working-class beauties: sloed, black and lively, with a hint of Asia about them. Her skin was fair, smooth, and unblemished; her face oval and full. As Grisha watched, she smiled at something and two dimples appeared in her cheeks.

Grisha was captivated. He heard little of what the chief engineer had to say until he wound up his remarks by saying, "Fine, then; if you have no questions, Sofia Arkadievna will hand out work sheets. Team leaders please come forward." He indicated the dark-haired girl who smiled her dimpled smile and began distributing the papers to the team leaders. Grisha pushed forward among the other boys until he came face to face with Sonya. She looked directly into his eyes, a mocking half-smile on her face. He blushed and stammered. She laughed.

"Well, comrade, who are you?" she said in a voice loud enough for all to hear. "Leader of the dummies?"

The other apprentices laughed, and Grisha's blush turned a deep crimson. He stammered again, coughed, and finally managed to say: "I . . . I'm leader of Team 21, comrade. Please . . ."

The girl tossed her head and laughed again. "He talks!" she said. The boys laughed. Grisha shrank back, mortified.

Sofia Arkadievna saw his distress and touched his arm gently. "Here you are, Comrade Team Leader," she said in a soft voice. She winked playfully as he took the papers. "You'll be in my section. We'll be the machinery division shock workers."

Grisha smiled dizzily, took the papers, and fled in a haze of befuddled pleasure. He was in love.

He worked the rest of the day with distracted energy, clearing out the dirt and construction debris in the lathe shop to prepare it for receiving the new machinery. He worked late into the night and did not see Sonya again until the following morning, when he arrived early to receive instructions for the day. He sat on a crate, staring wearily at the wooden floor, and did not hear her come in.

"Hey, silent one!" she said.

Grisha jumped to his feet, startled and embarrassed. Again he could not find his tongue, and again he blushed to a warm crimson. She was dressed for heavy work in a pair of men's coveralls and a blue shirt buttoned at the collar. Even in such clothing she managed to look feminine.

"Tsk, Grisha, you look tired," Sonya said.

"Ah, yes, I...I slept poorly last night, Sofia Arkadievna," he stammered.

She rolled her eyes in disbelief. "Sofia Arkadievna! Am I your mother? Am I a grand duchess?" She touched his arm and he shivered with pleasure at the intimacy. "Please call me Sonya if you must be formal," she said. "But if you like me, even a little bit, please use 'thou' and call me Sonichka, all right?"

"Oh yes, Sonya...Sonichka, thank you, of course I will," Grisha said, blushing even more violently. Behind him the arriving apprentices snickered and whispered.

"Glory to God!" She laughed and squeezed his arm. "Much better, Comrade Team Leader. Let's get to work."

She gave Grisha his assignment and the two of them walked through the area where Grisha's team was to move lathes into position on the factory floor. Working from a large blueprint, they began measuring and marking the clean, oiled wooden floor for placing the machines at specially reinforced positions. When they had finished, she handed him the blueprint.

"Take this and just follow it," she said. "I have to spend the morning doing paperwork for Nikolai Ivanovich, so I'll depend on you, Comrade Team Leader."

Grisha nodded happily. The other apprentices snickered again. Sonya turned before she left. "Listen, Grishenka, I'll bring something to eat, some bread and kvass. We'll have lunch here and look things over. Will you have lunch with me?"

"Oh yes, of course, Sonya...Sonichka," he replied, grinning and blushing and shuffling his feet.

"See you," she said, and left for the chief engineer's office.

When she was out the door, the shouting, shoving apprentices crowded around.

"Hey, lover, she's too much for you.... Hoo hoo, look at him turn red...."

"Shut up," he shouted, glaring around the room. "We've got to get those machines"—he pointed to the stack of crates at the end of the room—"onto those marks, and by God we'll do it ahead of plan if we have to stay all night."

He bullied and shouted and raced around the shop, organizing the apprentices and wheedling them to work faster. They began tearing off the packing crates and moving the heavy equipment into position with crowbars and brute force.

"Grisha, what the hell," one of the boys puffed as the team leader joined him in shifting a two-ton machine onto its floor marks. "Why don't you play a guitar under her window? You keep courting her like this, we'll all get ruptured."

"Push, God damn you!" he snarled. The boy shook his head and leaned against the lathe. Grunting and cursing, they moved it two more feet to the marks.

When the noon whistle blew, five of the lathe frames were in place. There were ten to go. Grisha was satisfied with the progress, knowing it would normally have taken the whole day to do this much. He knew Sonya would be impressed. He was inspecting the placement of feet on the marks when Sonya came into the shop. He walked across the floor to meet her.

"Heavens, Grisha, five in place already?" she said. Grisha threw back his shoulders and strutted along behind her as she examined the lathes. She shrugged, took the blueprint from Grisha and studied it. She frowned over the drawings, looked at the lathe frames, and shook her head. Grisha's elation evaporated.

"Dear, dear," she said finally. "I'm afraid they're all wrong."

"All wrong?" he yelped. "But they're on the marks!"

"They're in the right places, dear Grisha, but they're backward. See?" She spread the paper over one of the backward lathe frames. "Here's the chuck head here, and the motors here," she said, pointing to spots on the blueprint. "I'm afraid they'll all have to be turned around."

"Oh God, I'm sorry," he murmured, humiliated. He was grateful the rest of the team had left for their midday meal. Sonya patted his cheek.

"Oh, this is no problem, Grishenka," she said. She slipped her arm into his and pulled him away from the blueprint. He looked around and saw her face, tilted to one side and looking up at him with merry dark eyes. "Look, you got them all uncrated and this many in place...well, almost in place. I thought you'd have to take two days just for that much. Your boys work fast. It won't take long to turn them around.''

"I guess so," he replied. "But I feel like such an idiot...."

She put her finger to his mouth. "Probably because of hunger," she said. "Hungry men all feel like idiots. Let's have some lunch."

They made an empty crate into a table and she brought from a bag a jar of kvass and black bread. To his surprise, she also produced a heavy clasp knife from the pocket of the coveralls, the kind of knife only a man would be expected to carry. She snapped it open and sliced pieces of bread. He was, indeed, extremely hungry. He wolfed down the first slice.

"You see? Starving," she said. "No wonder you read the blueprints wrong; the brain had no food."

The lunch—and the attention from the lovely engineer's assistant—restored his spirits and helped him shrug off the howls and gibes of the apprentices when he had to tell them to turn the five lathes. By working an hour past quitting time, they got the first five machines reversed and shoved the remainder into rough position. He dismissed the team and set to work by himself gathering the packing boards into piles and sweeping up the nails, paper, and other debris left from the day's labor. As he swept up the last of it he heard voices at the other end of the room. It was late twilight, and through the gloom he could just see the chief engineer and Sonya. He set the broom aside and smoothed his hair.

"Well, young Comrade Malmudov, I think the lathe shop will be first on line, hey?" Chudov shouted. "Nice work, my boy. You'll have them in by the end of the week and we'll have the electricians here first thing Monday. Too bad the other shops aren't as fast."

"Thanks, Comrade Chief," Grisha said, pleased.

Chudov came closer and Grisha saw that he looked haggard, worn out. His shock of gray hair hung limply over on one side of his brow and his eyes were red-rimmed. There was a grayness in his face and the skin seemed to sag.

"You look tired, Comrade Chief," he said.

"Oh, not too tired," Chudov replied. He bent over one of the lathe frames and put a leveling glass on it. "No more tired than usual, and as soon as we get going here, I'll be able to take a rest." He peered at the glass.

"Look, I'll check the levels, Chief," Sonya said. "You go get some supper before they close the canteen."

Chudov nodded gratefully. "Sure. Fine. I think I'll do that my dear, thank you," he said. "I missed lunch today." He handed her the glass and walked away down the row of machines. He stumbled, recovered his balance, and walked on.

"He looks like hell," Grisha said. "What's the matter? Is he sick?"

Sonya laid the leveling glass on a lathe frame and examined it soberly before she answered. "He's been working hard," she said. "And he's worried."

"Worried? About what?"

"I saw..." she began, then stopped. She gave Grisha a look of serious intensity. "What I'm telling you is not to be repeated, not to anybody, understand?"

"Why yes," he said, surprised. "Yes, of course."

"You can help him." She set the glass aside. "I saw a letter today from the Party Committee. It said the factory is falling farther and farther behind plan...."

"Well, that's true," Grisha said. "But it's nobody's fault and it'll be going soon, so what..."

Sonya looked at him steadily. "That wasn't all," she said. "The letter said there've been reports about hostile class elements, possible wrecking, things like that...."

"What?!" He laughed incredulously. "Who said that? That's stupid!"

"Shh!" She put her hand to his mouth.

"But, Sonichka," he whispered. "We don't have any wreckers here. What do they..."

"Listen, Grisha, how do we know who's a wrecker and who isn't?" she said. "I don't know. You don't know. But they have ways of knowing and we have to depend on the Party to lead us. Our Party knows the best way." She sighed and shrugged uncertainly. "But anyway, I don't think Nikolai Ivanovich is at fault, I really don't."

She took Grisha's hand. "We have to help him, Grisha. Talk to the others. See if you can get them to put in some extra time Saturday afternoon and Sunday and get the other shops ready faster. Especially the milling shop and the foundry. The electricians will be here Monday, and when they're finished we can start production.''

Sonya squeezed his hand and the gesture made him lightheaded. "I'll do what I can, Sonichka," he said. "We'll get it done."

She smiled and turned back to the leveling glass. Grisha followed her nervously from machine to machine in the gathering gloom, and the fifth one turned up uneven.

"It's too low on the chuck end," she said. "Look, get a crowbar and we'll put it right."

"But it weighs two tons," he protested. "And it's getting dark. We'll need a couple of men. We'll do it first thing—"

"Oh, come on," she said, impatiently. "I'm not some duchess from the finishing school. Get a crowbar! Get two!"

He shrugged. "You're the boss, Comrade Engineer," he said.

He fetched two crowbars and a candle. He lit the candle and by its flickering light they loosened the bolts and, grunting and heaving, raised the lathe frame with the crowbars. Sonya expertly jammed her bar under the heavy base flange and flipped it over so the lathe was held an inch off the floor.

"Let's get the shims under here," she said. "Let's start with five millimeters."

Grisha fetched the shims and fitted them in place beneath the lathe.

"Now," she said. "Let's drop it. Easy...easy..."

Grisha strained against the crowbar, and he saw muscles ripple in Sonya's smooth arm as she pushed on his bar with her left hand and grasped the other bar with her right. With a quick motion she pulled her crowbar upright.

"Easy now," she said. "Down, down..." They eased the two tons down onto the shims and worked the tips of the crowbars out from under the flange. It thudded softly into place.

"Let's have a look," she said. She carefully laid the level along the frame and peered at the glass while Grisha held the candle. "Perfect," she said, clapping her hands in delight.

They reset the bolts, put away their tools, and left the shop, chattering happily about the day's work.

"Really, I was amazed you got the whole thing done, Grisha," she said. "When you put them in backward, I thought you'd lose a whole day, but you made it." She slipped her arm through his, and they strolled through the darkness toward the barracks.

"Walk me home?" She flashed a coquettish, dimpled smile. He grinned and moved a little closer. He felt the movement of her body where his elbow touched. Grisha let his hand drop and he found hers. She took his hand and squeezed it. His heart hammered and his stomach tingled and it was the happiest moment of his life.

F. E. DZERZHINSKY
HOME FOR CHILDREN

LENINGRAD

May 3, 1940

To Pupil Malmudov, G. N.

This is to notify you formally of your acceptance as a worker-student in the founding class of the Proletarian Victory Diesel Engine Factory now under construction in Leningrad.

You are congratulated on your entrance into the ranks of the great Soviet Working Class, which stands in the vanguard of the entire world proletariat in its struggle for freedom and dignity.

The F.E. Dzerzhinsky Children's Home pridefully sends you into the world of adult Socialist responsibility, confident that your work will reflect honor upon our home and upon its teachers.

I Salute You,

Vulkova

R. Vulkova
Superintendent

*Dearest Grisha,
The "F.E.D" is going to miss you terribly. Who will lead our young Pioneers? Don't forget us. Work well! I kiss you,
Your comrade
Vulkova*

7.

Grisha helped persuade the other apprentice crews that they should work extra hours to get the Proletarian Victory Factory ready for the electricians. He did not mention the letter concerning Chudov but he made it clear the extra work would help the respected chief engineer.

"He's killing himself," Grisha said. "We're hardly sweating. Only ten hours a day. We can do twelve, and work on Sunday."

The Komsomol Guidance Committee set a goal of two weeks for making the factory ready for production on at least a limited scale. It was an ambitious goal, for the apprentices had yet to be trained in the use of the machines they were expected to tend. They had learned to install a lathe but they had only the vaguest notion of how to operate one. The skilled workers who would teach the apprentices had not even arrived at the factory. They would be coming from other plants to form the skilled cadre of the work force, but they would come only when their skills were ready to be used.

Grisha, Sonya, and all the Komsomol teams worked to near exhaustion during the two weeks. Grisha was up by five-thirty every morning and was on the job by six o'clock after a quick breakfast of bread and butter and tea. The team took a half-hour break at noon and never knocked off earlier than six in the evening, often much later. Grisha usually stayed in the factory another three hours after his team returned to their barracks, planning with Sonya the next day's work. There were no days off.

There was little between Grisha and Sonya during those long days that could be called romance except in the evenings, when they walked hand-in-hand to the barracks. They never lingered long outside; they needed every second of sleep they could get. Yet Grisha remembered the time as one of heady and exciting romance. He did not dream about her at night— he was too tired; and he did not daydream about her in the daytime—he was too busy. But she seemed always to be somewhere at the edge of his mind, thoughts of her tucked between the assignment schedules and the blueprints. He could not remember a waking moment when a thought of Sonya, some thought, was not alive in the back of his consciousness.

At the end of eight days, work on installation of the lathe shop was completed and Grisha sat down with Sonya and two other engineers to work out a new assignment in the foundry for Grisha's team. It was new work, and it took until midnight. When it was done, Grisha walked Sonya to her barracks, holding hands and saying little. But instead of the usual quick good night, Sonya took both of Grisha's hands and held them, standing with one shoulder against the wall of the building.

"Grishenka," she began, then stopped, looking into his eyes. There followed a long silence, and Grisha wanted to say something, but no words came. He looked into Sonya's dark and somber eyes. They sparkled with dual pinpoints of light reflecting from the bare bulb over the barracks entry. He was confused, helpless; her eyes came nearer to his. They came very near, then vanished in a blur as she kissed him full on the lips. She pulled his arms around her waist and he held her gingerly. She put her own arms around his neck and with gentle pressure she pulled him close so he could sense the softness of her breasts against his shirt and the smooth, rounded mounds and hollows of her belly, thighs, and pelvis. A feeling of dizziness overwhelmed him, and with it an excited tingling in the pit of his stomach. It was an exquisite sensation similar, oddly, to the physical feeling generated by fear, one he had known many times. But this was different—intense, exhilarating. Their lips pressed harder together for a moment, then came apart; Sonya slipped her hands from around his neck and held his face in her two palms. Their eyes were close together and wide open.

Grisha tried to speak but his throat was too dry. His tongue felt paralyzed. His heart hammered. He swallowed, licked his lips. "Sonya . . . Sonichka . . . I think I . . . I love you, Sonichka."

"And I, you," she said. She slid her hands down from his face and rested her palms on his chest. She leaned her forehead on his shoulder, bringing her black, shiny hair close to his face. The smell of her hair was wildly feminine, causing the dizzy, tingling sensation to rush back. They stood thus for a few minutes, saying nothing. Then Sonya backed away slightly and looked up at Grisha with a weary smile.

"Grishenka, the state plan is no friend of lovers," she said. "We have to sleep. Tomorrow'll be a hard day."

"Tomorrow's already here," he said, smiling. "It's after midnight." He paused and looked away. "I'm very happy, Sonichka," he said at length. "I'm so happy I don't even feel tired."

She kissed him lightly on the cheek. "Tomorrow at six, Comrade Team Leader," she said, and she was gone, the barracks door swinging behind her. The smell of her hair lingered in the cool night air.

Grisha turned and began walking alongside a drainage ditch toward his barracks. Suddenly he broke into a run, sped into a wide turn, and leapt the ditch. He barely cleared the embankment, did a cartwheel, and came up with a leap.

"Hurrah!" he shouted into the night. The sound of his voice echoed among the darkened buildings. Then he ran all the way to his barracks, fell into his bunk with his clothes on, and dropped off to sleep within two minutes.

IN THE END, the work teams failed to meet their two-week deadline because of delays in the shipment of foundry equipment, but the skilled workers arrived and they began teaching the apprentices how to operate the machines. Near the end of July the foundry, after three failures, cast the first engine block.

In the lathe shop, Grisha and fifteen other youthful apprentices worked under the instruction of three skilled lathe operators. Grisha's instructor was a wiry little red-haired man named Dmitry Igorievich Kosolapov—Dyma to his friends.

Even more striking than his red hair were Dyma's freckles, an amazing crop that covered face, neck, and hands. When he took his shirt off he revealed freckles all over his chest, shoulders, and back. The freckles became a shop joke, which Dyma himself enjoyed and nurtured. He had a quick peasant wit and he kept up a steady patter of wisecracks as he skipped from lathe to lathe.

"Hey, Dyma," one of the apprentices yelled one morning. "You got freckles on your ass?"

Without a moment's hesitation Dyma spun around, popped his suspenders from his shoulders, and dropped his trousers. He mooned the apprentices with a rear covered completely in freckles. The shop exploded in laughter.

"You laugh at these freckles, boys," Dyma shouted, pulling his trousers up. "But, by God, it's no joke. It's a hell of a handicap." His eyes twinkled.

"I've got 'em all over my pecker..."

More laughter.

"...And, see, when I take it out, the girls think I got the clap...."

The men dissolved in laughter, tears streaming. Dyma joined the laughter.

With all his patter and jokes, Dyma was a good machinist and an able teacher. He was patient and alert with the apprentices, bringing them along so quickly that within ten days of his arrival he had all of them at work on production crankshafts and flywheels. Dyma himself turned the flywheel destined to go on the first engine of the Proletarian Victory Factory.

At first, production was slow and painstaking, with much waste from inexpert cutting. The various parts of the factory were uneven in delivering parts to the line, and there were frequent stoppages and general frustration. Nevertheless, on August 5, the first completed engine emerged from the line. It was an event of major importance, and a ceremony had been organized to greet the machine. The factory's work force gathered at the end of the assembly line and a huge cheer went up as a worker ceremoniously screwed down the final bolt.

The engine was rolled out on a special dolly, draped with a red bunting and topped by a red-and-white banner reading, "Forward to the Victory of Communism!"

The Leningrad regional Party secretary made a speech, and he announced that the chief engineer, Chudov, had been appointed to the vacant post of director of the factory in recognition of his success in getting it into production despite the difficulties and delays.

The news of Chudov's elevation brought a burst of spontaneous applause from the workers, which the new director acknowledged by stepping forward and bowing in an old-fashioned Russian way. He took a place on the engine dolly, bracing himself by gripping the valve cover. The crowd fell silent.

"Comrades," he began. "The Comrade Secretary has been kind in giving me praise for bringing our factory to production, but I cannot accept it. The credit goes to the young workers of our factory, especially the Komsomol cadres who led the workers in the difficult tasks of construction and installation. This is a factory of youth. The average age of the workers on our roster is nineteen, even younger than the age of our Soviet Republic. This is a socialist factory, built by socialist youth, manned by workers born under the red flag of socialism."

Chudov gave the valve cover a firm slap. "This is our first engine, and it represents the latest improvements in diesel engine design. It will power tractors to build socialism, and it will power tanks to protect socialism. You may be proud, we all may be proud, of this fine engine, this fine factory, these fine young workers.''

The workers applauded and cheered and pressed around the gleaming new engine while Chudov and several other men took the bunting down and prepared to start it. Grisha and Sonya pressed as close as they could, craning their necks over the crowd. The Party secretary moved to one side, smoking a cigarette and chatting with factory officials. Grisha heard him say, "Do you think the thing'll start?"

One of the officials winked. "We didn't take any chances, Comrade Secretary," he said. "We gave it a test before we rolled it out."

The secretary chuckled and turned to the engine. Chudov shouted: "All set, let 'er go!"

The starting motor growled and Chudov stood on the dolly with his hand on the throttle. The starter growled for about ten seconds while the workers watched in breathless silence, praying for a clean start. The engine coughed, coughed again, and then kicked over with a gratifying roar and a cloud of blue exhaust. The workers cheered and Chudov stood proudly beside the engine, inching the throttle forward until the diesel's roar drowned out the cheers. He set the throttle and jumped down from the dolly.

He walked toward the Party secretary, hand extended. The Party secretary smiled, put the cigarette into his mouth, and reached out to accept Chudov's handshake.

As the men's hands touched, there was a sharp crack and a zinging ricochet whine. A young man near the

engine seemed to leap backward unnaturally, high and
sideways. At the same moment the engine shook
wildly on the dolly; the crowd reflexively scrambled
away. Grisha was shoved backward and Sonya
screamed.

The engine and its dolly flipped over with a heavy
crash that shook the concrete floor like an earth-
quake. It wound down, shivering and whining. It fell
silent.

The silence lasted perhaps three seconds, blue
smoke rose in the air, and the crowd burst into a bed-
lam of shouting and screaming.

Grisha looked around and saw that Sonya was no
longer beside him. He looked frantically over the
crowd and saw her black hair near the fallen engine.
He lunged through the crowd to her amid a hubbub of
voices:

"My God, look at it."..."Is he all right?"..."Don't
know, something came loose."...."Oh, Jesus, look at
his chest...."

Grisha pushed through the packed crowd and
stopped in horror. A young man, the one who had
leapt so strangely, lay sprawled on the floor near the
fallen engine. His chest was ripped open, bones visible amid the bubbling mess of gore. The youthful face
was gray, and his eyes were open, but they were glassy
and unseeing. He was dead, or near enough to be beyond help. Sonya bent over and picked up a hand to
feel for a pulse. She held it a moment; then she
reached down and closed the boy's staring eyes.
Somebody stepped forward with a canvas tarpaulin

and she helped spread it over the body. She rose and walked to where Grisha stood, stepping carefully around the scuffed black boots sticking out from the bottom of the tarpaulin. She was weeping by the time she reached Grisha.

"Oh God, Grisha, no," she wailed, burying her face in her hands. "How could this happen? Why should this happen? The poor boy, he didn't know what hit him."

Grisha put his arm around her and looked at the wrecked engine. The flywheel was shattered. It had somehow broken and a piece of it had shot away, smashing into the youth's chest. Grisha saw another piece of the flywheel on the floor and a hole where it had ripped through the sheet-metal base of the dolly with the force of an artillery shell. The flywheel was the one turned by his teacher, the freckle-faced Dyma, and Grisha had watched Dyma make it. It had been a smooth, beautifully machined and beautifully balanced piece of steel. He could not understand how it could have shattered so disastrously.

The crowd broke into small, stunned groups. Word of the broken flywheel spread. Chudov, pale and haggard, helped carry the body of the young man outside to a van. Grisha could not see the Party secretary anywhere, and he heard later that the secretary left the factory immediately after the accident.

The failure of the diesel and the death of the young man cast a pall over the factory. Most of the young workers were simple peasant boys and they viewed the accident as an unlucky omen, a sign of disapproval from heaven, and there was a rash of requests of transfers to other factories. The workers in Grisha's lathe shop, especially Dyma, were listless and silent.

Still, the factory managed to continue work. In the first two days of production they completed five engines that tested perfectly, with no flywheel problems. The factory began to settle into workmanlike efficiency.

Within a week the gloomy atmosphere improved. Dyma cheered up and resumed his antics. The lathe shop hummed and he moved from machine to machine, mixing instruction with fun.

Grisha was laughing at one of his jokes when one of the other apprentices came into the shop and went directly to the lathe where Grisha and Dyma were working. The apprentice, eyes wide with concern, whispered that Chekists were in the building, their black car outside the main entrance. They were in Chudov's office.

Grisha shrugged. "So what?" he said.

But Dyma turned pale. He shook his head. "That's bad, Grisha," he said. "Very bad." He turned to the lathe and worked in silence.

Grisha frowned. Abruptly, he turned and walked out of the shop. He was on his way to the administrative section when he met Sonya in the hallway. She was red-eyed.

"Sonichka, what . . . ?"

She shrugged and looked away. "They came in half an hour ago," she said, her voice thick and husky.

"They dumped everything into sacks, all the records and papers in the office. They took him away."

"Took him away?" Grisha was incredulous. "They arrested him? What in hell for?"

Sonya shook her head. "He made no protest, Grisha, no denial. He just said, 'Why?' And the officer said, 'For wrecking, sabotage, treason, and murder."

Grisha felt the beginning of rage. "My God, they can't blame him for that accident! It was just something that went wrong!" He banged the wall with a fist and his voice rose. "The stupid bastards, what the hell do they think they're doing?"

"Shut up!" Sonya cried sharply.

Grisha, surprised, looked at her. Her eyes flashed.

"It was an order, Grishenka. They know things we can't know. Don't question them." Her shoulders fell and she shook her head.

"Anyway, he didn't defend himself, and why not? You have to wonder why not. He was a foreman for the Putilov Works before the Revolution, everybody knows that. He had a history of oppositionist activity. He told me himself he was a Right SR until 1925."

She said it sadly, as if the matter were settled. Chudov had once belonged to a disgraced political party.

Grisha looked at his feet and shrugged. Politics. He knew nothing of politics. Maybe so, he thought. He told Sonya he would see her after work, and he returned to his shop.

AS HE NEARED THE SHOP he sensed something was wrong. He heard the lathe motors running but no sound of cutting tools at work. He went through the door and saw two men in gray suits standing near his machine. Grisha knew immediately who they were. They were talking to Dyma, who looked shrunken and washed out; even his freckles had turned a sickly light color. All the other men stood at their machines, watching in silence. As Grisha walked slowly along the row to his machine, the men in suits grabbed Dyma by both arms. His head snapped as they jerked him into position between them. They dragged him along the row of machines toward Grisha, who stepped to one side and watched in horror. Dyma's eyes bulged with fright; as he passed, he cast a sidelong glance, a look that exposed the whites of his eyes. It was a look Grisha had seen on goats tethered for slaughter. It sickened him.

The policemen and Dyma disappeared out the door. The workers left their machines and gathered around the man who had been nearest to Dyma and who could hear what had been said.

"They say he's an accomplice of Chudov," the man said. "They say he used a cracked flywheel on purpose."

He repeated what the policemen had said. He said Dyma denied the accusations.

One by one, the workers returned to their lathes. They resumed their work. They did not talk again of Dyma.

8.

Kuznetsov Arrived at the Red Banner Factory early enough Monday morning to brew himself a glass of tea before the other office workers arrived. He sipped the tea and opened a folder containing his weekly production and maintenance reports, going over in his mind what he would say during the morning factory committee meeting. He was worried. It was the fourth week in a row that the winding shop was below the planned quota, and it seemed certain that the winding-shop troubles would put the factory at least 8 percent below quota for the third quarter of the year. That, plus the first-quarter failures, could cause the factory to end up below quota for the entire year. If that happened, there would be plenty of hell to pay.

Kuznetsov went over the figures, calculating on a clean sheet of paper percentages, costs, man-hours, and wire footage. A deliveries summary at the end of the production report showed well enough what the problem was: The Chelyabinsk Metallurgical Combine had fallen thirty-one days behind in its schedule for copper-wire deliveries, and Arbitrazh had already stepped in to settle the disputes arising from the combine's failures. In its turn, the Chelyabinsk Combine protested to the Arbitrazh officials that the Ministry of Mining had failed to meet the planned deliveries of copper ore, and that some old copper smelting equipment in Karabash had been shut down for overhaul.

But what the hell, Kuznetsov thought. In the end it's me who gets kicked in the ass for not making enough generators. He fervently wished he had never been made chief engineer. He couldn't even spend the money he'd been making when he was a line supervisor at 180 rubles a month, and now he was making more than 200 rubles and he was putting most of it in a savings bank. He loathed the decisions, explanations, statistics, disputes, responsibilities, and paperwork that had burdened his life since his promotion. He was lonely enough in his solitary bachelor's life, living with his solitary, unbearable thoughts, and now he had lost the camaraderie of the machine-shop floor.

Kuznetsov's secretary, Svetlana Igorievna, peeked in the door. "Good morning, Comrade Chief," she sang out, waving cheerfully before she disappeared in the direction of the samovar in the outer office. "Will you have some tea, Alexander Nikolayevich?"

Kuznetsov smiled. He was grateful for the sound of her friendly voice. "No, thanks, Sveta; I have some already," he said. "The water's hot."

Svetlana reappeared, gingerly handling a steaming glass of tea that had a paper napkin tied around it to keep it from burning her fingers. She pulled a chair up to a table in the corner of Kuznetsov's office and began putting together the duplicate copies of the chief engineer's morning reports. He watched from the corner of his eye while she dunked lumps of sugar into the tea and sucked at them.

He shook his head in disbelief. "Sveta, my dear, your teeth will rot out and you'll die a diabetic if you keep on like that."

Svetlana tossed her head and laughed, a brownish pile of tea-soaked sugar visible on her tongue. "We all have our vices, Chief," she said. "Some people are drunkards, some people smoke too much, some people eat all day. I suck sugar cubes."

She paused. "And what's your vice? Got any?"

He smiled. "None," he said. "Not one. I am the perfect man, the last one left."

She laughed and popped another sugar cube into her mouth.

He shook his head. "But I'm afraid the factory committee won't think I'm so damned perfect. The winding-shop problem will be my death. I'll have to tell them we're below quota again. Listen, Sveta, call Arbitrazh this morning, during the meeting, and see if there's any chance of getting the deliveries up. If there's anything hopeful, send me a note. I could use a little good news in that meeting."

"And if they don't have any good news, Chief?"

"Well, then don't send any notes. Bad news I don't need."

"Right, Comrade Boss," she said. "Listen, by the way, Marya told me some more wire got stolen over the weekend."

"What, again?" Kuznetsov pounded the desk with an open palm. "What the devil have they got those watchmen for, anyway? How much this time?"

"She didn't say. She says it looks like one of our own did it. She said Repin came in and looked it over. And he thinks the thief knew the plant, knew what to do, and where to look."

"Repin?" Kuznetsov frowned. "Why Repin?"

"Dunno, Chief," Svetlana said, shrugging. "Security's his job, I guess."

"Yes, guess it is," Kuznetsov said, frowning over his papers. "I guess it is."

He checked over the figures on the wire inventory and he sighed.

"Well, Sveta, maybe it's a blessing. We'll spend the whole meeting on security, and they won't have so much time for needling me on the quota."

Kuznetsov gathered his papers into a brown folder and rose from his desk.

"I'm off," he said. "Don't forget to call Arbitrazh. Do it in about ten minutes, because I'm sure they'll make me first on the agenda, as usual."

"Right," Svetlana said, waving cheerfully. "Good luck, Boss."

Kuznetsov put the folder under his arm and walked down the hall to the conference room. He smoothed his hair and tucked his shirt front into his trousers, pulling at the waistband. He buttoned all three buttons of his suit before he entered the meeting room.

The only persons in the room were the factory director and Repin, both of whom sat at the far end of a long, heavy oaken table, chatting in low voices. The table was covered with a green baize cloth and was surrounded by straight-backed chairs. Pencils, pads, glasses, and green bottles of Borzhomi mineral water stood neatly along the length of the table. When Kuznetsov walked in, Repin and the director stopped talking. They looked up.

"Good morning, Alexander Nikolayevich," the director said. Repin smiled and nodded.

"Good morning, comrades," Kuznetsov said, walking stiffly to the table, his stomach pressing against the three buttons of his suit. Repin turned back to the director and said something in a voice too low for Kuznetsov to hear.

"Quite right, Genya," the director said in reply. "Exactly right. We'll simply have to deal with it."

Kuznetsov took the chair to the right of the director, who sat at his customary place at the head of the table. Repin sat at the director's left, facing Kuznetsov. The director, an elderly and amiable man who was much liked by the factory staff, chatted politely about the weekend and the weather as the other leading factory officials began taking their seats around the table. Repin, with his thin smile and chilly eyes, listened to the director for a moment and then turned to talk with the chief accountant.

Kuznetsov cleared his throat and leaned toward the director. "By the way, I hear we had some more wire stolen over the weekend," he said. Repin broke off what he was saying to the accountant and looked sharply at Kuznetsov.

"Yes," the director said, frowning. Repin's gray eyes remained on Kuznetsov, who shifted uneasily in his seat.

The director shook his head. "We lost around forty thousand meters, it looks like."

"My God!" Kuznetsov exclaimed. "What the hell will they do with all that wire? And how could they carry it? That's heavy stuff!"

Repin smiled. "It appears they used a truck, or maybe they used a car and made a couple of trips."

Kuznetsov jotted down the figure "40,000" and began some calculations. The director brought the meeting to order by tapping his pencil on a glass.

"Let's get to business now, comrades," he said. The table fell silent. "We'll start with Comrade Kuznetsov's production report, then have the financial report from Comrade Ivanov, and then Comrade Repin's political report." He paused. "Comrade Repin also proposes to give us a special report on plant security." The director nodded to Kuznetsov.

"Well, to come straight to the point, comrades, the deficiencies connected with the winding shop have not yet been resolved," Kuznetsov began. "This has had an effect on the program of the factory as regards the overall fulfillment of the plan for the week."

Kuznetsov glanced down the table. Unsmiling eyes looked back at him.

"Specifically," he continued, studying the papers before him, "total production of Class IV generators for the week was two hundred and eighty-three; of Class III, one hundred and seventy-two total. At the same time, the rotor shop exceeded the plan by six percent, producing three hundred and twelve for Class IV and one hundred and ninety-six Class III. Also, the casing foundry met the quota in both categories. In the winding shop, however, production of completed windings was two hundred and ninety-two in Class IV and one hundred and eighty-one in Class III, and the conclusion is that the overall underfulfillment can be traced to the winding shop—that is, seven percent below plan in Class IV and five percent below in Class III."

Kuznetsov paused to pour a glass of water and sip from it.

"That is, comrades, the overall underfulfillment in finished generator production is the same as the underfulfillment in the winding shop."

Kuznetsov stopped speaking and took another long swallow from the water glass.

"How does it look for the quarter, then?" Repin asked, frowning and twirling a pencil. "Isn't this the fourth week in a row we've underfulfilled?"

Kuznetsov cleared his throat. "We don't have a chance of meeting the quarterly quota," he said. "For the quarter, I calculate we'll be down about eight percent, Evgeny Maximovich. Maybe less if we can get another seven hundred and fifty thousand meters of wire delivered before the end of the month.''

The director wrote something and looked at Kuznetsov. ''What's the trouble, still Chelyabinsk?''

''That's part of it, Comrade Director, yes,'' Kuznetsov replied. ''Arbitrazh hasn't acted yet. I expect to find out today if—''

''What are the chances?'' the director asked, interrupting him.

Kuznetsov stole a glance at his watch. Sveta would have sent a note by now if there had been good news.

''It doesn't look good, comrade,'' he said. ''There's been a pretty serious problem in smelting because of the overhaul in Karabash. It'll be October before smelting starts again and it'll be January before we see any wire from that copper.''

Kuznetsov opened a folder and took out a sheet of paper. He read off figures on the order backlogs.

''So,'' the director said. ''What do we do?''

Kuznetsov shrugged. ''As you know, I spent most of last week either at the ministry or at Arbitrazh. I can tell you everybody's raising hell. Everybody needs copper wire and isn't getting it, and we need more than anybody else.''

He thought for a moment. ''I wager that's why we're getting these thefts, comrades. Other plants are getting it under the table from the thieves, or maybe stealing it themselves.''

''Obviously,'' Repin cut in coldly. ''How badly have the thefts hurt our production?''

"Including the latest, we've lost enough for about twenty Class IVs and about half that many Class IIIs. Overall, speaking in terms of the quarter, the thefts account for about one percent of the underfulfillment, no more.

"It takes a lot of wire for windings, but not so much for lots of other industrial processes," he continued. "The thieves know we've got lots of wire, and I suppose they figure we don't need it as badly as some other factories do."

"That's not for thieves and traitors to decide," Repin cut in. "Our state planners know where the needs of industry lie. I don't believe it's useful to suggest enemies of the state know what's good for the state."

The room fell silent, and Kuznetsov sensed that all eyes were on him. He began to stammer an objection, but stopped. The words "traitors" and "enemies of the state" stunned him into silence.

The director cleared his throat and asked the accountant for his report, breaking the tension in the room. The accountant's voice droned, reciting figures and amounts and percentages. Kuznetsov heard little of it. He stared at his hands and wondered how much Repin knew or how much he suspected. The oily personnel director was baiting him; the relatively small amount of thievery in the yard did not justify such strong language. The accountant finished his report and the ice-edged voice of Repin began the political report. Repin went through the usual recitation of Red Banner political meetings and the factory's plans for participating in the annual Communist Subbotnik, the Day of Volunteer Labor.

He finished the report and sat a moment in silence.

"But there are wolves in sheep's clothing amongst us, comrades," he said. He paused and repeated it. "Wolves in sheep's clothing.

"Again, last weekend, as was mentioned earlier, we had losses of wire from the warehouse section. I spent the whole day here yesterday inspecting the areas of the thefts and receiving reports from the security workers; I can only conclude that the thief, or thieves, must be from among our own collective, our own workers.

"The thieves had knowledge of the habits of the watchmen," Repin continued. "That made it possible for them to enter unobserved and to take away the wire, either in a truck or by car, before the security workers visited the area again. Unfortunately, it was established that one of the security workers..." He consulted his papers. "...Watchman Demidin, V. E., was insufficiently vigilant; that is, he was drunk. He has been suspended from the security section and transferred to the custodial section."

Repin paused, frowning.

"As for the thefts," he said, "I've asked for assistance from the Committee for State Security...."

Kuznetsov looked up, startled.

"Er, excuse me Evgeny Maximovich," he said. "Why the KGB? This is plain thievery; isn't it a matter for the People's Militia?"

Repin stared coldly at Kuznetsov. "I think there's
more to this than 'plain thievery,' Kuznetsov," he said,
rudely omitting the "Comrade" before the name.

Kuznetsov froze and fell silent. My God, he
thought. He knows. He must know.

With a sinking sensation he speculated on how long
it would take for the KGB to trace his personal documents and find proof of their falsity. He had lived so
long under his new identity that there were multiple
layers of documentation that would have to be peeled
back to find the false ones, but careful investigators
would do it. And the KGB employed very careful investigators.

The director wound up the meeting with routine
announcements and the officials began gathering papers together. Kuznetsov sat for a moment, then rose
and walked wearily toward the door.

"Sasha!" Repin called. The personnel director was
still at the table, pulling his papers together. Kuznetsov turned.

"Sasha, you don't look so good," he said. "Feeling ill or what?"

"Not good, Genya," Kuznetsov replied uneasily.

Repin's icy tone during the meeting vanished. He
rose and put a sympathetic hand on Kuznetsov's
shoulder. "What is it, old man, the tummy?"

"A bad breakfast and too much tea in the morning, it gives me indigestion," Kuznetsov said, tapping
his chest.

"Chest pains?" Repin said, concerned. "It might be more than indigestion! You ought to see a doctor about it."

"Er, thank you, Genya," Kuznetsov said, thinking ironically that he had indeed seen a doctor, just the day before, and that's what started the chest pains.

Repin clapped him on the shoulder and smiled. "You need a little rest, my friend," he said. "Why don't you come out to the dacha with us next weekend? If the weather looks good, that is. What do you say? You're dying of boredom in that little room of yours. Come on."

Kuznetsov's uneasiness increased. So did the pain in his chest. It made him feel dizzy. Repin had never been to his apartment, but he spoke as if he had been in it. Perhaps he had.

"Oh no, thank you..." he began, but stopped. There was a fascination in the game Repin was playing. He decided to take a chance.

"Well, maybe it would be good to get out . . . if the weather's nice," he said.

Repin squeezed his shoulder. "Good!" he said. His smile almost held a touch of warmth. "Splendid! We'll plan on it, my friend. We'll cook shashlik and take a boat on the Volga. Ludmilla will love to pamper a bachelor." He gave Kuznetsov's shoulder another squeeze, looking intently into his eyes. Then he strode off down the hall, a merry bounce in his step.

"Workers of the World, unite"

LENINGRAD SOVIET

CERTIFICATE OF MARRIAGE

THIS IS TO CERTIFY THAT ON THE ___20th___ DAY OF __May__ OF THE YEAR ___1940___ ,

> *Malmudov, Grigory N.*

and

> *Vinogradova, Sonya A.*

were joined in marriage, having dedicated their Socialist union to the building of a free Communist future for the toiling masses of the world, to the creation of a Soviet family of the new type.

Witnessed __Yeliseyev, V. Y.__
Witnessed __Grelukova, S. Y.__
Certified __Shvartz, I. V.__

People's Magistrate, Leningrad Soviet

9.

Grisha courted Sonya through a long and memorable summer. After she returned to her institute studies in September, he took the tram into the heart of Leningrad every Sunday to sit with her in the library while she labored over her engineering texts. As long as the weather remained fair they took evening walks through streets and parks, stopping in quiet places to kiss and to talk in low, tender voices.

But as the affair of the heart blossomed, the affair of the flesh was painfully frustrated: She lived in a dormitory room with a dozen other women students; he lived in a workers' barracks with thirty-five other men. There was no place for love, so while the weather lasted they petted and caressed in the park on Sunday evenings. Grisha often ran for the last tram nearly crippled by a groin pain diagnosed as "lover's nuts" by his barracks mates, who raucously and obscenely prescribed the only cure.

When the weather turned cold, Grisha and Sonya
spent more time in the library and less in the park. On
a Sunday in December they left the library and walked
arm in arm to Sonya's dormitory. They stopped at a
tree, put their arms around each other, and stood a
long while in shivering silence. Grisha wore a padded
cotton jacket but the cold cut straight through it.
Sonya, in an old woolen coat too small for her,
stamped and shivered in a fruitless effort to keep the
chill away.

"Sonichka, let's get married," Grisha blurted.

Sonya looked up in surprise. "Married!" she exclaimed. "Married? It wouldn't make the winter any
warmer, and it wouldn't get us out of the dormito-
ries," she said.

"Why not?" he said, pulling her closer. "We'll look
around; we'll find someplace to live."

"No chance, not at this time of year, Grisha," she
said, shaking her head. "I checked. There's no chance
until spring."

"You checked?" he said, surprised. "Why did you
check?"

She smiled and kissed his cheek. "I checked just in
case you would ask, dear Grisha," she said. "A girl
has to be ready for such things."

Grisha shook his head, amazed. "I've been building my courage for weeks, Sonya. I thought of all the
ways to kill myself if you said no. And all the time
you've been looking for an apartment."

They both laughed and hugged each other. They stopped shivering and stood leaning against the tree, oblivious to the icy breeze blowing off the Neva.

"Then you'll really marry me, Sonichka?" he whispered. "When we have a place to live, I mean…"

"Of course," she said, smiling. "I thought you'd never get around to asking."

"I was terrified," he said. "If you'd said no, I'd have thrown myself under a tram. I'm too young to die."

They laughed together.

"The housing committee of the city Soviet says there'll be apartments available in the spring for newly married couples," Sonya said. "In May. How about May 20?"

"For what?"

"For a wedding day, blockhead!" She grabbed the flaps of his cotton shapka and kissed him. He struggled free.

"Wedding day?" he spluttered. "Good God, Sonya, all this time I've been practicing how to propose and you've already set the date. Yes! May 20! A great day."

He paused. "We'll have to get our application into the housing committee," he said. "I'll ask for time off tomorrow, I'll…"

"Already done," she said. "I made the application in November. They promised we'd have a room by May 15."

Grisha threw up his arms in mock despair. "So what's left for the lucky groom?"

They laughed and snuggled together. After a moment they fell silent. Sonya shivered involuntarily. He walked her to her dormitory and after a long kiss in the doorway he hurried off at a run to catch the last tram.

GRISHA AND SONYA were married on schedule, May 20, in an impeccably proletarian ceremony. Grisha, stiff and uncomfortable in a blue suit and starched white shirt, offered Sonya his arm when she arrived at the district office in a rattling Ford taxicab. He self-consciously complimented her on her lacy white dress.

Two dozen factory and school friends followed them into the office of the magistrate, a plump and kindly middle-aged woman who rose from her desk and greeted them with a nod and a smile.

The ceremony was a simple one. The magistrate began it by dedicating their union "to the building of Communism, to the creation of a new Soviet society."

"You're both Komsomols," she said. "You have already taken your positions as leaders among the flower of the Soviet working class. From today, you undertake fresh duties to add to the vital burdens you have already shouldered: You undertake the duty of building a Soviet family of the new type that will march unswervingly toward the creation of a Communist society; a family that will love and follow our glorious leader, Comrade Stalin, and submit to the guidance of our Party. May you not fail in that duty."

The magistrate pushed forward the registry book on her desk, and the couple signed. Two witnesses from the wedding party added their names, and finally the magistrate wrote her name at the bottom. Grisha and Sonya silently exchanged plain silver rings and turned back to the magistrate.

"In the name of the Leningrad Soviet of Workers' and Peasants' Deputies, I pronounce you husband and wife," she said. The couple kissed. The ceremony was over.

The wedding party surged forward to congratulate and kiss them, and then filed out of the magistrate's office and through an anteroom crowded with two other parties waiting for their turn. They walked to a restaurant where the best man had arranged a long table laden with smoked sturgeon, cucumber salad, pressed chicken, caviar, boiled eggs, two kinds of bread, mutton shashlik, wine, and vodka. The guests drank the toast to the wedding couple, crying, "Bitter, bitter, bitter" at the first taste of wine in accordance with old Russian custom, declaiming it drinkable only after the newlyweds kissed. They laughed, sang, danced, ate, and drank while Grisha and Sonya sat in subdued anticipation, smiling politely and exchanging secret glances.

When courtesy permitted, the newlyweds rose and made their way to the street. A car, a large American Packard hired from the city Soviet, awaited to take them away amid cheers and ribald jokes of their friends. The guests returned to the table; Grisha and Sonya heard later that they remained drinking and

dancing until the restaurant manager ordered them out
at closing time.

Sonya and Grisha held hands in silence in the back
seat of the big Packard as it delivered them to their
new apartment on Pestelya Street. Sonya led the way
up a single flight of stairs in an old gray building. She
opened the door of the apartment; only a single bedroom containing a tall, old-fashioned wardrobe and a
massive wooden bed dominated by a carved headboard. In the headboard were two framed ovals that
once had contained portraits of Czar Nicholas II and
Czarina Alexandra. The frames now were empty. The
bedroom was in an apartment that had once belonged
to a czarist government official and his family; it was
now divided into a communal dwelling for five families who shared a bathroom and a spacious kitchen
with a coal-fired cookstove.

Grisha and Sonya entered the room and closed the
door. Sonya gasped.

"Oh, look!" she cried. "A wireless radio!"

"My wedding gift to the bride." Grisha smiled.

"How handsome it is," she said, running her hand
over the smoothly varnished wood of the case. "How
do you make it work?"

Grisha turned a small knob on the front of the set.
A dim yellow light glowed behind the dial. He waited
a few seconds until the radio made a distant hissing
sound. It grew louder, and he turned the tuning knob.
The machine squawked and spat until he found the
Leningrad station, which suddenly burst from the
cloth-covered face with a roar. A man's voice thun-

dered, and Sonya covered her ears. Grisha fumbled for the volume knob and turned it down. They stood fascinated, listening to a news report from the Leningrad Central Radio Studios. When it was over, the station began a broadcast of the Moscow Conservatory Orchestra playing the Tchaikovsky Symphony No. 6, the *Pathétique*.

"It's so beautiful," she said, kissing her new husband. Grisha shrugged and looked at his new wife. They kissed again, long and deeply.

Sonya pulled away and took him by the hand. She guided him silently to the vast wooden bed. They made love for the first time, awkwardly and tenderly, to the mournful sweet dirge of the *Pathétique*.

THAT WARM LENINGRAD SUMMER was the happiest time in Grisha's life, before or after. It was an unusual summer, a succession of glorious days interrupted only by brief afternoon rain showers that cooled the air and left a heady and fragrant scent in the city. Grisha spent his weekdays in the machine shop and Sonya spent hers in the library, preparing for her examinations. Sundays they spent in the parks or rowing on the Neva.

Nights they spent in the fine big bed, whispering, giggling, loving, and listening to hour upon hour of music from the varnished radio.

They did not permit political concerns of those days to spoil their happiness, yet political concerns were always there. War had begun in Europe. Rumors of war between Russia and Germany swept through

Leningrad almost daily, but the glorious weather, the pearly "white nights" of the northern summer and their doting preoccupation with each other pushed such rumors from their minds.

Nevertheless, in the second week of June, Grisha came home looking gloomy.

"Sonichka, there's nothing but war talk at the factory," he said. "Vadim says the factory committee's been told to draw up plans for emergency evacuation, lock, stock, and lathes. What do you think?"

Sonya rolled her eyes. "What does Vadim know, for God's sake?" she said. "He's not even a member of the committee. He's a vodka-soaked gossip!"

"Now, Sonya," he said. "He's not so bad. He's just a talker. Anyway, he's going around with the secretary to Viktor Petrovich. She knows about—"

Sonya cut him off. "What nonsense!" she said. "That slut and her boyfriend should be brought up before the Komsomol committee, Grisha; I'm surprised you'd even listen to them!"

Grisha turned away, angry. Sonya took his arm. "I'm sorry, darling," she said. "But we've both seen the Party directives on this, and it's not right to question the line. These rumors are harmful."

Grisha dropped the subject, but he brooded silently as he listened to the evening news broadcast. The announcer read a statement that made reference to rumors of German troop maneuvers on Soviet borders; it denounced them as a "clumsy propaganda scheme by the forces arrayed against the Soviet Union and Germany and which are eager to spread and intensify the war in Europe.''

It said the treaty of nonaggression between the Soviet Union and Germany was scrupulously observed by the Soviet Union. ''All the rumors according to which the Soviet Union is preparing for a war with Germany are false and provocative,'' it concluded.

''You see?'' Sonya said, triumphant. ''So much for your Vadim's evacuation stories. Would they put out a statement if the Germans were about to attack? There you are. The Party knows what it's doing.''

''Ah, my political agitator,'' he said, smiling. ''I'm sorry. You're right.'' They fell together on the bed and made love, the radio playing softly.

They did not talk about war rumors again until Saturday, June 21, when Grisha came home and found Sonya sitting on the bed flipping through the evening paper and listening to the radio. Her face was dark with worry.

''Oh, I'm glad you're home,'' she said as he came through the door. ''The whole city's buzzing with the damned war stories. It's so upsetting.''

''Yes, I know,'' he said. ''Same at the plant. By the way, it's true they're making evacuation plans. Viktor Petrovich himself had a meeting and told us what to take and what to leave behind. He said it's just routine civil defense planning, but he looked like he was taking it pretty seriously.''

Sonya was silent. She flipped the paper onto the floor. ''There's nothing in the papers and nothing on the radio,'' she said. She lay back on the bed, frowning up at the ceiling.

Grisha sat on the edge of the bed and put his hand on her thigh, smiling. Sonya's frown vanished.

Laughing, she pulled him down on her and they rolled across the bed, laughing and grasping each other. They settled into a long, passionate kiss and spent the rest of the evening making love among the tousled sheets and pillows. They forgot about war, rumors, and Germans.

LENINGRAD MILITARY COMMAND

Aug. 1, 1941

ORDER TO REPORT

To: Malmudov, Grigory Nikolayevich
  Worker, Proletarian Victory Diesel Engine Factory

Comrade Citizen Malmudov:

You are ordered to report on Aug. 3, 1941, to the regional Training Command of the Leningrad Regional Military District, Moskovskoye Chaussee, for induction into the Red Army of Workers and Peasants.

You are ordered to bring personal documents and personal rations for two days.

Failure to report is an offense against the People and any persons failing to comply with the Order to Report will be subject to strict punishment as a military deserter.

Shashuisky, L.N., LT COL

10.

The night of Saturday, June 21, 1941, was one of those endless, glowing, glorious white nights for which Leningrad was famous, nights that went gradually from twilight to dawn with no true darkness in between. Sonya and Grisha snoozed in the white night's ivory luminescence until nearly eleven o'clock. They awoke refreshed, rose, dressed, and went out to stroll in the soft light.

They walked arm in arm along the Neva embankment as far as the Winter Palace, meeting other young couples along the way. It seemed that all of Leningrad, Leningrad in love, was out on this night. Grisha and Sonya murmured softly, talking of work and love and the river, and heard the similar soft murmurings of other couples.

The broad Neva shone pale under the midnight glow, and from the Palace Bridge they heard a brief burst of high-pitched laughter from a young woman and the lower chuckle of her young man's response. They walked along the embankment as far as the Admiralty, whose tall spire stood sharply silhouetted by the glowing sky. Grisha took Sonya by the waist and lifted her to the embankment wall. He vaulted up beside her.

Sonya sighed. "Oh, Grisha, isn't it a pretty night?"

Grisha smiled and slipped his arm around her, feeling her shiver from the chill of the night air. He touched his lips lightly to her hair and breathed the familiar womanly smell. She moved closer and they sat for several minutes in silence.

Suddenly, automobile tires squealed. They glanced toward the sound and saw a long black sedan careen around the corner near the statue of Peter the Great. The car gained speed and with another squeal of its tires it turned into the Admiralty archway. A guard on duty at the archway snapped a salute and the car sped into the courtyard.

Sonya shivered. They looked at the Admiralty and noticed for the first time that the windows were ablaze with lights. Normally the Admiralty was dark after six o'clock. In the archway a single headlight appeared and a sidecar motorcycle roared out into the street. As it turned onto the embankment, Grisha caught a glimpse of gold navy officer's epaulettes on the man in the sidecar.

Sonya shivered again. "I'm getting cold," she said. "Let's go home, Grisha."

They did not speak of the Admiralty or of the motorcycle. He took her by the arm and they walked quickly back the way they had come, heads down.

They were passing the Hermitage when another car shot past and turned into Palace Square, headed for the General Staff building. Grisha glanced at Sonya. Their eyes met.

"Sonya, Sonya," he whispered. "There's something wrong."

She looked toward the corner where the last car had disappeared. She shook her head slowly. She started to say something, but instead tightened her grip on Grisha's arm.

"Let's go home," she said.

They walked in silence to the apartment and did not turn on the lights when they got inside. They undressed and climbed into bed by the glow of the white night.

THE MORNING spread over Leningrad with the promise of a glorious Sunday, the sky blue and cloudless. As early as seven o'clock, crowds of Leningraders began pushing onto trams and trains, headed for the beaches on the Gulf of Finland. The street noises first woke Sonya and Grisha at eight o'clock, but they lolled in bed for an hour, arms around each other, dozing, before Sonya finally made a move to rise.

"Why get up?" Grisha murmured, squinting through one eye. She sat cross-legged on the bed, her hair tousled, blinking. A warm, sleepy smile played across her face.

"Look outside, it's a beautiful day," she said, getting out of bed and pulling the windows wide open. "Everything's *normal*."

Grisha thought of the frightening sense of calamity the night before. He heaved himself from bed and went to the window. He stood behind his wife and put his arms around her. Leningraders in light summer clothes, many of them carrying picnic baskets, hurried along the sidewalks to the tram stop at the corner. A tram rumbled along the street, making the building tremble. Its wheels screamed as it rounded the corner. The normality of the noise reassured them.

"Well, no war," Grisha said, slipping a hand onto Sonya's breast.

"Grisha!" she squealed, squirming away from the window. "People can see!" She blushed. Grisha laughed.

"To hell with 'people,'" he said, reaching for her. She fled from the window and fell, laughing, on the bed. Grisha fell down beside her and they kissed and laughed until they collapsed, panting, amid the rumpled bedclothes. They lay there catching their breaths. Sonya pulled herself up into her familiar cross-legged position.

"Enough, Grisha," she said. "We can't be newlyweds forever."

"Why not?" he replied, reaching for her. She spun deftly out of his reach.

"We'll wear out the damned bed," she said, laughing. She hopped to the floor. "We're going on a picnic. We've got the whole day. Let's take the train to Peterhof. Please, Grishenka!''

Grisha yawned. ''Damned czarist museum. Oh, all right, duchess,'' he said, swinging his legs to the floor. ''Let's go!''

They dressed, and Sonya tidied the bed while Grisha put sausage, bread, butter, and onions in a bag. It was nearly ten o'clock before they were ready to leave. Sonya had opened the door, but Grisha stopped her. ''Hold it a minute,'' he said. ''Let's get the news.''

''The devil with the news,'' Sonya said. ''Come on!''

''Just five minutes,'' he said, clicking on the radio. Sonya sighed and closed the door.

She sat on the bed while Grisha tuned in the Leningrad Central Studios. Music drifted into the room, played for a few minutes, then faded.

They waited for the familiar voice of the Leningrad announcer opening the news report, but instead they heard a new voice. It was the somber Yuri Levitan, whose heavy bass was to become grimly familiar to Russians as it announced the crises, deaths, and victories of a terrible war. But on June 22, Sonya and Grisha were hearing Levitan for the first time. They looked at each other, puzzled.

''ATTENTION, ATTENTION,'' Levitan's voice boomed. ''THIS IS MOSCOW SPEAKING.'' A pause.

''COMRADES! A REPORT FROM THE PEOPLE'S COM-MISSAR FOR FOREIGN AFFAIRS, COMRADE MOLO-TOV!''

Another pause. The radio clicked and sputtered in the silence. Grisha and Sonya looked at the cloth screen on the speaker as if they expected Molotov himself to step through it. Finally, the flat monotone of the commissar's voice broke the crackling silence.

"Men and women, citizens of the Soviet Union..." he began. "At four A.M., without declaration of war and without any claims being made on the Soviet Union, German troops attacked our country, attacked our frontier in many places, and bombed from the air...."

Grisha dropped heavily onto the bed beside Sonya. They looked at the radio, then at each other. The metallic voice of Molotov droned on, sounding incredibly matter-of-fact, even at the end of the statement, when he said:

"The government calls upon you, men and women citizens of the Soviet Union, to rally more closely around the glorious Bolshevik Party, around the Soviet government, and our great leader, Comrade Stalin. Our cause is just. The enemy will be crushed. Victory will be ours."

The radio fell silent, except for the crackle of static. Then the sounds of a Tchaikovsky symphony began. Grisha and Sonya sat looking at each other in stunned, pale silence. Finally, Sonya stood.

"So," she said, her voice trembling. "War. It's really war." Grisha said nothing.

"Dirty fascists!" she cried. "Why?"

She went to the window. People were still walking along the street, carefree and laughing, carrying picnic baskets.

"German bastards!" she mumbled. Turning, she ran to Grisha and put her arms around him. "They'll regret this, Grisha," she said in a low, angry voice. "God damn them, they'll be sorry they ever came to Russia!"

Grisha held her, stroking her hair and her shoulders. She began to weep silently. She raised her head and looked at him, tears streaming down her cheeks.

"Grisha, don't enlist," she said.

"Enlist?" he said. "In the army?" He hadn't thought about that, but now he did.

"But, Sonya, they'll need recruits," he said. "I'll have to join up. I'll go today!" The thought excited him.

"No! Grisha, no!" she said. "They need engines for tanks more than they need targets for German guns. Stay at your job!"

"But I can't stay here when there's a war on!" he said.

"You must stay here." She grabbed his shirt and held him. "You mustn't go to the war!"

"It's not like you to talk like this," Grisha said softly, taking her head in his hands. "You're the Komsomol enthusiast, Sonichka; you're the one who talks about duty. This is duty time, my love."

She put her head on his shoulder and wept. They held each other in silence. Finally she wiped her eyes and nodded.

"Yes, Grisha, it's duty time," she said. "We might as well go and do it now. No sense waiting until tomorrow. The sooner we start, the sooner it'll be over."

They put away their picnic food. She would go the the Komsomol Committee and begin organizing. Organizing what? She didn't know how to organize for a war.

Grisha put on his working clothes. If Viktor Petrovich was right about plans to evacuate the factory, there would be no time to lose.

As they started out the door, Grisha took her hand and held her back. "You said we can't be newlyweds forever, Sonya," he said. "The Germans just ended our honeymoon."

She nodded grimly and touched his cheek. "This will pass, too, love," she said. "We'll get this war over and we'll start the honeymoon again. Maybe we'll be newlyweds forever."

They left the apartment and kissed good-bye at the corner. Grisha heading for the tram stop and Sonya setting off on foot for the institute. She was still wearing the sandals and light cotton dress she had put on for the trip to Peterhof.

THE WAR BROUGHT CHANGES more drastic than they could have imagined. Grisha did not enlist and march off to war. He was not permitted to. He and his lathe-shop coworkers set to work on double shifts tearing down the factory they had worked so hard to build. It was to be moved, the entire plant, to a new location beyond the Ural Mountains as part of an industrial complex producing tanks and trucks for the war.

Grisha, as a Komsomol leader and leader of the apprentices in the lathe shop, worked as long as twenty hours a day, sleeping night after night on the shop floor because he was too exhausted even to drag himself over to the apprentices' barracks. The machinery was painstakingly disassembled and crated for shipment, the crates marked so the factory could be reassembled quickly on arrival at its new location. Truckload after truckload of crated machines rumbled out of the factory yard for the Moscow Station where trains left daily for the long haul eastward.

From June 22 until late July, he returned to the house on Pestelya Street only five or six times. Even then, he did not always see Sonya, who was putting in long hours at the Komsomol Committee.

She had been made the head of the student civil defense unit, assigning fire teams to rooftop duty with bags of sand to extinguish fires from German incendiary bombs. She also organized squads to erect sandbagged protective coverings for the city's historical monuments. She herself spent two days building a cover for the statue of Peter the Great near the Admiralty.

Only rarely did they find time to spend a night together in their big bed. And when they did, they simply collapsed and slept heavily, waking sore and weary.

The war did not stop sex, but it sharply altered the normal rituals of love and courtship. There was no more time for the gentle flirting usual among students and youthful workers; when there was a moment for passion, it struck like a tornado, whenever and wherever the opportunity or the urgent need arose. More than a few of Leningrad's 1942 babies were conceived hurriedly beneath a bush in a public park or during a quick stand-up coupling in a darkened passageway.

The lovely long days of June soon gave way to foggy, wet ones in July and then to dry, hot ones in August. The Germans bombed sporadically, beginning the day after Molotov's somber announcement. Dire rumors swept the city daily. It was said that the Red Army was being driven back along a broad front, and that the Germans were making for Leningrad and Moscow with dizzying speed.

German planes dropped leaflets that boasted of imminent victory and told Leningraders to overthrow the commissars and surrender. Few of the leaflets were picked up, partly from hatred and partly from fear of arrest.

Nevertheless, the German message traveled quickly through the city, spreading like ripples in a pond, from frightened grandmother to food-store clerk to factory hand to truck driver. The rumors filled the vacuum left by Sovinformburo, which permitted only news of victory at a time when the real news was of defeat. When Yuri Levitan's powerful voice announced a victory in fighting near Minsk, Soviet citizens gasped in dismay. The report meant that the Germans already had penetrated as far as the Byelorussian capital, and at that rate, they would be in Moscow and Leningrad before winter.

By the end of July, Grisha had seen the last truck-load of equipment roll off to the Moscow Station. On August 1, the factory workers were summoned to the foundry, a great, echoing chamber stripped of its furnaces and machinery. The director announced that two-thirds of the workers, the most experienced and skilled ones, would follow the machinery to the east. The rest, mostly younger men, were to go to the Leningrad Military Command for induction into the armed forces. He posted lists; Grisha's name was on the list for induction.

Most of the youths sent to the army were elated—they were sick of tearing down the factory and they wanted to fight, not flee to the Urals. They wanted guns in their hands.

They got them, and quickly. Orders were distributed that very day, and Grisha's directed that he report on August 3 to the training headquarters on the Moscow highway southeast of the city. He had two days, and he hurried home with the news. Sonya was not there, so he went to the Komsomol office and found her working on "Operation Attics," a program for getting flammable materials out of the city's attics.

"Sonya!" he cried, pulling her away from her maps and assignment sheets. "I'm in the army. I report day after tomorrow!"

She gasped. "Oh God, Grisha, only two days," she said.

"Yes, come home immediately," he pleaded. "Get some time off."

She hesitated. "I can't leave right now, Grishenka," she said. "We have four hundred and fifty people reporting here in the morning, and I have to have assignments ready for them."

"How long will it take?" he asked, disappointed.

"Seven o'clock," she said. "I promise. You look worn out. Go home and get a little rest. I'll be there at seven."

Reluctantly, he left the headquarters, but he didn't feel like resting. Instead, he went to a food store and bought a bottle of sweet Soviet champagne, and a 250-gram can of caviar. Then he stood forty-five minutes in a bread queue to get 500 grams of black bread due him on his ration card. It was one of the ironies of Leningrad wartime life that such luxury items as champagne and caviar were not included in the food rationing. Until the real famine set in during the nine-hundred-day siege, it was easier to buy wine and beluga caviar than to buy onions and lard. In later years, when he would have murdered for a single moldy onion, he often thought of that caviar and champagne in the threatened city.

Back in their room, he prepared painstakingly for Sonya's arrival. They had not been together for nearly two weeks, and it was the first time since the start of the war that he had time to think seriously of sex.

He dusted the furniture—especially the curlicues of the big wooden bedstead—swept the floor, and gathered up the odds and ends of clothing they had tossed off during hurried visits home. He set a table in the center of the room, covering it with a white cloth, a wedding gift that had never been used. On the table he set two candles—less a romantic luxury than a wartime necessity: The authorities enforced the nighttime power blackouts by the simple expedient of cutting off electricity to residential areas.

As seven o'clock approached, Grisha took out his blue wedding suit, brushed it carefully and put it on. He cut the bread into thin slices, spread them with butter and caviar, arranged the slices on a plate, and sprinkled them with chopped onion. In the center he put a bowl of sour cream and the bottle of champagne.

Seven o'clock came and went. He impatiently paced the floor. Seven-thirty came, seven forty-five, eight o'clock. He was starting to blow out the candles when he heard her key in the door. She came in, haggard with fatigue.

"I'm sorry, Grisha darling..." she began. Then she saw the candles and the table and Grisha in his wedding suit. Her face relaxed into a grateful smile.

"Oh, God, how nice," she said. "You did all this?" She kissed him. "You look so handsome...."

She looked down at herself and moaned. "But look at me, Grishenka, what a horrible mess I am." Her dress was rumpled and she had a soiled white kerchief on her head. Odd strands of dark hair fell in disorder from it. "I've got to make myself presentable."

"Vain woman," he laughed. "You're beautiful as you are. You're a woman of the working class."

"That may be," she said, "but you look like a man of property. I want to be pretty for this night."

She pulled a handful of clothes from the wardrobe and fled down the hallway to the communal bathroom.

He waited impatiently until she reappeared, clean and radiant. Her face was shiny from a scrubbing and she wore a clean cotton dress. Her hair was freshly combed, loosened from its accustomed bun and falling provocatively over her shoulders.

"How do I look?" she asked, spinning around so that her hair flew.

"Devastating," he said, pulling her chair out from the table. "Now, if Madame would care to take her seat..."

As she slipped into the chair, Grisha bent and kissed her lightly on the neck. She reached back and held his head close to her for a long moment.

They laughed and chattered while he opened the champagne and poured bubbling glasses of the pale yellow wine. They raised their glasses for a toast.

"To the victory," he said.

"To the victory," she replied. "And to us."

"To us."

They drank the toast and devoured the caviar, ravenous in their hunger. When it was gone they sipped the champagne slowly, talking of the war news, the fire watches, and the army. Grisha showed Sonya his induction orders and they discussed what he should take with him and where he might be sent after basic training. Sonya talked about the next day's project of sending 450 Komsomols out into the city for a block-by-block examination of attics.

He poured the last of the wine and they fell silent, looking at each other, feeling high and happy.

"Right now I think we both have more important work to do," he said. "Our great wooden bed has been neglected, my dear; we should remedy that."

Sonya stood without speaking and went to the bed. He followed, taking her in his arms for a hard, passionate kiss. They tore their clothes off jerkily, shadows leaping as the candles flickered, and they fell into the bed without turning down the cover. They made love, gasping and groaning, until they collapsed, slippery with sweat. The wine and the love had driven away fatigue, but as the orgasm subsided, weariness took charge; they fell asleep in a tangle of naked limbs and rumpled pillows. Grisha had a faint memory of Sonya covering him with a blanket in the night.

They awoke early the following morning, naked and embracing closely beneath the blanket, feeling refreshed, strong, and hungry. They made love once more, quickly and vigorously, then bounded out of bed. They washed, breakfasted on bread, butter, and tea, and rushed off together to the Komsomol headquarters.

It was the last time in his life that Grisha saw the inside of the room on Pestelya Street. It was the last time he slept in the great bed, and the last time he made love to his wife.

11.

Kuznetsov could not manage breakfast Saturday morning because of the tense anxiety that knotted his stomach. For nearly thirty years he had avoided close contact with other people as a matter of cautious habit; now, in a week's time, he had nearly begun an affair with a neighbor woman and was committed to spending a weekend with the one man who was most likely to suspect his secret.

He got up early and brewed tea, drinking glass after glass until he felt clammy and nauseated. By the time Repin arrived at ten o'clock, he felt too ill to go.

"Well, hey, all ready?" Repin shouted when Kuznetsov opened the door.

"Well, I'm not feeling awfully well, Genya..." he began.

"Tch, Sasha, you're not looking awfully well, either," he said. "You're sleeping badly, all washed out. Never mind, a little rest and sun, and you'll be a new man. You have a hat? Get it. Let's go, let's go!''

Repin dragged him to the door, Kuznetsov stammering helplessly.

Repin was in unusually high spirits as they climbed into his new green Zhiguli. In the back seat sat Repin's wife Ludmilla, a stout woman who looked ten years older than her husband. She wore a dark print dress of a shiny synthetic material and a pair of sunglasses with pointed rims that gave her the appearance of a fat and sinister cat. Beside her sat the Repins' son and only child, Anatoly Evgenievich, stiff and upright in starched white shirt and black woolen trousers. He was fourteen.

"Good day, Ludmilla Borisovna," Kuznetsov said, settling into the front passenger seat. "Good day, Tolya."

"So formal!" she exclaimed, pursing her lips in a coy smile. "You're such a proper Moscow gentleman, Sasha. Please call me Lyuda, or I'll feel like an old dowager."

"Forgive me, please...Lyuda," he said. He half turned so he could face her, twisting his neck uncomfortably. He was not accustomed to riding in passenger cars.

She did, indeed, look like a dowager, with heavy lipstick and rouge daubed over a flaking layer of makeup, the whole effect heightened by the imperious slant of the sunglasses. They were very dark glasses, tinted a shade of deep green. Kuznetsov could not see her eyes, but two eyebrows etched black with pencil arched above the glasses, rising and falling as she spoke. He turned to young Anatoly.

"And what are your summer plans, Tolya?" he asked. "I suppose you'll be glad to get a break from school."

Anatoly looked at Kuznetsov with gray eyes as cold as his father's. He cleared his throat. "Quite the contrary, Alexander Nikolayevich," he said. "I will take extra courses in the summer to prepare myself for ninth form. I look forward to it very much."

His voice quavered with the unpleasant timbre of adolescence.

"I am re-reading Marx's 'Critique of the Gotha Programme,'" he said, his voice breaking at the word "critique."

"Tolya will be a real political worker when he grows up," Repin said. He put the car in gear and shot out from the curb.

"God have mercy!" Ludmilla shrieked. "Not so fast, Genya. Be careful of the cars on the left side, they never look. Look out!"

Repin neither replied nor slowed, but his wife kept up a constant patter of warning and advice. Kuznetsov felt a surge of nausea as the car turned onto Gorky Street and sped away from the center of the city. He rolled his window down and took a breath; the air made him feel a little better. He politely complimented Repin on his car.

"Thank you, it's an excellent machine," Repin said. "It's much better than the Fiats they make in Italy. After we made the contract with the Italians, our engineers discovered a number of serious deficiencies. They made changes."

"I see," Kuznetsov said. He regretted having drunk the tea, which sloshed in his stomach.

Repin chattered on about the car—speed, mileage, horsepower, turning radius—and his wife shot warnings from the back seat. The car sped past the Dynamo sports complex, across the V. I. Lenin Bridge, and out the Leningrad Highway, where high-rise apartment buildings gave way to crooked wooden houses and communal wells. Traffic had been heavy in the city, but after they passed the airport, the four-lane road became two lanes and the traffic thinned. The Zhiguli sped along at a steady fifty miles an hour.

The only delay came just outside Klin, near a large sign announcing that the pretty little town was Tchaikovsky's birthplace. A big scrap-metal truck had jacknifed and overturned, blocking the road. A harried State Automobile Inspection officer waved traffic through a narrow gap beside the wrecked truck. A second truck was hooking up a cable to drag it from the roadway.

"You see, Genya, you see?" Ludmilla said. "That's from too much speed; you must drive more carefully!"

Repin ignored her, and as soon as they cleared the wreckage he pushed the speed back to fifty.

A few miles past Klin, Repin turned onto a dirt road and the Zhiguli bounded among grain fields and stands of pine and birch woods. They came upon an old church nestled in the edge of one of the woods. Its roof had long ago caved in, but a great bulbous onion dome was still in place. In the churchyard, iron St. George crosses rusted over untended graves. A flock of crows roosted in the pine trees around the church, setting up a raucous chorus when Repin's car approached. Kuznetsov shivered involuntarily at the funereal birds and their coarse voices. Repin stopped.

"By God, Sasha, just look at those crows," he said. "They look like a bunch of priests, eh? Priests standing guard over their church." He laughed.

"Ugh, let's go, Genya," his wife said. "It's too spooky!"

"Yes, it's a gloomy place," Kuznetsov said. "I don't like it."

"Superstitious?" He laughed. "It's just trees and birds. Come on, let's go see how old the graves are."

He opened his door.

"I... I'm not superstitious, but it's a pretty depressing place, Genya," Kuznetsov said. In the ruined church they saw words and pictures scrawled on the walls. One was large enough to read from the road:

"Valya sucks it."

Repin chuckled. "All right, we came to enjoy ourselves in the country." He closed the door and sped away, Ludmilla shrieking for him to slow down.

"The dust is coming in, Sasha," she cried. "Close your window, please!"

Kuznetsov reluctantly wound the window closed and the air turned stuffy. The rough road, the stuffiness, and the oily smell of Ludmilla's perfume overpowered him. With great difficulty he kept from spewing the tea over himself and the car.

They slowed down at an iron gate and he gratefully rolled down the window while Repin showed a document to a grizzled old gatekeeper.

As they drove through, Kuznetsov glimpsed a sign on the gatekeeper's kiosk and his nausea returned. The sign read:

HUNTING AND RECREATION CENTER
COMMITTEE FOR STATE SECURITY

Kuznetsov glanced uneasily at Repin. "Genya, aren't these dachas for the KGB?" he asked.

"Yes, true," Repin said. "But we personnel workers in the larger institutions have privileges. The KGB club is very generous about it. We do a lot for them, know what I mean? They like to have good relations with personnel officials."

Kuznetsov nodded. He was now quite sorry he had come. All Soviet citizens felt ill at ease around the Chekists. He certainly had more reason than most.

Repin turned into a street lined with rows of tidy, brightly painted cottages. They stopped in front of a cottage with the number 14.

"This is it," Repin said. "Home for the weekend. I'll get the key."

Repin set off on foot for the office and left Kuznetsov to help Ludmilla and Anatoly unload baggage and boxes of food. In the boxes was a plentitude of pickled cucumbers, dried mushrooms, bottles of wine and vodka, melons, cheese, sausage, and bright mandarin oranges from Georgia. Mingling with the inviting odors of the food was a cool forest scent blowing from a stand of birch and pine trees behind the dachas. On the other side, beyond a green meadow, the Volga River glimmered under a noonday sun. Kuznetsov's nausea gave way to the appetizing smells. He was hungry.

"Nice day, Lyuda," he said.

"Whew, hot one," she said. Her red lips wrinkled in a grin. Beads of sweat oozed through the makeup. "I'm ready to get into the water."

Kuznetsov imagined what she'd look like, untrussed and undressed, wading into the Volga.

Repin came back down the street with a key and they carried the supplies into the dacha's small kitchen. It had a tiny refrigerator just big enough to hold the perishables, a two-burner hot plate and a sink. There were also a bathroom and a shower, a parlor, and two bedrooms, each nearly as large as his room in Moscow. The furniture was of a dark, highly polished wood and had hard horsehair cushions. It was an attractive little house, and Kuznetsov felt comfortable in it.

"Well," Repin beamed. "Nice, eh?"

"Very nice indeed," Kuznetsov replied.

"The Chekists work well, and they play well," Repin said. "They have rowboats, shooting ranges, and there's a nice beach across the river. We'll get together a picnic and row over there."

Kuznetsov nodded gratefully at the mention of food. They changed to bathing suits and Ludmilla filled a basket with sausage, beer, bread, onions, mineral water, and cheese. She had donned an orange two-piece bathing suit that embarrassed Kuznetsov. Her flesh was stark-white and remarkably lively. At every step her breasts heaved and her thighs jiggled. Her stomach fell downward in three heavy folds; slashing upward diagonally from the waistband of the bathing suit was a lurid surgical scar, five inches long.

Repin, muscular and tanned, gray curly hair on his chest, could have been her son. Skinny Tolya could have been her grandson. The boy wore tight swimming shorts that came to a point where they stretched over his penis. He stood self-conscious in his near nakedness, tall, sallow, and thin, head unbending on a narrow neck.

Kuznetsov himself felt profoundly foolish in a shapeless pair of salmon-covered swimming trunks pulled up to his navel. His skin was fish-belly white except for his chest, which showed a light tan from the previous weekend in Luzhniki Park with Dr. Fomina.

They left the dacha and walked, single-file, along a path through the meadow to the docks, where Repin made arrangements for a boat. Kuznetsov took the first turn at the oars, struggling with the unfamiliar action of guiding a small boat through the water. After a while Repin shook his head.

"Sasha, you're a hopeless landsman," he said. "Let's change places or we'll never get across this river."

Kuznetsov willingly turned the oars over to Repin, who pulled expertly, straight for the beach. Kuznetsov sat in the stern beside Ludmilla with her catlike sunglasses and oily perfume. Young Anatoly sat stiffly in the bow, silent and unsmiling, his knees pulled together, eyes hidden by a pair of round sunglasses.

They pulled the boat ashore at the beach and waded into the chilly Volga water for a pre-lunch swim. Kuznetsov had wondered what might happen to Ludmilla's heavy makeup in the water, but his question remained unanswered: She avoided getting it wet as she paddled heavily back and forth, head held carefully clear of the river's water.

After the swim, they ate sausage and bread and Kuznetsov drank three bottles of strong Moscow beer. The food, drink, and swim made him feel normal again. He lounged on a blanket and chatted amiably with Repin and his wife. To his relief, Repin made no mention of the factory, the Party, or the Chekists. He talked of fishing, hunting, soccer, and cars. The sun shone brightly, and Kuznetsov relaxed.

The afternoon sun was beginning to cast long shadows before they took a final dip and gathered their things for the pull back to the KGB recreation center. Kuznetsov felt the feverish tingle of sunburn and realized, too late, that he had been careless. Ludmilla and Tolya, too, were turning from pale pink to red, and only Repin's well-tanned body appeared that it would survive the afternoon without an unpleasant burn.

"I'm afraid we'll be sorry for staying out too long, Lyuda," Kuznetsov said ruefully. Ludmilla pulled off the dark glasses. Two smallish black eyes, set close together in a fleshy face, blinked at him.

"God have mercy, you look like cooked shrimp, Sasha!" she squealed. "Oh, Tolya, you too, darling. You'll be so sorry tomorrow!"

Repin shook his head. "Lyudochka, my dear, you're as bad. I don't envy any of you."

Ludmilla tried to look down at her belly, craning her neck to see past the plump breasts that blocked the view. Her hands pulled at the flesh of her stomach, leaving white fingerprints in the pink expanse.

"Eek!" she shrieked. "Look at me! Genya, why didn't you tell me?" She looked reproachfully at her husband.

"I didn't notice, darling," he said. "But, fortunately, there's a cure." He held the boat while the others piled aboard, then climbed in and took the oars.

"Vodka, taken cold and in quantity, relieves sunburn," he said. "A wise Tatar told me."

Kuznetsov laughed. "What do Tatars know about sunburns?" he asked.

"Not a thing," Repin said. "But they know about vodka."

They unloaded the boat and climbed up the embankment to the meadow. A volleyball net had been strung there, and a group of men and women were playing. A dozen or so others sat around the net, drinking beer and kvass and cheering the players. One of them noticed Repin.

"Genya, how's it going?" he shouted. Others glanced around and waved as they recognized Repin, who headed toward the court. Kuznetsov reluctantly followed.

"Greetings, comrades," Repin said. "How the hell can you play volleyball on such a lazy day?"

"I don't," the man said. "I just watch." He looked at Kuznetsov with curiosity.

"Excuse me, Maxim Borisevich, this is my colleague from Red Banner, Comrade Kuznetsov. Our chief engineer. Sasha, Maxim Borisevich is deputy chief inspector for the second section in the Moscow region."

The deputy chief inspector looked at Kuznetsov with interest. "Ah yes," he said, smiling and shaking Kuznetsov's hand. "I think you've mentioned your chief engineer. A pleasure, Comrade Engineer."

Repin introduced Kuznetsov to several other volleyball spectators. He felt feverish and chilly under the stares of the Chekists. But he smiled and murmured the requisite pleasantries: "Hello," "a pleasure," "nice to know you."

"My dear fellow," one of them said. "I hate to say it, but you've been roasted like a leg of mutton. Repin, what have you done to your friend?"

"Yes," Kuznetsov said, touching his pink forearms and belly. "Little too long on the beach."

The Chekist laughed. "Ah, but your friend Repin here, he has a cure."

"I've heard," Kuznetsov said. "A wise old Tatar..."

"That's the cure," the Chekist said with a chuckle. "He gave me that cure once. For a sprained ankle. The ankle felt better for a while, but the rest of me barely survived. Be careful!"

The Chekist slapped Kuznetsov good-naturedly on the shoulder. He winced. "Sorry, brother," the man said, laughing and shaking his head.

Repin waved to the Chekists and led the way back toward the dacha, Kuznetsov following along behind. The KGB men spoke in low voices for a moment, followed by a burst of laughter.

At the dacha, Kuznetsov excused himself and went to his bedroom to lie down. He stretched out on the bed and studied the ornate glass light fixtures, pondering his situation.

Repin, he felt certain, suspected something. He also felt certain that the personnel director had communicated his suspicions to some of the Chekists. The one man, especially—the deputy chief inspector, second section—had heard of him. He thought of his wife, his daughter, of the consequences for them.

How long? he thought. How long before they peel back the layers and find that everything is false?

The Chekists, with their playful, confident eyes, looked at people as a scientist would examine a biological specimen, a butterfly pinned to a board. Kuznetsov felt like that butterfly: caught, skewered, no longer in control.

He looked down at the glowing skin of his belly and touched it gently. It was, indeed, a sunburn. He felt a strong need for Repin's Tatar cure. He sat up carefully and dressed. Ludmilla and Tolya were napping in the other bedroom and Kuznetsov found Repin in the parlor, reading a newspaper.

"I'm ready for your famous cure," Kuznetsov said.

"Fine, by God," Repin said, looking up from his paper. "I thought I'd have to take it alone if you didn't get up soon."

He went to the kitchen and returned with two glasses and a frost-rimmed bottle of Stolichnaya vodka fresh from the freezer. He poured two glasses of the clear liquid, so cold it flowed like syrup.

"Your health," Repin said.

"And yours," Kuznetsov replied. They tossed back the vodka in one gulp.

"Brrrr!" Kuznetsov shivered. "That'll freeze a man's throat! But good. Mmm."

Repin poured fresh measures of the icy vodka and the two sipped lightly, chatting about sunburns and the news of the day.

Kuznetsov downed the second glass, feeling its warmth spread through him.

"By God, your wise Tatar knew what he was talking about," he said. "I'm on my way to getting cured."

Repin laughed and filled their glasses a third time.

Kuznetsov's pink glow had deepened by the time Ludmilla, again trussed, stockinged, powdered, rouged, and combed, appeared from her bedroom and

announced that she was starting the shashlik and that
Repin should light the grill. Kuznetsov leaped to his
feet and bowed to her.

"Lyuda, my dear, what can I do?" he asked.

Ludmilla fluttered the lashes of her dark little eyes.
"You could slice the onions and cucumbers," she said
with a titter.

Kuznetsov followed her sedately into the kitchen,
where she tied a yellow apron on him, reaching around
from behind so that her breasts pressed against his
back. He decided she might not be such an unattrac-
tive woman after all.

Kuznetsov helped himself to the icy bottle of vodka.
He refilled his glass and poured one for Ludmilla before he sliced the cucumbers for the salad. Young Anatoly looked in. He announced primly that he intended
to take a walk before dinner. Repin came in, winked
at Kuznetsov, and poured himself more vodka. He
topped up Kuznetsov's glass, too, and said the fire was
ready.

They cooked spitted meat, onions, and peppers over
glowing charcoal on the open porch of the dacha,
drinking and laughing as the shashlik sizzled. Less
than a fourth of the bottle remained when Repin
poured the last round before dinner. The alcohol had
put Kuznetsov in a warm and witty mood; Ludmilla
laughed at everything he said.

Anatoly complained of his sunburn, and Ludmilla
ordered him to remove his shirt so she could rub co-
conut oil on the livid red of back and shoulders.

"Poor boy," she said, slathering the oil over the fevered skin. "Poor baby."

When the shashlik was cooked, Repin brought out two bottles of red Hungarian wine. "Egri Bikaver," he said. "It comes from the commissary here."

Kuznetsov gravely examined the label, which depicted a bull's head. He tried to read the Latin letters.

"Mmm," he said. "What does this Egra Bik—"

"Egri Bikaver," Repin said. "It means 'Bull's Blood.' Excellent Hungarian wine."

"Bull's blood!" Ludmilla squealed, wrinkling her nose. "What a name! It sounds awful."

"We'll like it, my dear," Repin said, uncorking one of the bottles. "It's strong and robust like our comrade here. It's good for the red organs of the body." He winked at Kuznetsov.

They sipped the wine and pronounced it good, although Kuznetsov could not detect that it tasted differently from any other wine. They ate the shashlik straight from the spits, Kuznetsov devouring two of them and sharing another with Ludmilla. He lost track of how many glasses of wine he drank, but noticed Repin pouring the last of the second bottle as they cleared away the remains of the shashlik and salad.

Ludmilla brought out dishes of ice cream with sweet blackberry jam and cups of thick black Turkish coffee. The coolness of the ice cream and the strong, bitter taste of the coffee cleared his head. He recognized with satisfaction that he was drunk. He looked at Repin, at the sedate Anatoly, and at black-eyed Ludmilla and felt content, among friends.

"Well, Comrade Engineer," Repin said. "Have enough?"

"Yes, yes," Kuznetsov said, patting his stomach. "Plenty." He nodded to Ludmilla. "She's pampering me, Genya," he said. "I don't know how you survive such tender treatment. Lucky man you are."

Ludmilla giggled, embarrassed, and began to gather up the dessert dishes. Kuznetsov rose to help, but she pushed him back into his chair. Repin went away and returned with Armenian cognac in a dark brown bottle.

"We'll top it off with a bit of this," he said.

"I'll surely hate myself in the morning," Kuznetsov said. "But what the hell . . ."

Repin chuckled and poured two tumblers half full of the cognac. "Yes, what the hell," he said. "We only live once."

Repin took out a pair of cigars and offered one to Kuznetsov. He seldom smoked, but the occasion and the mood called for acceptance. He took it, inexpertly bit off the end and took a light from Repin. Clouds of blue smoke floated out into the night.

"Excellent cigar, Genya," he said.

"Cuban," Repin replied. "The commissary here has a supply of the best Havana cigars. If you were an American you couldn't get one of these."

Kuznetsov felt a twinge of his old unease at the remark, but Repin went on talking about the quality of the KGB commissary and the feeling passed. He sipped at the brandy and relaxed. He felt dreamy, as if he were floating. He grinned at Repin.

"Times are good now, Sasha," Repin said. " 'Life is better, life is gayer.' Old Stalin said that in 1936, but now it's true. What do you think?"

"Yes, it's true," Kuznetsov replied. "Times are better. Can you imagine us during the war smoking Havana cigars and pouring good brandy into a belly full of meat and ice cream? No, comrade, we'd have been happy with stale bread and a rotten sprat twice a day."

Repin nodded silently and puffed at his cigar. "What were you, Sasha, infantry?"

"Mm-hm," Kuznetsov said. Through the haze of smoke and brandy his old caution asserted itself. "Infantry, southwestern front." That was what his documents showed, but the brandy was making it difficult to remember. It had been years since it had been necessary to recall those manufactured details.

"Fought the whole war down there?" Repin said.

"Uh hm." Kuznetsov said, frowning at the cigar. "Heavy machine gun company..."

Repin nodded. "Those were hard times, but we came out of it all right in the end," he said. "Cost us lots of lives, but we came out of it. I lost my wife in the war."

Kuznetsov glanced at Repin in surprise.

"Married Ludmilla after the war, in '53," Repin said. "I was just a kid, in Leningrad, and my...her name was Olga...she was working in the Kirov plant and I was at the front. I got into the city on leave. Had some potatoes and four cans of that good American meat. Spam. Remember it? Wonderful stuff.

"Anyway," he continued. "I was taking it to her. But I was too late. Dead. Dystrophy and dysentery was the diagnosis, which was another way of saying she starved to death. She died at work, collapsed in the factory. In those days people died like that. We had a kid, too, but she had died already, in the first winter of the blockade. Wasn't it hell there?"

Kuznetsov nodded, and saw that Repin's gray eyes were clouding. They didn't look so cold now.

"Very sorry, brother," he said. "Yes, it was hell. I . . . I lost my wife, too. . . ." He stopped. His mind cleared for a moment and he realized he was getting into a dangerous area. ". . . In Stalingrad," he added, and fell silent.

"What say?" Repin snapped out of his reverie and looked sharply at Kuznetsov. "I thought you were a bachelor all your life."

Kuznetsov struggled to clear his mind. He had to get out of this conversation.

"Well, technically that's true," he said. "She wasn't really my wife; it was hard to get married in those days. But . . . well, you know how it was."

"Oh yes, of course," Repin said. "There were plenty of marriages in those days that didn't go into the registry books."

Kuznetsov sighed, relieved, and took a puff from the cigar. Thoughts of Sonya came to his mind. He could see her in the big bed in Leningrad.

"Tell me about her," Repin said.

Now it was Kuznetsov's eyes that clouded. "A fine woman, Genya, really." He sat up in his chair and burped. "A real Russian beauty, as they say. Smart. Engineering student at the institute, right at the top of her class."

He felt dizzy and his nose was running. He tugged a handkerchief from his pocket, blew his nose, and wiped it clumsily. He stuffed the handkerchief back into his pocket and downed the brandy. Repin filled his glass again.

"After we got married we lived in an old apartment with a fine big wooden bed...."

"You said it again, my boy," Repin said. "Are you keeping secrets about this youthful marriage?"

Kuznetsov frowned and thought a moment. Must stop talking, he thought. Must get off this subject.

"Well, you know, like I said, I just thought of it that way," he muttered. "Anyway, she died in Leningrad and..."

"Leningrad?" Repin said.

"Stalingrad," Kuznetsov said. "Stalingrad. Genya, I'm getting a little drunk. I'm not thinking straight." He swallowed more brandy. "Letsh, let's get off this old subject, eh?"

"Right, of course, let's not talk about the bad old days," Repin said. "You like my Zhiguli?"

"Damn, yes," Kuznetsov replied, relieved to talk about something else. "Elegant machine. I'd like a car like that."

"Would you?" Repin said. "I could get you on the list."

"How?"

"I have friends. These people out here." Repin made a sweeping gesture. "They can arrange it."

"Really?" Kuznetsov thought of driving around Moscow in his own car.

"The question is, can you afford it?"

"Sure I can afford it," Kuznetsov said, waving a hand. "How much?"

"Oh, about five thousand rubles."

"Sure," Kuznetsov said. "I've got that." His head swam and his eyes refused to focus on the overhead light. He looked at Repin, and they still would not focus. There were two Repins, two grins, and four gray eyes.

"Lish...lish...looka here, Genya," he said. "Know what I'm gonna get?"

Two Repins shook their heads, still grinning.

"Dacha!" Kuznetsov blurted. "Daaaacha! Just like this. Gonna get one o' these daaachas."

Later, Kuznetsov could remember Repin asking if he knew how much a dacha might cost, but after that he lost track of the conversation. He could not make words and phrases properly and he remembered the double Repin head grinning at him.

There was something about bedtime; both Repin and Ludmilla helped him stand; one arm over his shoulder and one over hers; bumping into the door to the parlor; falling down in the parlor, laughing; getting up again; stumbling into the bedroom; groping at Ludmilla's breast with his left hand; squeezing it as they dropped him into the bed.

And that was all he could remember.

12.

Kuznetsov became aware of his situation in gradual
stages. First, he knew only that he was awake, but he
did not know where. Then he knew that he did not feel
well. Then he knew that he was in Repin's dacha. He
closed his eyes and lay still for some minutes, trying to
judge the seriousness of his illness, the dull, fuzzy ache
in his head, and the distress in his stomach.

At first it seemed it was not so bad. But then he
opened his eyes and started to move. Pain struck in a
dozen places at once and he closed his eyes again. He
lay still. The bed seemed to sway like a boat. He tried
to roll over, but the motion nauseated him. He needed
to pee, but he wasn't sure he had the strength to reach
the bathroom. He decided to go back to sleep. No
good. The bladder; the nausea; the throbbing head.
Gingerly, he raised himself to a sitting position at the
edge of the bed. He swayed, groaned, and put his

hands to his temples. Cautiously, he struggled to his
feet.

"Ooh, Christ Jesus, help me," he murmured.
"What have I done to myself?" With a choking belch
he stumbled to the bathroom and vomited. The gagging coughs resounded through the little cottage.
When it was over, he stood up, tears rolling down his
cheeks and his head pounding. He urinated in a prolonged, blessed stream that eased his stomach and
cleared some of the fuzz from his brain. When he finished he looked at himself in the mirror. He groaned,
looked away, and ran cold water into the sink.

With the shock of water on his face he began to remember.

"Aaach!" He inhaled some of the water and
coughed. "Hell hell hell hell shit!" he muttered. He
remembered talking about his wife and the war. He
rubbed his forehead. Repin had all his personnel records; they said nothing of a marriage. He tried to recall the conversation. He couldn't.

He reached for a towel, hands trembling. Snatches
of the conversation came back to him, his explanation about the marriage, Repin's story of a wife in
Leningrad. Leningrad! Christ, they could have served
in the same unit!

He shakily worked up a lather with his shaving
brush and spread the foam on his stubbled cheeks. He
opened the razor, stropped it weakly and brought it up
under his nose. He scraped downward, but his hand
trembled and he nicked himself. He tried again, and
nicked himself again. Finally he got most of the hag-

gard, bloated face shaved. He washed away the lather and dried his face, pressing bits of toilet paper on the nicks. The stubble showed darkly where he had missed shaving, but he ignored it. He started to unbutton his pajamas, wondering how he had gotten into them. Then he remembered being helped into the bedroom by Repin and Ludmilla. Then he remembered fondling Ludmilla's breast. The nausea returned and he held his head over the sink, gagging, but nothing came.

He tried again to unbutton the pajamas, but this time he felt the stinging pain of the sunburn.

"Oooh, shit!" he groaned. The skin across his back, shoulders, and thighs felt tight and blistered. He left the pajamas on and stumbled back to his room. As he crossed the hallway he heard Repin and Ludmilla talking on the porch. They laughed and he pushed the door shut.

He removed the pajamas gingerly and dressed, sucking on his teeth when the shirt rubbed against the burned shoulders and back. At that point he noticed two teeth were missing. The bridge! It had come out in the night. He looked around the room, but it was nowhere in sight. He pawed through the bedclothes, felt his pockets, peered under the bed. He went back to the bathroom and looked in the mirror at the unsightly gap on the right side of his mouth. He searched the sink and medicine cabinet. No teeth.

He sighed heavily and went out to the porch, dreading the necessity of facing the Repins and worried about the missing bridge. It was American-made, but he was not sure anybody could recognize that fact today. Soviet dentistry had relied over the years on American technology. As he stepped onto the porch, Repin stood up, laughing.

"How does the head feel, my boy?" he said, slapping Kuznetsov on the back.

"Yike!" he cried. "Oh, shit, Genya, God-damned sunburn!"

Ludmilla gasped, and he muttered an apology.

"Please excuse me, Sasha," Repin said, still grinning. "I forgot. You must have a bit of a head today."

"A bit," he said, easing himself into a chair. He surveyed the array of sausage, beets, bread, cheese, and boiled eggs with bilious distaste. "I'm afraid I drank too much."

"We heard," Repin said, chuckling.

"Sorry," Kuznetsov said. "Lost some teeth too," he added, pulling his upper lip back to show the gap. "Seen them?"

"Dropped out in the living room when you took a spill," Repin said, opening a handkerchief and bringing out the bridge. "I saved them for you." He looked at the bridge with interest before handing it to Kuznetsov.

"Nice pair of teeth," he said. "Who's your dentist?"

Kuznetsov took a deep breath and carefully replaced the denture before answering. He bared his teeth and tapped the dental work.

"Just the local polyclinic," he said. "They do good work there."

"Hm, I'll have to pay them a visit," Repin said.

Kuznetsov reached unsteadily for a bottle of yogurt, but his hand trembled and he nearly upset it. Ludmilla grabbed the bottle before it spilled. He glanced at her, and she smiled coyly. He looked away.

"You really do look like hell, Sasha," Repin said, shaking his head. "When you looked in the mirror you must have tried to cut your throat."

Repin and his wife laughed. Kuznetsov picked away the bits of toilet paper covering the nicks.

"I think I considered it," he said. "I feel like the Armenian cavalry's been through my mouth at a gallop, and the horses shit on my tongue. Excuse me, Lyuda."

She giggled. Repin roared with laughter. He pounded Kuznetsov's back. Kuznetsov clenched his teeth and moaned.

"I knew you'd feel this way," Repin said. "I've arranged a cure."

"God save me, Genya, no more cures, please," he groaned. "I can't survive another one of those Tatar cures."

Repin laughed. "This one's a cure that won't kill, I promise," he said. "I reserved the banya for us. Ten o'clock, in just half an hour. We'll sweat the poison out."

Kuznetsov nodded gratefully. A good sweat in a Russian bath would indeed improve his condition. He drank the yogurt, thankful for its coolness, and then

sipped two glasses of tea while Ludmilla cleared away
the breakfast. He had no stomach for solid food.

Anatoly did not like sweat baths and stayed behind
to read, but to Kuznetsov's dismay, Ludmilla began
gathering together her towel and straw hat. The three
of them set off along the road to a rough wooden
building with smoke billowing from a stone chimney.

"It's a splendid banya," Repin said. "Running water, hot and cold. And the hot room will take your
whiskers off if you sit high enough."

Repin opened the door and a blast of warm air
rushed out. He and Ludmilla retired to the dressing
area, leaving the entryway for Kuznetsov.

Kuznetsov hung his clothing on wooden pegs,
wrapped a white towel around his waist and when Repin shouted "Ready!" he went through to the hot
room. There, he found Repin sitting naked on an upper bench, the sweat already starting from his forehead. Ludmilla sat one level lower, wrapped in a towel
that covered her great bosom and broad hips. He
edged past her and took a seat on the same upper level
as Repin, nearly choking in the dry heat near the ceiling. Ludmilla smiled up at them and her makeup began to collapse under the heat. Glistening beads of
perspiration bubbled through the pancake, turning
everything into a chalky mud that eroded in rivulets of
sweat. Her hair came undone and straggled from its
sweep in a jumble of oily ringlets. She poured a pan of
cold water over her head, shrieking as it ran between
her breasts and soaked the towel.

Kuznetsov looked away, pain and nausea sweeping over him.

He sat in the hot room until he felt drained and short of breath; then he showered. After a thorough scrubbing he returned for another bout in the dry, searing air of the top level. The heat began to drive away the sense of depression, and after an hour alternating between cold showers and hot sweats he began to feel normal again.

"Had enough?" Repin asked.

"Just a little more," he replied. "You and Ludmilla go ahead. I'll go when you're ready."

Repin and his wife left the hot room and Kuznetsov lay on the bench, breathing the air and listening to the spray of the shower outside. When the shower stopped he wearily got up from the bench and went out for a last cold shower. He dried himself, wrapped a clean dry sheet around waist and shoulders, and joined them in the dressing area. They sat on overstuffed chairs and Repin turned on a fan to dry the perspiration that still gleamed on their foreheads. A sense of well-being came over Kuznetsov as he settled into the deep cushion.

"Now the last stage of the cure," Repin said. He stepped outside and reappeared a moment later with bottles of Czech Pilsner beer, so cold that condensation glistened on the dark green bottles.

Kuznetsov looked uncertainly at the beer. His stomach was as yet unready for beer, but he was powerfully thirsty and he accepted one of the bottles. He

drank, and the icy liquid felt good on his tongue. He
pressed the bottle to his head.

"Thanks," he said. "That helps."

Repin sipped quietly and turned his gray eyes on
Kuznetsov. "Remember what we talked about last
night?"

Kuznetsov's bloodshot eyes met Repin's. He
thought carefully for a moment. He forced a smile.
"Not too well. Not too well."

Repin smiled. "I imagine not. But I thought you
might want to go into the subject a bit further, in the
clear light of dawn, so to speak. I think I could help."
Repin winked. "It can be useful to have friends in the
Cheka."

Kuznetsov's mind raced. He could not think clearly.

"Honestly, Genya, I was drunk as a priest last
night," he said. "I can't imagine what I might have
said."

Repin laughed and shook his head. "The car, my
friend. You wanted to buy a Zhiguli, remember?"

He shrugged, relieved, remembering the conversation about buying a car or a dacha. "Really, what do
I need a car for? I hardly know how to drive." He
laughed and took a sip of the beer.

Repin nodded and sat in silence for a moment,
peeling off bits of the label from his bottle.

"Well, Sasha, you should find some use for your
money, you know," he said. "The stuff's made to be
spent. No kids to leave it to."

"My tastes are too simple to spend it, Genya," he
replied. "I've gotten used to living in a certain way,

and it's hard to change. I wouldn't know what to buy." He studied the label of his beer bottle. "But maybe a dacha. A nice little place somewhere in the country, not too far from a train line. It would be nice to do that."

Repin leaned forward. "Yes, just the thing," he said. He wiped his nose with a corner of the sheet. "But that takes quite a bit of cash. How're you fixed?"

Kuznetsov put his head back and closed his eyes, comfortable in the after-bath warmth of his body. "Oh, I've saved a good bit over the years," he said. "How much would a place like this cost?"

Repin calculated. "I'd guess around twenty-five thousand, at least," he said.

"Hm," Kuznetsov murmured. He opened his eyes. "Well, that's quite a bit of money." He drained the beer.

"Could you handle that much?" Repin asked.

Kuznetsov shrugged. "Oh, I suppose so. But, really..." He chuckled. "...Really, it's just an idle thought. I doubt I'd ever reach the point of actually spending that much money." He looked up. Repin's gray eyes studied him coldly. He felt aware of his hangover. He wanted to leave.

"Well, what's the order of business?" he asked.

Repin was silent a moment. He stood and took his watch from a trouser pocket. "It's already after noon," he said. "We should have some lunch and get going before the traffic gets too bad."

Ludmilla roused herself from a snooze and began gathering her clothes. Kuznetsov retired to the entryway and dressed.

His headache had returned, despite the comforting bath. He was ready to leave. He wanted to be alone in his room.

LENFRONT

From: Commander, Leningrad Military Front
To: Malmudov, G.N., Private, Red Army

Greetings Comrade Red Armyman!

It is with Comradely pride that I confer upon you the Order of the Red Banner, Military, for conspicuous bravery in action against the enemy of the Motherland.

You are cited for:

Halting the advance of a company of fascist soldiers at the 13th milestone of the Ivanovskoye Highway on August 28th, 1941, and by your heroic actions disabling 28 enemy officers and men, four enemy mortars, two motorized vehicles, and one provisions wagon.

According to reports from your fighting comrades of the 210th Dn, 1023rd Bn, 1st co., you remained at your post without regard to enemy fire and in the face of grave danger to your life.

It is by such heroism and devotion to duty that the fascist invaders will be driven from the soil of the Motherland.

        I Salute You!

        V. Lebedev, Maj. Gen.
        for K.E. Voroshilov
        Commander, LENFRONT

13.

For Grisha, the war began less than a month after reporting for army duty. His eager hope of getting a gun in his hands and immediately going out to fight Germans proved false: When he reported to the training command there were not enough guns to go around. They were needed at the front. He was issued a uniform—a summer one—and for three weeks he prepared for combat by taking turns firing the only heavy machine gun at the training command. As soon as he learned the rudiments of the heavy machine gun, he was ordered to the front and immediately entered combat, fighting for his life in a blur of bewilderment, fright, hunger, dirt, and exhaustion.

He was assigned as heavy machine gunner in 1st Company, 1023rd Battalion, 210th Division, fighting desperately to prevent the encirclement and siege of Leningrad. His company commander put him in charge of a two-man machine gun crew, a pair of eighteen-year-olds named Vanya and Alyosha. They had been in the division a few days longer than Grisha, but his status as a Komsomol gave him seniority. For the first five days as heavy machine gunners they had no weapon and instead fired old single-shot rifles dating to World War I. Then they received a machine gun from a battalion that had been nearly wiped out in a battle to the west and had been sent back for regrouping and rearming.

Vanya and Alyosha, his mates on the weapon, were simple and likable youths. Vanya, tall and handsome despite a cruelly pockmarked face, had the duty of ferrying ammunition during combat. He had worked as a laborer at a housing-construction site when the war began. Alyosha, short and dark with a heavy peasant's face and a comically big nose, fed ammunition into the gun while Grisha fired it. Before he was drafted he had been, like Grisha, an apprentice in a large Leningrad factory that produced precision machine parts. They went into combat first in the Kolpino area and, later, at Ivanoskoye.

Soviet troops staged a major counteroffensive at Ivanovskoye that stopped the Germans temporarily and gave the 210th Division a brief respite from fighting. Grisha's company spent the night digging slit trenches about three miles south of the village; he was asleep at midmorning when he was jarred awake by the sound of his name being shouted by his sergeant.

"Malmudov. Malmudov! MALMUDOV! Get your ass over here. Now!"

Grisha scrambled out of the trench and hurried to a red-faced sergeant standing by a pile of ammunition boxes, hands full of papers.

"Yes, Comrade Sergeant," he said.

"God damn you, Malmudov, you asleep or what?" The sergeant did not wait for an answer. He pointed a dirty finger toward a stand of fir trees two hundred yards away. "There's an NKVD captain over there...." The sergeant flipped through the papers. "His name's Grif. Yes. Grif. Take your gun and your crew and report to him. Captain Grif. Get going!"

Grisha scurried off, calling for his mates.

"Boys, get the gun and ammo, let's go!" Vanya and Alyosha scrambled out of the trench, dragging steel ammunition boxes with them. Grisha picked up the gun and hoisted it onto his shoulder. They walked briskly across the field toward a knot of two dozen uniformed men. Most of the soldiers wore the green epaulettes of NKVD troops.

An NKVD captain in a clean new uniform stood to one side with three bedraggled and unshaven officers in dirty uniforms with black infantry insignia on their epaulettes. They were arguing, their voices rising in anger. One of the infantry officers, a major, was speaking:

"...I'llhave to get that order from somebody higher up, God damn it, I don't have to take this shit from you...."

"Listen Major," the NKVD captain said. "I'm doing my duty and following orders, and you'd be wise to do the same."

"Go to hell," the angry major shouted. "I want to see your superior officer, Captain, and I want to see him now!" The major had a German machine gun slung across his chest, and he gestured threateningly with it.

The NKVD captain glared at the major, ignoring the weapon. When he spoke, his voice was so low that Grisha had difficulty making out the words.

"My orders, Major, are to take your division's weapons and march your men to the rear for screening. If you resist, I can have you shot. And I will do it. Make no mistake."

The captain and the major glared at each other, and Grisha took the opportunity to report himself.

"Captain Grif?" he said.

"What the hell do you want?" the captain snapped, not taking his eyes from the major.

"Private Malmudov, Comrade Captain, reporting as ordered with machine gun and crew," Grisha said, standing stiffly to attention.

A sergeant approached and the captain glanced at him. "Sergeant, take charge of the gun and crew," he snapped. Grisha followed the sergeant, relieved to be clear of the enraged officers.

"Right, Malmudov, just wait here until they get their bile out," the sergeant said, pointing to a place at the edge of the fir trees.

"What's up, comrade?" Grisha asked.

"Dirty job to do, my lad, and we need a machine gun," the sergeant said. He spat on the ground and pulled his cap off. His hair was graying and he looked to be about forty-five to fifty years old. His eyes were weary.

The sergeant ran his fingers through his thick hair. "You ever been detailed to an NKVD outfit before, boy?"

"No, comrade," Grisha replied.

"Mmm. Well, I'll tell you what's what. This major here, he's the senior surviving officer of the 113th. They just busted out of a German encirclement." The sergeant kicked a clod of dirt. "They been cut off for thirty-eight days, and about eighty percent or so are dead or missing or captured. There's about three hundred of 'em here, including stragglers from other outfits that picked up with 'em along the way. They lost most their weapons and all their transport. About all they got out with them was their divisional colors." The sergeant motioned in the direction of the trees. "They're waiting through there, till the officers get this little matter settled."

"So what's the dirty work?" Grisha asked.

"You heard the captain, my boy," the sergeant said. "We disarm 'em and send 'em back for a grilling. And you heard the major. They ain't gonna like it."

"But, Comrade Sergeant, why's it necessary..." Grisha began.

"Don't ask why, dummy, you're a private soldier," the sergeant growled. But then he gave Grisha an answer.

"Who knows?" he said. "Maybe some of 'em are German agents. There might be some traitors. Cowards. Deserters..."

"But, Comrade Sergeant," Grisha said, confused. "Why would traitors and deserters come back to our own lines?"

The sergeant waved both hands, exasperated.

"Shit!" he said. "I should have known better'n trying to explain things to God-damned privates! What do you know? Huh? Grif's a captain. He's been to NKVD school. He knows how to find traitors. Right?"

Grisha nodded and fell silent, but the sergeant kept talking.

"Poor fuckers," he said. "They thought they'd get a hero's welcome, bread and salt and vodka. Pretty girls." He shook his head. "Poor fuckers."

In the distance, the officers' voices rose in anger. The NKVD captain shouted to the infantry major:

"Get your hands up!"

Grisha turned and saw Grif with his service revolver pointed straight at the major's head. The major, white with fury, slowly raised his hands. The two officers behind him, bewilderment showing through the dirt and stubble on their faces, raised their hands as well.

"Throw down your weapons!" Grif shouted. "Sergeant! Come disarm these scum! Sergeant!"

The captain waved his pistol under the major's nose. The sergeant ran to the officers, first taking the major's German machine gun and then pulling the service revolvers from the holsters of the other officers.

"Now then, show your papers!" the captain demanded. "Your documents, on the ground at your feet. Quick!"

The two officers behind the major reached into their soiled tunics with trembling fingers and tossed their papers out before them. The sergeant picked them up and handed them to the captain.

"And yours, Major?" The captain pointedly left off the "Comrade."

"They were taken from me," the major said. His voice was hoarse with rage.

"Oho! Oho!" The captain put his revolver back into its holster and stood before the major, arms folded on his chest. He nodded slowly. "Well, well. And who, may I ask, took your documents from you?"

"I . . . I was captured by the Nazis, they took 'em," he stammered.

"Ah yes, I see," the captain said. "They took your documents, your paybook, and your Party card, and then they said, 'Look, such a fine major, we'll send him right back to his friends, we'll . . .'"

"That's bullshit," the major snapped. "I killed my guards and escaped. They were going to shoot me. You have no right, Comrade Captain . . ."

"Shut your mouth!" the captain snarled. "Get those hands up!" He pulled out his revolver again and pointed it at the major's chest. "And don't call me 'Comrade,' you worm. Sergeant!"

The captain turned and shouted again. "Sergeant, put these so-called officers under close arrest!"

The sergeant ordered a rifleman to watch the three worn-out officers, and Captain Grif strode over to where Grisha and his crew waited with the NKVD troops.

"All right, here's what you do," he said. "The division'll be ordered to stack arms and form up in battalion units. Sergeant! You take ten men and put them in front of the units. Corporal Griboyedov! You take ten men and get into position behind the units. You..." The captain pointed at Malmudov. "You, what's your name?"

"Malmudov, Comrade Captain!"

"Yes, Malmudov! You set up your machine gun on that little knoll just through those trees. The sergeant will show you the place. But don't do it until the men have formed ranks and stacked their weapons. Then you move fast, set up, and be ready to fire. But you don't fire unless I, personally, give the order. You understand?"

Grisha looked dumbfounded. "I... But, Comrade Captain, why would I fire on our own..."

The captain's eyes bulged with rage. "God damn you, don't question orders!" he shouted. "Do like you're told or I'll have you shot!"

Grisha leapt to attention.

"Now," the captain said. "Do you understand now?"

"I understand, comrade," he said, standing rigidly to attention, barely breathing.

"Fine," Grif said, continuing his instructions. "I'll tell the men their arms are to be taken and that they'll be sent to the rear for retraining and re-forming. If they're going to give any trouble, it'll be then.

"At my signal, Sergeant, you and your men start gathering the weapons. Then the men will be told to put their papers at their feet. You and Griboyedov take two men each and go through the ranks checking the papers. Those with documents come back here to be mustered and processed. Those without—keep them on the spot until the troika comes to deal with them. Any papers that look the least bit fishy, keep 'em standing there for the troika."

He pointed a long finger at the sergeant.

"Anybody gets through with fishy papers, we'll find 'em later, and you're responsible. Understand?"

Captain Grif paused.

"Any questions?"

Another pause. Nobody moved.

"Then let's go!"

Grisha and his crew mates exchanged silent, frightened glances as they loaded up their gun and ammunition. They followed the sergeant through the trees, but before they reached the clearing on the other side, the sergeant told Vanya and Alyosha to wait in the woods with the weapon, and he ordered Grisha to follow him. In a few seconds they came out into a large clearing. A ragged crowd of Red Army men sat and stood in disorderly groups. They had been given a ration of rough army tobacco—shag, the men called it, a mixture of tobacco and dried leaves. An acrid smell arose from the clearing.

They were in a shocking condition. Their uniforms were tatters, stiff with dirt. Many wore filthy bandages. All were unshaven. More than anything else Grisha noticed their eyes, glowing feverishly from dark sockets. The burning, staring eyes gave the men a gaunt and half-dead look. Most were carrying their personal weapons, and Grisha spotted a number of German rifles and various other kinds of non-regulation weaponry, including Lugers and potato-masher grenades.

A murmur arose from the crowd as the NKVD captain appeared. Those who were sitting rose slowly to their feet. All turned to the captain. He cleared his throat.

"Comrades!" he shouted. "May I have your attention, please?"

He waited for the voices to die down. "I have orders for you. Will the officers and NCOs please instruct the men to stack arms and form up here in battalion ranks?"

The troops murmured again and a milling movement began. The captain eyed them carefully. From among the soldiers a young man with a lieutenant's stars stepped forward.

"Comrade Captain," he said. "Ah... Is Major Shelepin coming, or..."

The captain smiled and interrupted him. "The major and the two captains have gone to headquarters to report, comrade. Are you senior?"

"I..." The lieutenant looked around him, confused. "Well, I guess I am." He was a youth of perhaps twenty, and suddenly he found himself in command of a division. He looked around helplessly.

"Fine," the NKVD captain said. "Then kindly form up your men, Lieutenant." He continued smiling.

The lieutenant nodded and turned. In a quiet voice he spoke to the men around him. "Well, boys, you heard. Let's stack arms and form up."

An older soldier stepped up to the lieutenant and spoke softly. He was frowning.

"Yes, I know, Kolya," the lieutenant said. "But I think it's best to do as he says, eh? Let's go."

He patted the older man on the arm. The soldiers gathered up their weapons and began to stack them in the clearing. They formed straggled ranks. The "battalions" were not battalions at all, but platoons or, at most, under-strength companies. The entire division was reduced to the size of a normal battalion.

In front of the unit, a soldier took position with the divisional colors: a red flag, ripped and stained, with the almost illegible words: "113th Red Banner— Workers and Peasants' Red Army."

When the men finished stacking arms, the NKVD sergeant turned to Grisha and pointed to a knoll behind Captain Grif.

"Now, get moving," he said. "Set up, load, lock, and aim that weapon straight at the colors. And listen. If you shoot without the captain saying to shoot, you've had it; and if the captain says to shoot, and you don't shoot, you've had it. You understand? Move!"

Grisha ran back into the woods and motioned Vanya and Alyosha to follow him. He hoisted the gun to his shoulder and they ran to the side of the knoll. As quickly as he could, Grisha mounted the weapon and fell down behind it. Alyosha slammed a belt of cartridges into the breech and closed it. Grisha locked with a metallic snap and trained the sights on the tattered red flag.

The troops stirred and muttered. The youthful lieutenant spoke up. "Comrade Captain, what's this?" he asked. He stepped forward three paces. "What's this machine gun here for?"

"Silence!" Grif shouted. "Silence in the ranks! And step back, Lieutenant, or I'll have you arrested." The lieutenant hesitated, then stepped back into his position.

"I have orders!" Grif said. "It is my duty to give you these orders, and it is your duty to obey them." The murmuring subsided but the men looked angrily at each other and at the NKVD captain.

"Comrades!" Grif said. "You are to be congratulated for bringing the divisional colors through enemy lines. I congratulate you!"

He surveyed the troops and continued.

"It is now necessary to give you proper rest and re-equipment. It is ordered that you shall be transported to the rear for this purpose." The captain paused again. "Naturally, weapons are not needed in the rear. They are needed here, at the front, and it is necessary that your weapons be reissued to fresh troops now taking positions on the front lines."

The murmur rose again; a voice cried: "But it's a disgrace! These are our arms!"

"Silence!" Grif demanded, glancing at his sergeant and at Grisha's machine gun. Another voice rose from the ranks.

"These are our weapons; we won't surrender them!"

The troops began a spontaneous movement toward the stacked arms, but the NKVD sergeant and his ten men rushed forward, rifles aimed at the bellies of the soldiers in the front ranks.

"Malmudov!" the captain shouted. Grisha tensed over the machine gun sights.

"Malmudov, if anybody makes a move toward the weapons, open fire!"

Grisha stared in over the gun sights. The bedraggled men's dark, haunted eyes glared at him. He grasped the weapon so tightly his knuckles turned white.

"God, God," he prayed. "Don't let anybody move! Don't let them move!"

Grisha held his breath, watching the sullen soldiers over his gun muzzle. The soldiers looked at the machine gun, at Captain Grif, and at the weapons. A milling movement began among them, and a soldier with a bandaged hand moved forward. Instinctively, Grisha shifted the muzzle a few degrees to point straight at the bandaged soldier. The soldier saw the movement, and, equally instinctively, he stopped. He stood motionless, glaring at Grisha.

As quickly as it developed, the crisis passed. The troops receded into ranks and the NKVD sergeant's men began gathering up the weapons and carrying them away.

The division deflated as the weapons disappeared through the woods. The colors sagged and the men stood with dead eyes listening to Grif's shouted orders. Only one man, the one with the bandaged hand, continued to glare sullenly at Grisha. The others seemed to have forgotten the machine gun, or to have ceased to care.

"...Your documents at your feet, and step back one pace," Grif was saying. A shuffling movement rippled along the ranks, and "flop, flop, flop," the papers landed on the ground. Some of the men stood motionless, no papers at their feet.

"Sergeant!" Grif ordered. "Examine the papers!"

The sergeant and his men worked their way down the ranks, picking up the packets of documents, looking, questioning, ordering. A low, steady hubbub rose from the clearing, punctuated by angry rejoinders: "I don't know!" "I lost them." "They took them from me"; and "Shut up!" "Get over there!" "Stand back!"

After an hour, a group of about sixty soldiers whose papers were missing or not in order had formed up separately from the main body. The main body was marched away and the sixty remained behind, standing in ragged ranks surrounded by NKVD troops. The sun beat down, and sweat trickled across Grisha's back. One soldier, then two more, fainted in the ranks.

Those nearby bent to help them but the NKVD soldiers didn't move. A lieutenant, the one who had earlier identified himself as the senior officer, motioned to the NKVD sergeant.

"Can we have some water for the men, Sergeant? It's hot."

"I have no orders," the sergeant replied.

"Then I give you orders!" the lieutenant snapped. "Bring water!"

The sergeant spat on the ground. "I don't take no orders from so-called officers who lose their papers," he said. He turned and walked away. The lieutenant said nothing.

Grisha, Vanya, and Alyosha crouched by their weapon as the afternoon wore on. They wondered if the captain had forgotten them, but they dared not ask that they be allowed to return to their unit. They took bread and water from their rucksacks and ate a guilty meal under the burning eyes of the 113th Division's paperless soldiers.

After another hour a lieutenant colonel, a tall man in the uniform of the artillery troops, walked into the clearing with Captain Grif. A moment later, two NKVD majors appeared, accompanied by a lieutenant in a tank officer's uniform. The tall lieutenant colonel and the two majors sat down on a fallen log at the edge of the woods and talked briefly with Grif. Grif turned to his sergeant.

"All right, Sergeant!" he said. "Let's have 'em. In order of rank."

The NKVD sergeant pointed to the lieutenant who had demanded the water and motioned him out of ranks. The lieutenant marched to the troika and stood at attention.

"Name?" one of the NKVD majors asked. The major, a squat man with a shaved head, appeared to be in charge despite the seniority of the artillery lieutenant colonel. The other NKVD major, an Asian-looking officer with a black mustache, took notes. The artillery officer merely listened.

"Senior Lieutenant Barabanov, aide to Major General Bezborodov, commander of the 113th Red Army Division!" the lieutenant replied in a clipped, precise voice.

"Papers?" the bald major said, his voice a flat monotone.

"I have none, Comrade Major," the lieutenant said.

"Don't call me 'comrade.' Where are they?"

The lieutenant glanced down at the major. His voice lost some of its military precision.

"I was forced to hide them so the enemy would not know my staff position if captured, Comrade Major, I—"

"Don't call me, 'comrade,'" the major snarled. "It is an act of cowardice to throw away your papers; I am not a comrade of cowards!"

The lieutenant's face reddened. "I am not a coward!"

The major glared at him. "Barabanov, if that is your name, you have seen that most of the survivors of the 113th Division managed to get back with their

papers," he said. "I think it can be said that at least
an equal percentage of those who did not survive also
managed to keep their documents until death."

The major's voice was low and menacing. "You will
be held under guard until we can determine who you
are by questioning others in this division who retained their documents and their honor. If they vouch
for you, then you will be permitted to serve the Soviet
Union as a Red Army man in the ranks of a shock
battalion where your honor may be redeemed in
blood." The lieutenant's shoulders sagged. "If you are
lying," the major continued, looking down and writing on a sheaf of papers, "you will be shot. Next!"

The lieutenant marched off with an NKVD soldier
at his back, pale and stumbling. The next man, a ju-
nior lieutenant, marched to the troika.

The troika continued questioning the soldiers for the
remainder of the day, with the bald major doing most
of the talking. Most of the men were paperless, like the
lieutenant, and they fared as badly as he did. A few
persuaded the troika of the genuineness of their damaged or incomplete papers and were released to join
the survivors on the other side of the woods. But two
of those with suspect documents, an aging corporal
and a stocky young private, underwent a rigorous
grilling that did not satisfy the major. They were ordered to stand aside while their papers were sent by
runner to an NKVD headquarters.

By late afternoon the troika had finished with all
but those two. The runner had returned with a message from the headquarters, and the two men were

summoned back before the troika. The major stood
and regarded the two men angrily. He held up the
message.

"Your papers are forgeries!" he shouted. The older
man winced. The swarthy private did not move or even
change expression. He stood staring mildly at the major.

"Your papers are fakes!" the major said. "Where'd
you get them? Who are you?"

"Speak!" he snapped.

"I..." the corporal began. "I lost my papers,
Comrade Major. I took these from a dead man and I
changed the birth date...."

"God damn you!" the major roared. "Don't call
me 'comrade'! You're lying! You're a German agent!
You speak Russian like a fucking German!"

"Oh no, God help me, I'm Latvian!" the corporal
cried. He shook his head so hard his graying hair fell
into his eyes. "I'm a loyal soldier, I..."

"Shut up!" the major said. He turned to the short,
swarthy private. "And you? What do you say?"

The private smiled in a dreamy way. He looked
shell-shocked, and said nothing. The major grabbed
him by the collar and shook him. The private blinked.
Still smiling, he said in a low voice, "My papers."

The major looked at the private a moment and then
turned to the troika. They put their heads together for
a few seconds. The major nodded and turned back to
the two men.

"It is the judgment of the Special Military Tribunal that you are enemy agents, and it is the sen-

tence of the Tribunal that you be shot," he said. "Sergeant, see to it!"

The elderly corporal fell to his knees, wailing like a woman. The major spun on his heel and walked away. The rest of the troika and their aides followed him into the woods.

Two NKVD soldiers jerked the corporal to his feet. "I fought from Borisov," he cried. "I'm a loyal soldier. I'm no German. Please!"

The soldiers said nothing as they half carried, half shoved the weeping corporal toward the tree line. The private's expression of mild incomprehension remained unchanged. He marched away between the NKVD troops with a stumbling, club-footed gait. The group disappeared into the trees, but the old corporal's cries and protests continued. The crackle of a rifle volley echoed through the clearing, flushing birds from nearby trees, and the cries abruptly ceased. A moment later two sharp cracks from the sergeant's pistol ended the operation.

Grisha lay still on his belly, still gripping his machine gun. In the silence he realized he was squeezing the weapon so hard his hand hurt. He let go and pulled himself up to a sitting position behind the gun. Vanya sat staring in the direction of the firing squad, pale as death. Alyosha's head was lowered, and he had tears on his face.

The NKVD troops began marching the remaining soldiers away and the sergeant walked over to the knoll. He glanced at the tearful Alyosha and said softly, "All right, boys, your work's over. You can get back to your unit."

Grisha and his crew rose and dismantled the machine gun. Alyosha and Vanya took the ammunition cases and Grisha shouldered the weapon. Before he turned to leave, he looked a moment at the worn, angry old face of the NKVD sergeant. The sergeant snapped, "Come on, get going, there's a fuckin' war on!"

Grisha turned to go, but the sergeant stopped him. "Look, lad, somebody always has to do dirty work in a war," he murmured. "Today it was your turn."

Grisha nodded and walked away through the woods.

SOVTELEGRAF

MALMUDOVA, S. A.
#58 PESTELYA STREET, LENINGRAD

8 SEPT. 1941 1058GMT

IT IS MY REGRETFUL DUTY TO INFORM YOU THAT
YOUR HUSBAND, PRIVATE G. N. MALMUDOV, HAS
BEEN REPORTED MISSING IN ACTION. KINDLY
ADDRESS ALL INQUIRIES TO THE OFFICE OF
PERSONNEL, LENFRONT.

COMMANDER

LENFRONT

14.

Grisha Malmudov's war with Germany lasted less than two months. In the first week of September, an advancing German armored corps surrounded his division outside Mga, a key station on the Leningrad-Moscow rail line. On the fourth of September, Mga fell; with its fall, Leningrad lost its food lifeline to "mainland" Russia.

On the fifth of September, at eleven o'clock in the morning, Grisha looked into the barrel of a German rifle and raised his hands over his head. Alyosha was dead, his comical peasant's face blown away by a German shell; Vanya lay nearby, dying, a bubbling shrapnel hole in his chest. The machine gun was out of ammunition; ahead, to the right and to the left, German infantrymen cautiously picked their way among dead and dying Soviet soldiers.

The German soldier prodded Grisha with his rifle and marched him away to begin four years of fear, hunger, and degradation as a prisoner of war. He was glassy-eyed and shell-shocked when they captured him; he showed emotion only when an SS sergeant took from him a letter, folded in the triangle specified by the Soviet wartime postal system, and addressed to "Pvt. Malmudov, G. N., 210th 1023BN 1st Co."

It was written in a close, small hand, and it read:

Darling Grishenka:

I got your letter today about the Order of the Red Banner. Hurrah! All the comrades here at the CentCom cheered when I gave them the news that you're a hero! We're dying for you to get a leave so we can hear all about it. Your letter is much too modest.

I have a reward, too, but from another kind of battle. I'm pregnant. I suspected it, and now the doctor confirms it. Oh, Grisha, I don't know what to think. My head tells me to weep but my soul says to laugh and rub my belly with joy. So what to do? First I cry my eyes out, and then I rub my belly and then I cry again. I can't imagine trying to raise a child in such hard times, but neither can I imagine being without your baby growing inside me. Sometimes I wish we had used our heads instead of drinking champagne by candlelight, but if I had it to do again, I'd change nothing of that night.

But please don't worry about anything. I feel wonderful and my comrades here are looking out for me. I'm happy for this child, and I want you to be happy too.

We're working hard, and the city is determined to drive the fascists back to their dens and exterminate them. Morale is high. Our flat is mercifully intact, but I spend little time there. It's as before, sleeping on desks and living on cold tea, but work is our salvation.

Did you get my letter about Marya? I write every day but I don't know if the letters reach you. I got your letter about the sergeant getting killed, and I went to see his mother as you asked. She had been notified, but she was glad to have a message from her son's comrade and she sends you her gratitude and good wishes.

I kiss you a thousand times, Grishenka. Sometimes I wish I were a believer so I could pray for your safety. Sometimes I do it anyway. When I walk down the embankment I pray to a star, or to the Admiralty spire or to the Neva River. Please don't laugh at me.

I love you, I love you, I love you.

Your Sonichka

P.S. The doctor says the date is May Day!
What devoted Komsomols we are!!
XXX

The letter was soiled and wrinkled from being held in Grisha's blackened hands and from being read over and over again. The SS sergeant tore the Red Banner

medal from Grisha's chest and he did not move. The
German took his red-bound army paybook and his
Komsomol card and Grisha did not protest. But when
the sergeant reached into a tunic pocket and pulled out
the letter, Grisha tore the German's hand away and
lunged, sending him sprawling. But before Grisha
could regain his balance, a rifle butt caught him on the
side of the head and the world turned black.

Grisha could have saved himself the trouble. He had
memorized every word of the letter, and in the long
series of confinements over the next four years he
often recited it to himself. He treasured the words and
the worries. He fretted over the nagging questions it
raised, and he carefully counted off the days and
months until May Day, when the baby should come to
term and be delivered into a war-ravaged world.

He spent nearly all his waking hours thinking of his
wife and forming child. He imagined every detail of
her activities, her appearance, her words. As the
months dragged by, her womb grew in his mind's eye.
He saw it swell beneath a woolen winter skirt and saw
it rise and fall as she slept in the carved bed. He put his
hand on it and felt the baby's kick; he saw Sonya's
dark eyes laugh.

While the other prisoners groaned with the pain
of dysentery, the misery of the bitter winter, and
constant, gnawing hunger, Grisha sat quietly taking
himself through the routine of Sonya's Leningrad existence. He saw that she ate properly, that she did not
lift heavy loads, and that she got enough rest at night.

In the spring of 1942, he sat in a camp in Poland and imagined Sonya moaning in the pain of labor. In his dazed, half-mad brain the question of the child's sex was decided when he witnessed the delivery in every detail: the fat woman doctor with her white coat and bloody hands pulling the child, a girl child, from Sonya's womb. He was pleased to have a daughter.

Grisha feared he was losing his mind; but if it was insanity it was also salvation. The other prisoners regarded him as mad, a pitiable shell-shock case, and gave him special consideration. Even the German guards treated him less harshly. He was emaciated along with the rest, but his obsessive, single-minded preoccupation with his wife and child saved his soul. His spirit lived a life beyond the reach of privation and did not atrophy with his body. Prisoners died all around him, wasting away from loss of spirit. Grigory Malmudov survived because he lived, almost literally, on love.

He so well lived outside his circumstances that in later years he remembered only sketchy details of his imprisonment: a series of camps, each one much the same as the one before, except that the food became worse and less as the war dragged on. He first was taken to a camp in an area he thought to be western Poland. It was a vast, fenced-in, boggy field crowded with a stinking, exhausted, dysentery-ridden mass of Soviet prisoners. The Germans delivered stacks of lumber and the prisoners fashioned barracks that sheltered more than a hundred thousand men that bitter winter, some of them for only a few days before

they died. Every morning more prisoners marched in
on failing legs; every morning more corpses rolled out,
stacked naked and dead in the backs of the trucks.

Most of the dead succumbed to dysentery com-
pounded by starvation; some were shot. One night in
early spring a group of three hundred prisoners at-
tempted a mass breakout, but when the men cut the
inner wire and began pouring into the wide space between the inner and outer fences, the German guards
turned on floodlights and blanketed the area with
machine gun fire. When the shooting stopped, guards
walked among the bodies firing pistol rounds into the
heads of the wounded.

A few days later two plump corpses were included
in the morning truckload of skeletal dysentery victims—informers, strangled in their beds during the
night.

Through 1942 and 1943, Grisha lived in four different camps in various parts of Poland. But in 1944
he was packed into a boxcar with 150 other men and
shipped westward to work in German factories. Grisha
was taken by a small Munich machine shop turning
out parts for generators. He was the only Soviet prisoner there. The other dozen or so slave workers were
Czechs and Poles, and they worked alongside German machinists.

The assignment to slave labor in so small a factory
certainly saved his life. The prisoners were quartered
in a sturdy brick building that backed onto the wall of
the foundry, which provided ample warmth. Because
the plant was small, relations among the prisoners and

with their German overseers were more humane than
was the case in some of the large factories that employed thousands of slave laborers. The prisoners ate
humbly, but the food was more than adequate; they
began to regain the weight they lost in the camps.

The work was hard. The prisoners stood at their
machines twelve to fourteen hours a day, seven days a
week, trying to meet rigorous production quotas. If
they made mistakes or failed to meet the quotas, they
were whipped or deprived of food. But, on the other
hand, when they exceeded quotas, they were given re-
wards including such luxuries as tobacco and candy.

In the Munich factory, as in the camps, Grisha's
mind was never far from his wife and child. Standing
hour after hour at the lathe, his mind's eye saw Sonya
rear their daughter. He gave her pet names, "Pi-
geon," "Bunny," "Muffin," but he never was able to
give her a proper name. He wondered what name
Sonya had given her, but although he had assigned the
child a gender, an eye color, and even decided when
she would take her first step, he could not christen the
child of his imagination.

Never, in all his imaginings, did it occur to him that
the baby might never have been born, or that, having
been born, the baby might have died. Nor did it occur
to him that Sonya herself might be dead.

Yet for those in Leningrad during those years, death
was never far distant. More than a million Leningraders died during the nine-hundred-day siege of the city,
either from starvation or from the constant shelling of
German guns. The survivors often subsisted on shoe

leather, wallpaper paste, cats, rats, and meager rations carted in at great risk and with great difficulty over the frozen Lake Ladoga.

He did not imagine his family suffering through the winter of the first year of the siege, the coldest in a century. His Leningrad was the one he had known in the beginning days of the war, sandbagged and determined: His Leningrad had food shortages, not famine; its hardships were edifying, not degrading; life was austere, but secure. Had he known of the corpses lying ignored in the frozen streets, the cannibalism, the rows of bombed-out apartments, he would have lost his mind.

The hard routine of factory labor abruptly ended in the wild spring of 1945. For the first time in his captivity, events moved so quickly and fatefully that Grisha was able—was compelled—to tear his mind away from his dreams and deal with the reality of the present.

For weeks, the German workers in the shop had whispered rumors of impending defeat. Some of the German-speaking Czechs heard the rumors and passed them on to Grisha, speaking the makeshift pidgin Slavic designed in the camps.

Night after night, air raid sirens wailed; frequently, their warning was followed by the distant rumble of bombs falling into the heart of Munich and by the thumping of antiaircraft guns.

Grisha's factory was bombed one night in May, shortly before the prisoners were to be released from work—which saved their lives. A bomb smashed the foundry and the furnaces exploded, turning the prisoners' quarters into red-hot bricks and molten metal. The explosion blew out all the windows of the lathe shop, injuring many of the workers. Grisha suffered a cut on the shoulder from flying glass; one of the Czechs was cut so badly he bled to death. A German first-aid car came and orderlies bandaged the injured men. The damage stopped work in the factory, and although the prisoners were put to work making repairs, the Germans showed little real interest in returning to production. They were preoccupied and fearful of another bombing, and a few nights later a foreman brought the news that American troops had reached the outskirts of Munich. By evening, the rumble of an artillery battle could be heard from the southwest.

The prisoners slept in the shops after the destruction of their quarters, and on the morning after the artillery battle they awoke to find no German watchman outside the door. Nor did the German workers arrive to supervise the repair work. The prisoners waited in the shop, fearful and confused. The shelling had stopped, and a deathly silence hung over the normally noisy industrial zone. The prisoners had not been outside their factory since they had been brought there nearly a year before, and they dared not venture forth in their gray POW coveralls.

They climbed onto workbenches and peered through the shattered windows into the deserted street outside. By midmorning sporadic machine gun and carbine fire broke out to the southwest, and around noon a column of German tanks thundered into the street headed eastward. A few minutes behind them came disheveled columns of German soldiers, unshaven and exhausted. Within minutes the street filled with more soldiers, trucks, and motorcycles. It was full retreat, and the prisoners whispered excitedly but still dared not leave the silent factory.

The street fell empty again within an hour of the first appearance of the German tanks. The small-arms fire grew closer until it became a steady din and seemed to surround the factory. Rounds splattered against the brick walls and the prisoners jumped off the benches and crouched on the floor. Grisha wondered if, after all the fighting outside Leningrad and all the years in prison, he would die at the very hour of his liberation.

Outside, more vehicles roared past, followed by running feet and German soldiers shouting in confusion, then silence except for bursts of small-arms fire. The prisoners argued in whispers. Some wanted to slip out of the factory and find the Americans. Grisha argued against it.

"If an SS patrol sees us, they'll shoot our asses, brothers," he said.

"They're too busy to care about us," a Pole argued. "Anyway, there ain't no patrols. They've cleared out."

"We don't know that yet," Grisha said. "Anyway, nobody's interested in this place right now. I'm for waiting until the Americans get here."

One of the men had climbed onto the workbench and was peering cautiously into the street.

"Brothers, look at this!" he whispered. "I think the Americans are already here."

Grisha and the others jumped onto the bench and peeked over the windowsill. Two tanks of an unfamiliar type stood idling at the end of the street, then gunned their engines and moved slowly past the window under the frightened eyes of the prisoners. As they drew near, the prisoners could make out large white stars and the letters "U.S." stenciled onto the turrets.

"Amerikantsi!" Grisha cried. "Americans! Let's go!"

The men tumbled pell-mell off the bench and poured through the main door. They raced across the factory yard, out the gate, and into the street behind the tanks.

"Hallo!" one of the Poles shouted. "Hallo, Joe! American! Hallo!"

The second tank stopped sharply, rocking on its suspension as the turret spun. The prisoners stopped in their tracks ten yards from the mouth of a cannon barrel. The Pole who had shouted raised his hands and the others did the same.

"No shoot!" Grisha yelled. "No German! No shoot! *Kamerad!* Tovarishch!"

He turned frantically to the others. "How do you say 'friend' in English?" he asked. The tank engine grumbled at idle. Nobody knew the word. "Hey, no shoot!'' he shouted again, pointing to the letters stenciled on his gray coveralls.

A hatch on the turret popped open and the helmeted head of the tank commander appeared. A pair of blue eyes frowned at the prisoners and the American shouted something they didn't understand.

"Tovarishchi!" Grisha shouted.

The blue-eyed American stood up and shouted into the turret a sentence that began with the word "Hey!" and ended with "Russians."

"Yes, yes!" Grisha cried. "Yes, Russky! Russians! Russians!" He pronounced it as the American tank commander had: "Roosyans, Roosyans."

The American smiled and beckoned the men to come to the tank. They approached cautiously. Another hatch opened in the main body of the machine and another American poked his head out. The prisoners overcame their caution and began chattering at the Americans in three languages. The tank crewmen laughed and waved their arms.

"Hey, we don't speak it," they said. "*No comprendo*, guys. No savvy."

The blue-eyed American dropped down into the turret and came up a few seconds later with packages of Camel cigarettes and Hershey bars. He climbed out and passed them among the prisoners. They opened the cigarette packages immediately; the American snapped open a silver Ronson lighter and began lighting them up. He sat down on the tank body while the prisoners puffed hungrily at the Camels. He motioned in the direction from which the tanks had come.

"Headquarters company!" he shouted. "Head-quarters company! Understand? You go that way! Okay? Get it? Savvy?"

The men drew on the cigarettes and stared at the shouting tank commander.

"That way!" he shouted. "Go! That way!" He laughed, shook his head, and climbed back into the turret. "Good luck, fellas," he said as he disap-peared into the hole. "I gotta go." The hatches slammed shut and the tank engines roared. The turret spun and the heavy machine sped away down the street, its metal treads throwing sparks off the cobble-stones.

Grisha turned to the others and shrugged. "He said that way, so we go that way." They set off along the street in the direction the tank commander had pointed.

Within a few minutes they came to the main body of an advancing U.S. armored division and were es-corted by a pair of soldiers to a headquarters unit. There, they entered a maze of paper, questions, free cigarettes, canned meat, and confusion that lasted for weeks.

From the headquarters company they and several dozen other assorted ex-prisoners in gray coveralls were trucked across town to temporary quarters in a school dormitory that the Americans had turned into a military administrative center.

At the dormitory a harried German civilian speak-ing Polish and Czech gave them blankets, boxes of U.S. Army C-rations, and showed them where they could sleep. He said they would stay there only until they could be sent to a "place for processing."

They were trucked three days later to the "place for processing," a half-bombed building in central Munich filled with a polyglot assortment of non-Germans who constituted a category of humanity that rapidly grew to the hundreds of thousands as the Allies swept across Germany. These people soon acquired an official bureaucratese name: Displaced Persons, or DPs. They included Russians, Ukrainians, Poles, Czechs, Hungarians, Slovaks, Yugoslavs, and a smattering of Gypsies, Romanians, and Bulgarians. They were of all ages and both sexes, but the majority were male and East European. Most had been prisoners of war.

The Americans posted guards at the doors of the building and put up a sign, black-stenciled letters on a white plank, that read:

U.S. FORCES, EUROPE
DISPLACED PERSONS CAMP #323
Authorized Personnel Only

The occupants of DP 323 were not permitted to leave the building, but most had no interest in doing so. The Americans gave them food, comfort, and security that had been lacking in their lives for months and years. The Army brought truckloads of fresh bread, canned meat, cheese, chocolate, coffee, cigarettes, and clean clothing. They slept on comfortable cots, had access to showers with hot and cold water, and didn't have to work.

But idleness and rumor soon began to cause unrest in DP 323. The most persistent and frightening of the rumors concerned the prospects for returning home. After his first few weeks in the camp, Grisha began hearing reports of arrests and disappearances in the Soviet zone of occupation. The stories became more detailed and more frightening in the late summer of 1945, when more and more DPs began arriving from the Soviet zone. They told of lengthy interrogations and secret police kidnappings that took place in full view of hundreds of passersby.

Grisha listened to the stories in silence. Some of the bearers of the reports were strongly anti-Communist or anti-Russian or both, and he treated them with skepticism. But there was a basic consistency in the stories that worried him. In the idleness of the DP camp he had resumed his old habit of imagining how his family was living, and he yearned to return home to be with Sonya and his daughter.

In July a young Russian turned up in the camp and was assigned to the room Grisha shared with two of the Czechs from the factory. The man, a husky blond-haired youth with tired eyes and a faraway look, said he came from Novgorod and was a corporal in an armored division when he was captured in 1943. He had survived the POW camps and was sent to Germany to work as a slave laborer in a Berlin factory producing army boots.

When Soviet forces reached Berlin, he fled the factory and reported to the first Soviet unit he found.

They greeted him like a lost son, he said, giving him Russian cigarettes, bread, and kasha.

"But then they turned me over to the special detachment, the NKVD boys," he said. "They questioned me, and the first thing I know I'm locked in a cellar with a bunch of other guys. I spent a week there. They shot a lot of the guys, but I . . ."

"Shot!" Grisha gasped. "They shot our own soldiers?"

The blond corporal chuckled ruefully. "That's right, sonny," he said. "That's right. Ping!" He stuck a finger to the side of Grisha's head. "Pow! Lights out!"

Grisha stared in silence as the corporal lit a cigarette and continued his story.

"After they put me in that cellar they started grilling me," he said, blowing a cloud of blue smoke. "I told them everything that happened to me, and they said I was a collaborator. They said working for German war production was collaboration."

"Jesus!" Grisha said. "How is that collaboration? That's horse shit! We were slaves. They'd kill us if we didn't . . ."

"Well, the NKVD guys didn't care about that," the corporal said, rubbing his eyes. "There were a lot of others in the same boat, and after a week in there they started taking 'em out and shooting 'em."

"How do you know they were shot?" Grisha demanded.

"Shit!" the corporal said, shaking his head. "You see a guy taken out of the room, you hear 'em march down the hall, you hear a pistol shot, sometimes maybe a yell. The guy never comes back. You put two and two together. How do you think I know?''

"So why didn't they shoot you?''

"I escaped," he said. "They decided to move us someplace else, so they take us out of the cellar and start to put us in a truck. They're shooting collaborators, so I figured it's my last chance. They just had one guy at the back of the truck. There was another guard and the driver, but they were up front.

"I had these heavy boots from the German factory," he said, grinning. "I kick the guy's nuts as hard as I can; he goes down. I jump on him and another prisoner gets his rifle, runs up to the cab, and blasts hell out of the driver and the guard. We take off in all directions, NKVD soldiers shooting like crazy. I don't know how, but I got away. I hid out and just kept going west until I found some Americans, and here I am and I ain't never going back. I go back, those fuckers'll shoot me before breakfast.'' He put a finger to his neck. "Ping! I'm dead meat if I go back.''

Grisha slumped onto his cot and stared at the floor.

"You too, comrade," the Novgorod corporal said softly. "I'll take bets that they'd say you're a collaborator too.''

"I dunno," Grisha said, still staring at the floor. "Maybe not. I didn't work in military production.''

"What kind of place were you in?''

"They made generators.''

"Shit!'' the corporal snorted. "Generators, boots, it's all the same. Just getting captured nails your ass.

They say they even shot poor bastards they got out of the POW camps, most of 'em half dead anyway. If they don't shoot 'em, they ship 'em back to the Union, but they don't go home. They take 'em to a place where they cut down trees all day long, so fuckin' far into Siberia that the wolves are scared to go there.''

"How do you know that?" Grisha demanded.

"That's what they say." The corporal shrugged. "I can believe it. You ever hear about what happened to the guys who busted out of German encirclement?"

"Yeah," Grisha said. He shook his head. "Yeah, I heard.''

"Anybody who's been in German hands is a fishy-smelling piece of meat," the corporal said. "If you lived through the POW camps they figure right away that you're one of three things: You joined the Vlasov Army; you informed on your comrades; or you worked in German war production. If you're one of those three things, you're dead as the ham in this can." He held up an olive-drab can of C-rations and pointed his finger at it. "Ping!"

"How would they know I worked in that factory?" Grisha asked.

The corporal shook his head and laughed. "Sonny, you're a dumb ass," he said. "*You've* gotta convince *them*. You gotta prove you're just a poor dumb boob who never joined the Komsomol and never snitched on his pals and never made generators for German trucks.''

"What's being a Komsomol got to do with it?" Grisha asked.

The corporal glanced sharply at him. He stubbed out the cigarette in an empty C-ration can. "You a Komsomol?" he said. It was more a statement than a question.

"I was," Grisha replied. "Am," he added.

"You ain't got a chance, Comrade Komsomol," he said, rising. "They have tougher standards for Party members and Komsomols—they're supposed to die fighting. If you're Party and you surrender, you're dead to the NKVD. They'd shoot you before anybody else."

The blond corporal again pointed his finger at Grisha. "Ping!" he said. Grisha winced. "Lights out!"

"I've got a wife in Leningrad," Grisha said quietly. "I've got a baby I've never seen. I've got to go back."

"Hey," the corporal said. "Forget it. You'll never see your old lady and you'll never see your kid. I got a girl in Novgorod, too, if she ain't fucking some cop, but I'm forgetting about her. I'm going to America, get rich, eat Spam three times a day!" He laughed and left the room.

Grisha lay on the cot and stared at the ceiling. Silent tears streamed from his eyes.

210th Division

RED ARMY

28 Sept. 1941

Respected Comrade Malmudova:

Concerning your request for information on your husband, Private Malmudov, reported Missing in Action, I regret that the requirements of military secrecy prevent me from giving you full information.

I can say, however, that Private Malmudov acquitted himself with full honor as a Red Armyman, and that he was separated from his comrades while fighting heroically and bravely for the Socialist Motherland, true to his military duty.

We, his fighting comrades of the 210th Division, keenly feel his absence and we hope fervently for the day he stands again among our ranks.

With Comradely regards,

V.V. Shalopnikov,
Commander, 1st Co.,
1023rd Bn, 210th DN

15.

Grisha tried to tell himself that the Novgorod corporal's story was a lie. But he believed it. He had to believe it. Others came into the camp with information that corroborated it. There were ex-POWs who escaped from NKVD trains bound for the east and slave laborers who saw fellow workers rounded up by NKVD squads. There were Soviet soldiers who had deserted and who knew what was happening to ex-POWs and DPs. One man claimed he had met an NKVD defector in American hands who confirmed that virtually all Soviet citizens found in Germany were arrested and shot or sent to the USSR as prisoners.

For Grisha, all this was unacceptable and unsupportable, but he knew it was believable. His own experience with the NKVD unit that disarmed the survivors of the 113th Division outside Leningrad told him it was true. The 113th had fought its way out with its colors intact, yet its commander was arrested and possibly shot. How would they deal with a man who surrendered to the enemy and worked in a factory making parts for enemy trucks that might have been used to kill his own comrades?

In late July the issue came to a crisis. A U.S. Army team arrived at DP 323 on July 28, 1945, to begin processing the DPs. Within hours, word flew through the camp that all Soviet military personnel were to be turned over to the Soviet command in Berlin. Civilians from Soviet-occupied territory who had no family in the American zone would be returned to Soviet jurisdiction.

The news spread fear and sometimes panic through DP 323. One by one, the DPs went to interviews with the Army team, and one by one, they returned to gather their meager belongings for the trip east. Some, especially the Czechs and Hungarians, were delighted. Others protested vehemently. A few had to be dragged from the building by American MPs. But all went.

During the afternoon of the second day, the ex-corporal from Novgorod took the walk down the corridor to his interview. He grinned.

"Shit, they won't send us back, sonny," he said. "When I tell 'em what I told you, they won't send us back."

But the ex-corporal returned twenty minutes later, pale and shaken.

"I won't go, Malmudov," he whispered. "I ain't going back there!"

He fell on his knees beside the cot and rummaged through his clothes. He stuffed them in a sack. "Fuck, no, I ain't going," he kept saying. "Fuck, no, I ain't going."

An American MP came to the door and waited for the distracted youth to gather his gear. The Russian rose to his feet with a roll of toilet paper in his hand.

"Got to take a shit," he said, making a wiping motion with the paper. The American shrugged and stood aside. It occurred to Grisha that the ex-corporal would try to escape through the tiny window in the toilet. But he was far too stocky to squeeze through.

Minutes passed, and the American glanced uneasily down the hall. Another DP went to use the toilet and found the door locked. He rattled it and knocked.

"Oh, shit!" the MP muttered. He trotted down the corridor. Grisha followed.

"Open up!" the MP shouted, banging on the door. "Come on outta there!" There was no sound from inside.

The MPs stepped back and kicked the door. The lock snapped and the door slammed open.

Grisha followed the MP into the small toilet. He saw the blond hair first, then the blood on the walls and smeared on the tile floor. The MP tried to pick up the ex-corporal's body, but the head flopped back and a gaping hole opened in his throat, yawning like an extra mouth, drooling with blood and pink foam. The MP dropped the body to the floor. A straight razor lay beside the corpse.

The corporal had sliced his throat from left carotid artery to right carotid artery. He was dead.

The interviewers did not call Grisha that day or the next. On the third day an MP came and summoned him. He followed the soldier down the corridor and was shown into a room that had been turned into a makeshift office. Among the papers and boxes were three men in American uniforms, sleeves rolled up, laboring over forms and documents. One, a thin, brown-haired captain looked up as Grisha came in.

"Hello," he said in Russian, smiling pleasantly. Grisha nodded and greeted the officer. The captain wore rimless, octagonal glasses with gold earpieces. His eyes were weary and red-rimmed.

"You're, uh...Malmudov?" he said, riffling through some papers.

Grisha nodded.

"Name and patronymic Grigory Nikolayevich?"

He nodded again.

"Please, take a seat," the captain said, motioning Grisha to a box. Grisha sat down on it. "Um, now, Malmudov, I understand you're a member of the Soviet armed forces, is that correct?"

"Correct," Grisha said. "Private, 210th Division, 1023rd Battalion, First Company."

"Fine," the captain said. "In that case, if you'd be kind enough to sign some papers for me, I'll arrange for you to be taken to your people in Berlin."

Grisha swallowed and accepted the pen. The captain pointed to places on a form where he had made Xs.

"Just sign here and here and here...."

"Please..." Grisha began. "Please, Mister Captain. Is there...please...is there something else I can do? I'm afraid to go there."

"Sorry, Malmudov," the captain said. "There's nothing to be done. You've got to go back. We have a firm understanding with our Soviet allies concerning the repatriation of prisoners of war..."

"But, Mister Captain," Grisha blurted. "They'll shoot me."

"Why?"

"As a collaborator."

"Why?"

Grisha wiped perspiration from his upper lip. "I worked in a German factory. To the NKVD, that's collaboration."

"Well, Malmudov," the captain said. "The Soviet authorities know very well the conditions under which POWs were forced to work; I don't think..."

"I know they'll shoot me," Grisha said, his voice softened nearly to a whisper.

The captain shrugged. "Well, the situation is this: You must be repatriated and I can't do anything about it. Will you sign?"

Grisha sat in silence, looking at the paper.

"I must tell you, Malmudov, that if you don't sign, you'll be sent to Berlin anyway, and the Soviet command will wonder why you didn't sign. I advise you to sign."

Grisha sighed, took the pen and began signing where he saw Xs.

"How old are you, Malmudov?" the captain asked.

"Twenty-three."

"Where you from?"

"Leningrad."

"Born there?"

"No. The Ukraine."

"You're Ukrainian?"

"Yes."

"Family?"

"Yes, my wife..." Grisha swallowed. He did not want to weep in front of these strangers. "...And my baby..."

His voice broke and he blinked his eyes to stop tears from forming.

"Where are they?" the captain asked.

"Leningrad."

"When'd you last see them?"

"I saw my wife in 1941," Grisha said, struggling to maintain his composure. "I never saw my daughter."

"I see," the captain said. Grisha finished signing and the officer riffled through the papers. "Have you been in contact with your wife?"

Grisha hesitated. The question momentarily confused him. His contact had been spiritual, and it could not be explained.

"No," he said finally.

"How do you know you have a daughter?"

"I don't know for sure, Mister Captain," he said. "I just think so...."

"Mm hm." The captain studied the papers. "Where in the Ukraine?"

"Where I was born? West of Kiev."

"When did you leave there?"

"When I was nine."

"Family still there?"

"No. They're dead."

"Your whole family?"

"Yes, in the collectivization," he said. "My mother, father, uncle. My sister. All dead."

"I see, I see," the captain said. "And who raised you?"

Grisha was puzzled by the questions but he answered without hesitation. "The orphanage," he said.

"You speak Ukrainian?"

"Of course."

"Fluently?"

"Of course."

The captain nodded silently and regarded him for a long moment. Grisha felt a surge of hope.

The captain riffled through the papers again, then abruptly dropped them on the desk.

"Okay, Malmudov," he said finally. "I hope you'll have a chance to see your wife and your...um... daughter. Go back to your quarters and get your things. We'll have transportation for you in half an hour."

Grisha's heart fell. "Mister Captain," he said. "Where do you send me?"

"Look, Malmudov, please just do as you're told," he snapped. "I'll see what I can do, but in the meantime, for Christ's sake, just do as you're told."

"Thank you, Mister Captain," he whispered, and slowly left the office.

Grisha gathered his belongings into a laundry bag and waited with dwindling hope to be summoned for transportation to Berlin. But a half hour, then an hour, then three hours passed before anybody came to him. Finally he heard a tap at the door. Standing there, instead of the MP private he had expected, was the captain from the interview.

"Ready?" the captain said. He was wearing his Ike jacket and a garrison cap.

"Yes, Mister Captain," Grisha said, hurriedly grabbing his belongings.

"Just 'Captain,' please, Malmudov," he said. "Skip the 'mister.'"

"Thank you, Mister Captain," Grisha said, following the officer out of the room and down the corridor.

Outside, the captain led the way to a Jeep parked near the entrance, motioning Grisha to get into the passenger side. The officer took the wheel and they sped away.

Grisha was mystified. If they were shipping him back to Berlin, it wouldn't be like this, riding in a staff car like a general. He had seen the others when they left the building in the back of a big army truck.

The Jeep sped through the bomb-damaged streets of Munich, to the outskirts of the city and through a woods.

"Where are we going, Captain?" he asked politely.

"You'll see, Malmudov," the captain said, a slight smile showing through his fatigue. "You'll see in good time. Meanwhile, just keep your trap shut and your eyes open."

At that moment the captain turned off the main road and sped down a narrow lane through the woods. After a few hundred yards they came to a U.S. Army checkpoint. A sentry held up his hand and the Jeep skidded to a stop.

The captain handed a sheaf of papers to the sentry. The sentry looked at the papers, then at Grisha. He said something in English. The captain answered. The sentry handed back the papers, snapped a salute, and waved the Jeep through.

Another few hundred yards along the road they stopped at another sentry post, this one manned by two soldiers and equipped with a swing-away steel barrier. One of the soldiers, with the stripes of a sergeant, took the papers. He went to the sentry box and cranked a field telephone. He spoke into the mouthpiece.

"Mal-muh-duhv," he said. "Initials *G* golf, *N* nancy; last name—I spell—*M* mike, *A* able, *L* lima, *M* mike... Yeah. Okay. Got it?"

The sergeant returned the papers to the captain and pulled the barrier away. The Jeep shot through, swung around a curve, and spun over gravel as it approached a palatial villa set among the trees, a rambling, four-story building with lawns stretching off down a hillside. More than a dozen American Jeeps and Ford sedans stood in neat rows outside the villa on the gravel.

The captain parked the Jeep alongside the other vehicles and motioned Grisha to follow him inside.

At the doorway another sentry went through the same process of inspecting papers, calling on a field telephone, and spelling Malmudov's name. He passed them through to a richly appointed entry, hung with an ornate chandelier and decorated with paintings, gold leaf, and carved paneling. They went up a wide, carpeted staircase and into a room at the top of the stairs where an American sergeant sat at a carved gold-and-ivory table.

Again, the papers changed hands. The sergeant read the papers and spoke with the captain. He nodded, saluted, and sat down again at the desk.

"Well, Malmudov," the captain said in Russian. "Here's where I get off." He reached out to shake Grisha's hand.

"But . . . but Mister Captain," he blurted, alarmed. "What am I here for?"

"Just wait here and find out," the captain said, and he was gone.

Grisha stood awkwardly in the middle of the room. The sergeant said something without looking up. After a moment he looked up and said it again.

Grisha grinned, embarrassed. "No . . . no Ainglich," he said. "Is not spoke Ainglich."

The sergeant pointed to a chair and said it again. Grisha understood. He sat down. After a moment the sergeant picked up the papers that had come with

Grisha, knocked on the door behind him, and walked through. Grisha caught a glimpse of a carved table, a tall window, and a figure seated at the table. The sergeant came out a moment later, without the papers, and motioned Grisha into the room.

As he walked in, a tall, sandy-haired man in the uniform of a lieutenant colonel rose from the carved table and said in flawless Russian. "Well, Mr. Malmudov, and how are you today?"

Grisha was at a loss for words. He stood gaping at the tall, crisply uniformed officer. He still had his sack of belongings in his hand and he felt intensely out of place in the sumptuous room. The officer put a hand on his shoulder and guided him to a velvet-cushioned chair near his desk.

"Please have a seat," he said. "I'd like to have a chat with you. Will you have a drink?"

Before Grisha could answer, the sandy-haired officer poured out a glass of amber liquid and handed it to him. Grisha sat in the chair gripping the glass in one hand and the sack in the other.

"Here, let me take that," the officer said. He took the sack and deposited it on the floor by the door.

"Now, Mr. Malmudov," he said, pouring himself a drink and resuming his seat behind the desk. Grisha, overwhelmed by the opulent surroundings and bewildering situation, still had said nothing.

Finally, he found his voice. "Please, Mister Lieutenant Colonel," he said. "Why am I here?"

The officer smiled and sipped his drink. "First, let me introduce myself," he said. "I'm Lieutenant Colonel John Cabot, but I'd like for you to call me Jack. Our organization here is rather informal. And what shall I call you? 'Mister' sounds like a Chekhov play; 'comrade' is out of the question. May I take the liberty of calling you Grigory, or perhaps Grisha? It's an American habit, first names.''

"Why...yes, of course, eh, Jack," Grisha said, pronouncing the name as "Jek." It was odd to use such a name, because he remembered a Chekhov short story that had a dog named "Jek." The story was about two Russian boys who dreamed of going to California. Now this elegant officer had a dog's name.

"My friends call me Grisha," he said. "That's what you may call me if you wish."

"Fine, fine," Cabot replied. "Well, Grisha, try our American whiskey. We call it bourbon. Tell me what you think."

Grisha raised the glass to his lips, thinking how forward these Americans were. Already, Cabot had adopted the informal second-person singular "thou" verb form. Russians might be acquainted for years without assuming such a familiarity; this American was using it after two minutes.

He poured back the whiskey.

"Ach...sploo!" He gagged and coughed, spewing whiskey on his trousers. His throat burned. He looked at Cabot with alarm. The American laughed.

"Grisha, my friend, this is sipping whiskey, not vodka," he said, coming around to take the glass. He pulled a gleaming white handkerchief from his pocket and dabbed at the splattered trousers.

Grisha coughed, embarrassed. "Please, that's all right," he said. "I'll be all right."

"Here," Cabot said, pouring a fresh glass. "Now, the custom is to take just a bit at a time and savor it."

Grisha took the glass and held it awkwardly, not daring to chance even a sip. Cabot resumed his seat.

"Grisha, my friend, I understand you're, um, somewhat reluctant to be repatriated. Is that right?" he asked.

Grisha looked into the glass. "That's right."

"Why?"

"I'm afraid. We hear they shoot collaborators."

"You mean because you were forced to work for the Germans you'll be regarded as a collaborator?"

"That's what they say," Grisha looked up.

Cabot raised an eyebrow. "Well, 'they' are right, I'm afraid. We have evidence that a considerable number of repatriated POWs have been shot. A considerable number of others have been transported to camps in the north." He sipped at his glass.

"I understand you're a married man..."

"Yes, Jek," Grisha said. "I want to see her again."

"And you have a child?"

"I think so. She was with child..." He choked back tears.

"Wife's in Leningrad?"

"Yes." He raised the glass and sipped. The burning liquid helped him control his emotions.

"And you want to see her."

Grisha looked intently at Cabot. "Yes, Jek," he said. "Can you help me?"

"Yes, Grisha, I can help you," he said. "But I don't know if you'll like it."

"How?" he said, leaning forward in the chair. "Tell me how! I'll do anything."

"As I said, you might not like it, Grisha," Cabot said. "And it might not work. I can't guarantee it."

"How?" he said again, half rising from the chair and spilling some of the whiskey. "Just tell me!"

"I'll tell you, but there is a condition," Cabot replied. "After I have told you, you will have two choices: You may cooperate with us, and perhaps return to the Soviet Union without becoming known to the NKVD; or you may refuse to cooperate with us, in which case you will not be repatriated at all. After a certain amount of time, you will be given an opportunity to make your life in the West, but I will not be able to help you after you are outside my jurisdiction."

Grisha thought about what he was hearing. He sensed that there was something coming that would test his conscience; he felt as if he were bargaining for his soul with a shrewd and charming Beelzebub.

He nodded. "I agree."

"All right, Grisha," Cabot said.

He walked over to the tall, curtained window and looked out.

"Here's the deal: We will train you and outfit you for reconnaissance work in the Soviet Union," he said. "For this purpose we will provide you with all the necessary documents to make it possible for you to live and work in the Soviet Union as a normal citizen. You will only be required to obtain certain information, and to transmit this information to us by means of a radio, which will be provided to you. What do you think?''

That, or something like it, was what he had expected. It was difficult for him to think clearly. Until this day he had considered himself an average sort of citizen, perhaps even above average. Patriotic. A Komsomol. A Red Army man. But war changed things and he had been robbed of choices.

"I thought you were our allies," he said. "Why do you need me to be…" He hesitated. "…To be a spy?"

'It's simple, Grisha," Cabot said, returning to his chair and sipping the whiskey. "We're allies now, but Germany is defeated. Things change. Josef Stalin has ambitions for control of Europe. We must be concerned about a country as powerful as the Soviet Union. We must know if the Soviet Army plans to move west, and we must know in plenty of time to protect ourselves.

"We will ask you to watch the movements of large contingents of Soviet armed forces and make reports by radio. That's all. We don't ask you to provide us with information that would threaten the defense of your homeland; we ask you to give us information that will help us defend our own homelands."

Grisha thought for a long moment.

"You ask me to be a traitor to my motherland," he said. "Suppose I say I'll do that? Suppose you give me a radio and send me into the Union. I have already agreed to betray my country. So what's to stop me from betraying you? I go, I throw away my radio and go to the authorities?''

"Well, obviously, the authorities would probably deal rather harshly with you, Grisha," Cabot replied.

"Okay, okay," Grisha said, using the American word. "Okay, suppose I just throw away the radio and don't go to the authorities?''

Cabot smiled and traced a design on the tabletop. "Well, we've considered that. We would not be relying only upon you, but upon a number of individuals. We expected that a certain percentage of them will not cooperate once in the USSR, or will be captured..."

He paused.

"And there's another consideration," he went on. "You must keep in mind that we have a certain residual power over you. It is always possible that certain information might reach the Soviet authorities. That information might help them to ferret out certain people in the Soviet Union whose papers are not entirely in order. Do you understand?''

Grisha nodded slowly. There was a long silence.

"Well," Cabot said. "How about it?''

Grisha sat another moment in silence. He raised the glass of bourbon and drained it in a gulp, without coughing. The whiskey warmed his throat and his belly.

"I like to take it my way, Jek," he said. "Now, tell me what to do.''

TOP SECRET
OFFICE OF STRATEGIC SERVICES
UNITED STATES OF AMERICA
EUROPEAN THEATER OF OPERATIONS

Jan. 12, 1947

FILE MEMORANDUM

Re: (a) Performance of Operative
         (b) Assignment of Security Code

Ref: OSS Dir 122.4 of 15 Aug 45

Encl: (a) Biographic Summary of Kuznetsov, A. N.
         (b) Biographic Summary of Malmudov, G. N.
         (c) Original file of Operative Reports

(a) Performance of Operative.

> 1) Operative Malmudov, G. N., has completed nine months SovMilRep in region IV(A), EastEuro OpArea, under authority of OpOrder 267 of 12 Jan 45. He has taken employment in the Victory Tractor Factory. He has reported weekly according to assigned schedule and twice under emergency procedures.

> 2) Euro Evaluation, after cross-checking, assigned subject operative's reports Class A reliability.

> 3) In response to query, subject operative has reported negative attempts to contact spouse (see encl b) and negative intention.

(b) Assignment of Security Code

> 1) For purposes of improved security, subject operative is designated HEARTFELT, to be used in all future references. Only documents identifying subject operative by designated code name shall be maintained in the General Operative File.

> 2) Enclosures (a) through (c) shall be forwarded to Washington Operations Center for security storage. Any copies shall be destroyed.

Lt. Col. John Cabot
Commanding

TOP SECRET

16.

When Kuznetsov arrived at work Monday morning, his secretary, Svetlana, informed him that the weekly factory meeting was canceled.

"What? Why?" he asked. He was both surprised and relieved. It had been another poor production week and he did not relish the thought of reporting another failure to meet quotas.

"It's those Chekists," Svetlana whispered. "They've been prowling here since early this morning, going through records and looking things over. They're in the director's office now."

Kuznetsov raised his eyebrows but did not reply. It was alarming to have secret policemen so near. It was doubly alarming that Repin had not told him during the weekend that the Chekists would be in the building that day.

He hung up his coat and sat at his desk. A thought

struck him. "Sveta, has Comrade Repin arrived yet?" he asked.

"Oh, Chief, hours ago!" she said. "He came with those spooky policemen."

A heavy sense of foreboding settled over Kuznetsov. After he returned the day before from his weekend with Repin he had pondered his situation and had nearly concluded that his fears were groundless. He had decided that Repin did not actually suspect him. His reptilian manner and bureaucratic prissiness merely made it appear that way.

But the personnel director had been planning all along to bring the KGB into the building early Monday and had said nothing to his weekend guest.

Sveta brought him his first glass of tea, and he sipped slowly at it while he put together the production report for the director. He would want the bad news, meeting or no meeting. After an hour, he put the documents into a folder and went down the corridor to the director's office and left the folder on the secretary's desk. The door, normally open, was closed. The Chekists were still there. Kuznetsov shuddered and went downstairs to begin his daily inspection tour.

The factory tour was the best part of his day. It took him back to the factory floor where he had come from, and away from the paperwork and worry of the chief engineer's office. He had been an outstanding machinist, an expert on the use and maintenance of every machine tool in the plant. Ordinarily that would not have qualified him for the post of chief engineer at a time when such positions were occupied by ambitious young executives who held degrees from prestigious engineering institutes and who invariably belonged to the Communist Party or the Komsomol. But the director of Red Banner was an old-fashioned man who believed in promoting managers from the ranks of workers.

Because of that factory-floor background, Kuznetsov was well liked by the men in the shops, many of whom had worked with him before he donned a suit and tie and moved up to management.

"Hey, Chief," the lathe-shop supervisor shouted when he walked through the swinging doors. "You're early today; trying to catch us off our guard?" The supervisor laughed and clapped Kuznetsov on the back.

"Ouch!" he cried, grimacing. "Easy, Vanya, I got a sunburn."

"By God, Alexander Nikolayevich, you've been playing at the beach," he said. "Hey, boys! Kuznetsov's been to the beach with the big shots and got a sunburn!" The machinists laughed. Kuznetsov laughed with them.

The supervisor accompanied him down the rows of lathes, explaining technical problems. Kuznetsov listened with interest, and he made it a point to exchange a few words with the operators as he inspected their machines and their work. He took pride in knowing every man and woman in all the shops by name and patronymic.

The supervisor stopped at a lathe that was standing idle. Kuznetsov opened it, and examined the chuck. "Somebody put too many revs on this one," he said.

"That's what happened, Chief," the supervisor replied. "New guy, trying to make up time. I had a talk with him."

Kuznetsov thanked the supervisor and started off to the casing shop. A clerk caught up with him in the corridor. "Excuse me, Alexander Nikolayevich," she said. "Comrade Repin wants you in the winding shop."

"Thank you," he said. He frowned and changed course for the double swinging doors of the winding shop.

When he pushed through the doors he saw Repin with a group of men near the foreman's cubicle. Among them were the shop foreman and the security chief. He did not recognize the other two, who wore dark suits and ties.

"Alexander Nikolayevich," Repin said as Kuznetsov approached. "This is Comrade Saltykov, inspector from the Committee for State Security; this is his colleague, Comrade Chicherin. Comrade Chicherin is a specialist in industrial security. Comrades, our chief engineer, Comrade Kuznetsov." They shook hands.

Repin's hearty manner of the weekend had vanished. He was clipped, precise, and formal.

"I thought we might have a look at the area, and perhaps you'd answer some questions, Comrade Kuznetsov," Saltykov said.

Kuznetsov nodded, and the group started off single-file to the warehouse, making their way around the heavy winding equipment in the shop. The first man, Saltykov, clearly was in charge. He was tall and heavy, with a broad barrel chest that created a general impression of fleshy mass. But despite his burly appearance he spoke with refinement and courtesy.

Both Saltykov and his colleague, Chicherin, had a way of looking at people with a discomfiting intensity. It was a policeman's look, a piercing gaze that caused even the innocent to examine their consciences.

"This is where the last thefts took place, comrades," Repin said as they entered the warehouse. Repin pointed to heavy wooden crates, each containing ten thousand meters of wire. The KGB men examined the area with care. Saltykov looked over the crates and stooped to heft one. He could barely lift it.

"Damned heavy!" he said. "You'd have to have several men to move this stuff."

"Yes, and they'd need a truck or something to get it away," Repin said.

They moved along, the KGB men asking questions about storage and procedure. Kuznetsov followed in silence. Production, not warehousing, was his responsibility. He did not understand why they needed him.

Finally, Saltykov turned to Kuznetsov. "Well, Comrade Engineer, perhaps you'd be able to supply us with information on the uses of this wire?"

"Why, of course, comrade," he said. "Would you like to come up to the office? It will be a little more comfortable."

"Excellent," Saltykov said, and they headed for the management building.

"Sveta, four glasses of tea, please," he said as he showed the two KGB men and Repin into his office. He pulled out chairs for them and took his place behind his desk. Sveta came in with tea and sugar on a tray.

Saltykov sipped his tea and turned his policeman's gaze on Kuznetsov. "Well, comrade, what are the uses of this wire?"

"Well, next to silver, copper is the best metal for electrical conductivity, so it has thousands of electrical applications," Kuznetsov said. "Here, we use it for the windings in generators. We use quite a lot for that purpose, as you could see in the warehouse."

"I see," Saltykov said. "And the particular type of wire you have here, is it widely used?"

"Yes, I suppose it's fairly widely used," he said. His uneasiness subsided. He explained the wire's applications in making generators, electric motors, transformers, and various other heavy-duty electrical devices.

"This particular wire may be useful in certain types of circuitry, and of course it's essential anywhere a winding is needed for the creation of a field.... Really, there's a thousand uses for copper wire; ten thousand uses—"

"Thank you, comrade," Saltykov interrupted. He wrote in a black notebook. "And the price? How much does it cost?"

Kuznetsov made a mental calculation. "Well, we pay about five hundred and eighty rubles for each of those cases; that makes it about five and a half kopeks a meter..."

"That's the state price?"

"Yes, of course," Kuznetsov replied, puzzled.

"What would it be worth on the black market?"

Kuznetsov looked surprised. "Surely, I wouldn't know that, Comrade Inspector. I know nothing of the black market."

"Well, look," Saltykov said impatiently. "Just try to give me an idea what a thief would get for it. You yourself are running short of it. You're behind plan because of wire shortages, right?"

"Yes, that's right, comrade, but I wouldn't—"

"Just give me an estimate," Saltykov said. "Suppose you had a chance to get some under the table, enough to get back up to plan, how much—"

"Comrade Inspector," Kuznetsov said stiffly. "I don't buy materials 'under the table.' In fact, I don't buy materials at all. That is the responsibility of the purchasing department, and I have no doubt that at this plant we pay the state price under state contract."

"I see," Saltykov said, writing again in his notebook. "What is your responsibility, then, Chief Engineer?"

"Why, production, of course," Kuznetsov said.

"What is your background?"

Kuznetsov frowned and leaned forward on his elbows. "What does my background have to do with thievery, Comrade Inspector?"

"Please," the KGB inspector said. "I'll ask the questions. Are you a Party member?"

"No, I am not." Kuznetsov began again to feel the familiar pain in his chest, just at the breastbone. He swallowed and involuntarily pressed his knuckles against the spot of the pain.

"Why not?"

"I have never been much involved in political matters," he replied. "I'm a technical person, not a political one."

"The Party is interested in technology as well as politics," Saltykov said. "I'm surprised that the chief engineer of so large a plant is not at least a candidate member. Have you never applied for membership?"

"I have not."

"Has it ever been suggested that you apply?"

Kuznetsov glanced at Repin, who was studying his fingernails.

"Yes it has," he said. The pain worsened. He pressed the spot and took a deep breath. "Comrade Repin only recently suggested that I apply."

"What did you say?"

"Comrade, I fail to see what my membership in the Party, or the lack of it, has to do with the case at hand..."

"I wish to investigate all aspects of this case," Saltykov said. "We Chekists often find that where there is crime, there are other failings as well...."

Kuznetsov's chest tightened. He took a sip of the tea, which had gone lukewarm, and rubbed again at the spot of pain.

"Are you not feeling well?" Saltykov asked.

"I . . . I have a little indigestion," Kuznetsov said, taking his hand from his chest. "A little heartburn. It's nothing. . . ."

"Have you a degree?" asked the other KGB man, Chicherin, the specialist in industrial security.

"I have not," Kuznetsov said.

"Yet you're chief engineer," Chicherin said flatly.

"What are you suggesting?" Kuznetsov said.

"Just that in my experience, chief engineers usually are engineers, with graduate degrees."

"In my experience," Kuznetsov replied testily, "some excellent chief engineers come off the factory floor where they have learned firsthand the needs of the factory and the capabilities of the workers. This is a workers' state, a proletarian state, comrade . . ."

"Well," Saltykov said, chuckling. "You are a political man after all, even if you aren't a Communist."

Kuznetsov said nothing. Saltykov looked at his notebook. "Have you always worked here?" he asked.

"No. I've been here ten years," he said.

"And before?"

"At ZIL."

"What did you do there?" Saltykov was writing rapidly.

"Machinist. The motor shop, then auto generators. That's how I came here." Kuznetsov sipped his tea. The pain throbbed in his chest.

"Did you have training in generators at ZIL?"

"Only on the job."

The inspector's questions were coming at Kuznetsov rapid-fire, and he scribbled in the notebook. He had dropped the use of the "comrade" in addressing him.

"Have you ever had formal training?"

"I took some courses at the Moscow Institute of Electrical Engineering."

"Is that how you have the title 'engineer'?"

"Comrade Inspector," Kuznetsov shot back, "'engineer' is a job description, not a title. I am a machinist and I make no apology for that. I have certificates of qualification as a master machinist and as a master electrician; those are the certificates specified by the ministry as qualifications for the position of chief engineer. I might add that I—"

Saltykov interrupted him impatiently. "And what did you do before the war, Engineer Kuznetsov?"

The question caught him off guard and he did not reply immediately. His mouth was dry and the pain in his chest throbbed. He took a sip of tea. It was stone cold.

"I said, what did you do before the war?" Saltykov gazed impassively at Kuznetsov, his pencil poised.

"I am at a loss..." Kuznetsov said. "What can this have to do with the investigation..."

"As I said, we must explore every avenue," Saltykov replied evenly. "I am not accusing you, but I am interested in your background. Please, what did you do before the war?"

"The Ukraine," he said. He spoke mechanically, conscious of the pain in his chest and a ringing in his ears. "The Ukraine. I was born in the peasant class; I joined the working class at the age of fifteen on the southwestern railway project; then I worked at the Metallastroi Works in Stalingrad..."

"As?"

"As a lathe operator. Parts for large engines."

"And the war?"

"All this is in my file," Kuznetsov said. "Why is it necessary to go over..."

"Just answer, please."

"Southwestern front, 112th Infantry Division, machine gunner." He recited the details of his fictitious youth, surprised that he could remember them so easily so many years after they were drilled into his head by the young Americans in Munich. He had always thought his nerve would fail if it came to answering these questions. They had trained him better than he had imagined.

"You were in that division for the whole war?"

"Yes," he replied. "We fought at Stalingrad and we chased them to the Ukraine."

"Did your division go to the West?"

"No. We demobilized in Lvov. I got drafted into a labor battalion and we set up a steel factory there. Dobrov."

"I see. And how long were you there at the...what was that factory?" Saltykov scribbled in the book.

"Dobrov Works," he said. "A year. After that, they sent me to Kiev and I worked on the Victory Tractor Factory. It was rebuilding."

"How long there?"

"From '46 to '50. Then to the ZIL plant here."

Saltykov sighed and looked at his notebook. He flipped back a page, then another. He smiled and gave Kuznetsov that piercing policeman's look. He turned to Chicherin, and the specialist on industrial security nodded.

"I'd just like to go over your reasons for not joining the Party, Comrade Engineer," Chicherin said. "You were a good worker, were you not? A respected worker? And now you're chief engineer. You're a leader among the proletariat, yet you didn't even apply to become a member of the Party of the working class. I find that strange. Why not?"

Kuznetsov stared at his palms. "I suppose I don't think of myself as the Party type, comrade," he said at length. "I think Comrade Repin here will tell you that I'm a quiet person, a bachelor. In short, I don't do very well making speeches and so forth. I try to do my socialist duty, but a Party activist? It's not in my—"

"Communists do more than make speeches, Kuznetsov," Saltykov said in his flat voice.

"Yes, I know, comrade...."

"You may call me 'inspector,'" he said. "The form of address 'comrade' is used between Communists."

Kuznetsov fell silent. The pain in his chest subsided. He felt a lightness in his head and he seemed to
be viewing the scene from a distance, looking down
from somewhere above the room. The two policemen
folded their notebooks and stuffed them in their breast
pockets. They rose from their chairs.

"Well, thank you, Chief Engineer," Saltykov said,
making no move to shake hands. They started for the
door, but Saltykov turned.

"I'd like to take a look at your papers, if you'd be
kind enough to bring them down," he said. "Just give
them to Comrade Repin here...."

Kuznetsov spoke in a detached voice. "I have my
passport right here, if you'd..." he began.

"No, no, I don't mean your current papers," Saltykov said. "I mean your old papers. Your old working papers, from the Army and the Stalingrad plant,
and that Dobrov Works. I assume you have those papers?"

"Yes," Kuznetsov said in the distant, dreamy voice.
"Yes, of course. I will bring them."

They left. Saltykov thanked Svetlana for the tea as
he passed through the outer office. As the outer door
closed, Svetlana hurried into his office.

"Oh-oh, what creepy-looking guys they are, huh?"
she said, gathering up the empty tea glasses. "How
about the way they look at you? Some characters.
What'd they say, Chief? Want some more tea? You
going to lunch now? Chief?"

Kuznetsov sat at his desk. He stared absently at her.

"Chief?" she said. "Are you all right?"

He blinked. "Yes, Sveta, I'm fine," he said. "Please close the door when you go out."

The secretary looked at him, puzzled. "But, Alexander Nikolayevich, you don't look well. Can I..."

"No, Svetlana Igorievna, please!" he said sharply. "Please, just go and close the door!"

She stiffened. She marched out of the room. Kuznetsov sat staring blankly at the door. The pain in his chest returned.

PEOPLE'S COMMISSARIAT OF
DEFENSE

Jan. 3, 1946

Dear Citizeness Malmudova:

In response to your letters concerning your husband, Malmudov, G. N., Private, Red Army, I regret to inform you that no record can be discovered concerning his whereabouts.

Having considered the circumstances of his disappearance, as reported in the Battle Diary of the 210th Red Army Division, and having discovered no record of his presence among returned prisoners, the People's Commissariat has transferred his name from the list of Missing in Action to the list of Missing and Presumed Dead.

You are advised that in accordance with Ukase 14.5 of the Presidium of the Supreme Soviet, Moscow, dated Aug. 5, 1945, presumption of death of your husband entitles you to military benefits accorded widows of Red Army soldiers lost in the Great Patriotic War.

A list of those benefits is enclosed.

Respectfully,

Serpov, Y. Ye., CAPT
Personnel Division

17.

Kuznetsov went to find Sonya in the fall of 1948, a month after he received the message from his controllers releasing him from his obligation to report.

He had remained faithful to the agreement he made with Cabot. He found a small room in a house near a complex of buildings, barracks, warehouse, and vehicle parks making up the headquarters of the Soviet Southwestern Regional Military Command. He passed by it twice daily going to and from work, and from his apartment he could hear the engine noises that would be associated with any large-scale military maneuvers.

On two occasions he was awakened in the night by the roar of truck engines that marked the beginnings of major exercises. Both times he got up and walked through the shadows around the perimeter counting vehicles and noting the comings and goings of staff cars. Then he returned to his room and transmitted terse reports to the controllers in West Germany.

Those two inconsequential reports on what turned out to be routine training exercises constituted the sum total of his espionage. The rest of his work consisted only of transmitting check messages according to a staggered weekly schedule. He sent the checks without fail for nearly three years. Then one night the usual acknowledgment was replaced by a message telling him his job was over; he was to destroy the radio and make no further attempts at contact. He acknowledged the message, signed off, and buried the radio.

While he was faithfully serving his secret masters in Munich he also faithfully served his public masters in the Soviet Union. He received advancement and reward at the factory for his skill as a machinist. He set the factory example for high production and low waste, and when his shift was over he accepted extra duties organizing union activities and administering the recreation fund. He was invited to join the Party, but he declined; his documents would not survive the inspection that would be demanded.

He had only acquaintances, no friends. He neither smoked nor drank, and he never invited any of his coworkers or neighbors to his room. People who knew him thought of him as shy and quiet, if they thought of him at all. He sought and found obscurity, a life painfully similar to German captivity. As he had then, he turned his mind frequently to thoughts of Sonya and his daughter, by now a pretty little girl in pigtails and pinafore.

Despite his longing to see his family he could not contemplate a trip to Leningrad until after the Amer-

icans had released him from his espionage obliga-
tions. He knew he could not think of going to Sonya
while he was an active espionage agent. He could not
think of facing her in those circumstances.

But even after his release he did not know how he
would present himself to her. He was beginning to
understand the full implications of the decision he had
made in Lieutenant Colonel Cabot's office. He was
discovering the loneliness of a secret unshared and
unshareable. He was finding himself caught in the
subtle, unyielding web that a human society spins
around its members.

He had suspected its existence in Munich, but put it
out of his mind because he had been left with so few
choices. Now, in the reality of postwar USSR, the web
tightened around him. He had even fewer choices.

Within a few days of his arrival in Kiev he was able
to ascertain that Sonya was alive in Leningrad at their
old address on Pestelya Street. He learned this by
thumbing over past issues of Leningrad newspapers,
especially the Leningrad Komsomol newspaper. In a
1947 issue he found a report on the election of the
Leningrad City Committee of the Komsomol. Among
the new members was Malmudova, S. In another issue
her name appeared among the members of the presidium of the City Komsomol Committee.

The reports brought the joy of confirmation that
she was alive and well. But her rank and responsibilities in the Komsomol depressed him. She had become
an important leader, bound by Party discipline and
well known to people of consequence in Leningrad and
elsewhere. Knowing her enthusiasm and her person-

ality, he was sure she had been noticed by senior party
officials; she would soon be a member of the Communist Party itself.

There in the library, reading her name, he began to
understand the power of society's stern catechisms.
She was a much different person now than then, a
creation of her experience in the war. She was a full-
time professional political activist; no doubt a good
one. She was bound in the web.

Kuznetsov was also in the web, but one far different from hers. It had been woven by war, captivity,
and compromise; by his decision to revoke the irrev-
ocable. He'd chosen to become Alexander Nikolayevich Kuznetsov instead of Grigory Nikolayevich
Malmudov, to trade his old life for a new. Now he saw
the impossibility of bringing the two lives together.

The experience taught him the true meaning of fairy
tales of princes turned into toads. The tales are tragic
because the former prince knows what he is; his family and friends do not. The toad must observe his loved
ones from a distance, living his toad's life, doing what
is expected of toads. Their grief is softened by the
passage of time; his is not.

The forces confining Kuznetsov to his new life were
many: His red-bound passport had been seen,
stamped, recorded, checked, cross-checked, and an-
notated a dozen different times; his qualification papers listed places, dates, times, and names that were as
much a part of his identity as his Ukrainian accent;
foremen, coworkers, neighbors, housing officials,
store clerks, and, of course, the unknown Americans
listening at radio receivers in West Germany bound

him to his identity. These forces made heavy demands. They compelled him to be at certain places at certain times, to give certain answers to certain questions, to answer to one name rather than another.

Finally, there was the force of his conscience, and it was with his conscience that Kuznetsov waged his bitterest struggle. It asked him what he would tell his wife if he faced her in Leningrad. The truth? But the truth was that he was a spy with a false passport. Even if she were to accept him under such circumstances—and he hoped she might love him enough to do so—they were both too closely bound in society's web to make a life together. To stay with her in Leningrad among their prewar friends was plainly impossible; for Sonya to abandon her Party responsibilities to live in secrecy with him in Kiev would be extremely difficult. The Party did not easily release its servants, and there were no talented American experts to forge papers for her.

In any event, he could not conceive how he would present his story to Sonya, his dark-eyed and trusting young wife. And that being so, how much more impossible to tell the story to Malmudova, S., Komsomol secretary. As a Komsomol activist Sonya had stoically accepted the injustice of the prewar arrests in his factory, even defended them; she was conditioned to serve the Party faithfully. To compel her to choose between faithfulness to her Party and faithfulness to a renegade husband would be an act of infidelity on his own part. He could not ask her to make the choice.

He considered throwing himself on the mercy of Stalin's secret police, telling them everything. But that, too, was impossible. Not only would it mean that he

would die with no chance of seeing Sonya; it would
mean ruination and suffering for her in a fearful, sus-
picious nation that granted no benefit of doubt to the
friends and families of traitors.

In that respect, even suicide was out of the question. As a matter of routine, the authorities would examine the documents and background of a suicide
victim to find his next of kin. If their inquiries led to
discovery of his false documents, the full force of the
NKVD's investigative resources would be brought to
bear. Sonya would not be safe.

But if common sense told Kuznetsov that he could
not resume his life, his heart said otherwise. In his
heart, he could not let go of the thought of seeing her
sometime, somehow.

Thus, on September 5, 1948, with no clear plan,
Kuznetsov left Kiev by train in a driving rainstorm. To
guard against recognition in Leningrad, he had grown
a mustache which, to his chagrin and surprise, came
out red. He recoiled at the thought of being seen by
Sonya with such foolish hair on his lip, but its very
foolishness made it a better disguise. He decided to
keep it and perhaps shave it later when he decided
what to do in Leningrad.

By the time he reached the City of Peter and Lenin
he had traveled out of Kiev's dreary, gray pre-winter
mists and into a sparkling Leningrad autumn. The
glorious weather overcame his bleary fatigue from the
long train ride and he stepped into a sunny Vostan-
naya Square with a sense of elation. He walked briskly
across the square into Ligovsky Prospekt and into the
Oktyabrsky Hotel in search of a room.

In the old hotel's main lobby he waited patiently at the administrator's window in a queue of would-be lodgers wheedling and cajoling for a place to stay. Inside the window sat a sallow wasted-looking woman with sagging skin and sparse reddish hair. She stared with vacant eyes at the supplicants, brusquely dismissing the requests of all but a favored few.

Kuznetsov listened to the exchanges and learned that rooms were made available on a priority basis: highest priority went to those with official business in Leningrad; next came military men on leave, in order of rank; then workers with travel-authorization slips, which was Kuznetsov's category; and finally all other categories of travelers. The weary administrator made it clear that this last category would under no circumstances obtain a room in the Oktyabrsky Hotel.

Finally it came Kuznetsov's turn. He produced his travel-authorization paper and the woman unfolded it with indifference.

"Don't you have relatives here?" she asked.

"None," he said.

"Well, why did you come, then, if you don't have no relatives? If you've got somebody to see, stay with them; if you got nobody, then leave."

With a feeling of mild guilt, Kuznetsov told a lie. "It's not quite true that I don't have relatives here," he said.

The administrator snorted and pushed the paper back through the window. Kuznetsov stopped her.

"My relatives are all in the Piskarevsky Cemetery," he lied. "They died in the blockade. This is the first time I had a chance to come see them."

The administrator looked hard at Kuznetsov. She shook her head, making the folds of sagging skin swing back and forth. A momentary light shone through the bleak, indifferent eyes. She pulled back the paper.

"Two days, comrade," she said. "That's long enough to see those relatives. Room 1209." She scribbled on a piece of paper and pushed it through the window.

"Thank you," Kuznetsov muttered. He prayed that the lie would not bring him bad luck. He took the paper and turned to go.

"Comrade," the woman said. He looked back; her eyes glistened. "Say hello to my old man."

"I will, comrade," he said, feeling even more ashamed of the lie. "I will."

Privacy and a place to stay assuaged his guilt. He closed the door to room 1209 and sat on the bed trying to decide what to do. He was excited by his nearness to Sonya but terrified at the thought of making contact with her.

Finally, he undressed, wrapped a towel around himself, and walked barefoot down the corridor to the bath. He bathed and shaved carefully, trimming the ridiculous red mustache, and cleaning beneath his fingernails with the point of his penknife. Back in his room, he unfolded a dark woolen suit and put it on over an open-necked white shirt. He turned the shirt collar over the jacket, smoothed it, and added a flat cap, a new one he had bought in Kiev. He had never worn such a cap before the war; he hoped it might help prevent recognition.

He examined himself in the room's small mirror. He looked like a fool with the blazing-red mustache and the flat cap pulled down over his eyes. But he was sure no old friends would be able to recognize him unless they had a chance to look closely into his eyes.

It was nearly noon. He sat down to wait a couple of hours before going near the Pestelya Street apartment so he would avoid meeting anybody who might go in or out of the building at lunchtime. But the waiting made him impatient and nervous. After fifteen minutes he leapt to his feet and marched out. He walked briskly down the Nevsky Prospekt, looking closely at approaching faces. He saw nobody he knew until he reached the Fontanka, where a man with vaguely familiar features appeared on the crowded sidewalk. Kuznetsov stopped, turned, and stared into the window of a cobbler's shop. The man passed, and Kuznetsov continued to the river, turned right before the bridge, and walked along the Fontanka embankment toward Pestelya Street.

Once off the busy Nevsky Prospekt, he encountered fewer pedestrians. He took time to look at the buildings and was surprised that so little had changed. Here and there he saw empty spaces with board fences closing them from the street—buildings destroyed by bombs or shells. But most structures were not heavily damaged. The city's general appearance certainly was far drearier than it had been before the war. Most of the state's resources were given over to the restoration of industry, leaving nothing for the painting of buildings and the repair of sidewalks and streets.

As he neared Pestelya Street, Kuznetsov's heart raced and his stomach tingled with excitement and fear. He stopped and leaned on the railing at the embankment to calm himself. He walked on after a moment, and, taking a deep breath, he rounded the corner at Pestelya Street. He was shocked at what he saw. At least a third of the buildings on the north side of the street were gone, including one near the corner where one of Sonya's closest friends, Marya, had lived.

With a rush of emotion he stepped across and looked down the south side of the street where the peeling facade of Number 58 stood. The southern side of the street had fared better in the war. The German guns fired from the south, so the north-facing apartments were protected by the buildings behind them. Those facing south bore the brunt of the gunnery.

He started along Pestelya Street, heart pounding, but at that moment a woman emerged from a nearby doorway and walked toward him. She moved with difficulty on swollen legs, and he recognized her haggard face as that of the wife of a block warden they had known in the early days of the war. Kuznetsov, alarmed, turned back to the embankment and waited by the railing until she had hobbled around the corner in the opposite direction.

It was a shock to see her condition. She had been a plump and excitable girl of twenty-five then, rather pretty and irrepressibly cheerful. She could hardly be more than thirty-three, but she looked sixty, a lame, weak, haggard wreck. He realized with a sinking heart that his Sonya could have suffered the same ravage as

the warden's wife. He had consistently imagined her
being the same as she had been in 1941; but there had
been seven years and a terrible war since then. How
would he react if he knocked on the door of Number
58 and encountered a raddled shell of a woman like the
one he had just seen?

Deep in such thoughts, he began a slow walk to the
Kutuzova Embankment of the Neva. He walked along
it for a few blocks, then turned back toward Pestelya
Street. He pulled out his watch. It was ten minutes past
one; time to go to the apartment. His heart pounded
as he approached the corner and he breathed deeply to
calm himself as he approached Number 58. As he
neared the doorway, a man walked out of the building; Kuznetsov looked down and away, but the man
was a stranger. He waited a moment, then hurriedly
opened the street door and stepped inside. There was
nobody in the dark entryway, so he bounded up the
stairs two at a time, heart racing, noticing in the mar-
gin of his mind that it looked much as it had before the
war except for peeling paint and greater dinginess. At
the top of the stairs he turned, took three steps to the
corner of the hallway, and faced the door of his room.

It was the familiar door with the familiar metal card
holder and a white card in it. He looked at the name
in the holder and groaned aloud with disappoint-
ment. The name Malmudov was gone. In its place was
a new name:

Pobedontsov.

Kuznetsov could hardly contain his disappoint-
ment. She had moved, and now he would have to go
through the difficult and dangerous procedure of

finding her new address. That would mean surreptitious checks of directories, cautious inquiries, and guarded telephone calls. He felt angry and cheated. He glared at the new name, Pobedontsov, and slowly descended the stairway. He paused in the dark entryway at the bottom, considering what to do next. He heard the outer street door open, turned, and ducked down the passageway beside the staircase leading to the building superintendent's door. He stopped in front of the door as if waiting for a knock to be answered.

There were voices and footsteps of several persons in the entryway. They started up the stairs. A man's voice said, "It's all the same to me, darling; the zoo or a boat ride, it's up to you."

Then a child's voice: "The zoo! The zoo!"

"The zoo, then," the man replied. Kuznetsov peered up and caught sight of legs on the stairs: a man's, a woman's, and a young girl's. The feet had almost reached the landing when the woman said, "Uh, I don't think she's home."

Kuznetsov's heart stopped.

It's her!

He stared in disbelief at the superintendent's door. It was Sonya's voice, no mistake. He stood frozen, horrified, confused. Then, sharp and clear, he heard it again:

"Comrade, the superintendent's not there. She's out. There's no use knocking. She'll be back later!"

The voice was sharp, peremptory; but there was no question whose it was. It was Sonya. Panic swept him and he heard his own voice, hoarse, strained, muttering, "Thank you, thank you."

He plunged headlong down the passageway and into the street. As he shot through the door the familiar, lovely, beloved voice cried out:

"Kolya, what was he doing? Maybe he's a criminal!"

Kuznetsov flew out of the building at a dead run. He ran all the way to Nevsky Prospekt before he stopped, gasping for breath. He collapsed against the embankment railing and stared into the dirty water of the Fontanka. His heart pounded, exploding in his ears.

Who was the man? Was the girl my child? His child? Our child? Their child?

Who was the man?

Kuznetsov pounded his forehead with a clenched fist, attracting the stares of passersby. He groaned. A woman said, "He's drunk."

Sonya's words rang in his ears.

"Kolya, what was he doing? Maybe he's a criminal!"

He stood leaning against the wrought-iron railing for several minutes before he pulled himself together and made his way back to the Oktyabrsky Hotel, dragging his feet and staggering as if drunk. At the hotel, he fell on the bed and stared with dull, unseeing eyes at the ceiling.

Kuznetsov awoke a few hours later with the afternoon sun glaring into his room. He was sore and depressed, and his first waking thought was of Sonya and the girl and the man and her words:

"Kolya, what was he doing? Maybe he's a criminal!"

He sat up on the bed and went over the painful details. The man: a relative? No. The name on the door was Pobedontsov, not her maiden name. The only possibility that suited the circumstances was that she had remarried. Kolya Pobedontsov was the new husband.

But perhaps not. Perhaps he was a friend. A cousin. Sonya had had no close family before the war: both parents dead, an older married sister in Tashkent, a few aunts and cousins, infrequently mentioned. Why the name on the door?

He had eaten nothing all day, so he rose and went down to the hotel café to buy bread and tea. He gobbled it quickly and left the hotel. He did not think about what he was doing. He simply did it. He walked purposefully along the Nevsky Prospekt to the Fontanka and then to Pestelya Street. He looked up at Number 58 and saw there was no light in the window of his apartment.

"My" apartment, he thought. No. Not any longer.

He slipped behind one of the wooden fences in front of a destroyed building and waited in the shadows, thinking again of her voice, clear and commanding:

"Kolya, what was he doing? Maybe he's a criminal!"

The last light was fading from a clear autumn sky. He stood in the stillness, tensing when a figure walked along the street. The only illumination came from the lights at the entryways of the buildings and from a half-moon high in the sky.

A car turned into the street, and Kuznetsov realized as the lights swept his hiding place that it was a canvas-topped militia scout car with two uniformed officers in the front seats. He ducked. It would be disastrous to be caught loitering there, so near his Sonya. After the car disappeared, he squeezed out from behind the fence and began to walk away.

At that moment, in the glow of an entryway light across the street, he saw them: a man, a woman, and a young girl. He slipped back behind the fence.

The three walked slowly. The girl's lighthearted voice carried through the night air. The man said something and laughed.

Then, clear as a bell, Sonya's voice rang through the darkness.

"Kolya, you devil!" she said.

She laughed, a bright, strong sound that Kuznetsov remembered with painful clarity.

They came closer. In the light of Number 58 he saw them. He stopped breathing as he recognized the features of Sonya. She had not wasted; she had matured: her body was fuller, more matronly, but the dark hair was the same, the clear Russian face, the strong black eyes.

Holding Sonya's left hand was a slim girl with a bow in her hair. She laughed, and in the laughter was something of Sonya. She was about six or seven years old. She was his daughter.

Kuznetsov caught only the briefest glimpse of the man Sonya had called Kolya before they passed from the light and through the doorway. He seemed to have light-colored hair and was perhaps thirty years old. Her arm linked his, comfortably, familiarly.

Kuznetsov did not breathe until they disappeared through the door of Number 58. He watched the darkened window upstairs. A light came on. A minute passed. A figure, Sonya, appeared at the window, looking out. Another figure appeared. The man. He lowered his head and kissed her on the neck. Her mouth opened.

Faintly, as in a dream, her laughter carried into the street. Her head turned; arms went up; they faced each other; they kissed.

From the fence came the sounds of choking sobs. Three times. Then the dark figure wearing a flat hat and a red mustache broke from the fence and ran away down the street, footsteps echoing away in the darkness.

18.

Kuznetsov sat for several minutes with his hands pressed against his closed eyelids. Red, green, and yellow lights flashed in the blackness. The time had come. The secret would be his no more. It would be shared with the two Chekists; with Repin; with the state. With Sonya. With Sonya.

He saw the accusing policemen's gaze of the two KGB officers, heard Saltykov's voice, icy and even:

"You may call me 'inspector.' The form of address 'comrade' is used between Communists."

He wondered how much they knew. Perhaps everything. A few days of diligent investigation, checking records, and asking questions in the Ukraine and at the Ministry of Defense would be enough to tell them what they needed to know. Establishing his true identity would take a little more time, but they could do it.

They had time.

They were playing with him, as a cat plays with a wounded bird. They knew they had him. They knew

he could not escape. They could afford to play him, to
watch how he behaved, how he responded to their
blows.

He wondered how Sonya would react. He called her
familiar image to his mind: her smile, her dark eyes,
her shining black hair, the way she walked, talked,
laughed. She would be different by now, heavier,
probably, and gray hair mixed with the black.

He felt the looseness of the skin on his face, the
pouches beneath the eyes. He tried to put together a
face that would be Sonya at the threshold of old age.
But he could only visualize her as she had been that
last time, walking beside the man named Pobedontsov.

Kuznetsov sighed heavily and rose from the chair.
He leaned on the desk with his palms open on the
smooth surface. He turned to the window and looked
through the filmy curtain. In the yard below, a truck
stood at a platform and men loaded crated generators
onto it. They shouted and cursed as they worked,
sliding the heavy machinery off the dollies and shoving it into position on the truck bed.

"Hey, hey, hey, Lyolya, God damn it to hell, get
under it, get under it!" the dock foreman yelled.
"Now, push, push, push, more, more, more, more,
more, more!" The foreman waved the dolly into the
truck, directing the men with his shouts. "Hold it! A
little more, more more! Hold it! Good! Next one!
Let's go!"

Kuznetsov envied them. He wished he could trans-
form himself into one of the men working on the
platform, to be free of his burden and his guilt. He

would have a jolly fat wife cooking cabbage soup for him in a tiny, odor-filled flat; he would drink himself stupid every Saturday night and sober up on pickle brine every Sunday morning.

A bird flew past the window, swooped, and fluttered under an eave. Kuznetsov envied the bird as he envied the workmen on the platform. He wished he could be any other thing than himself.

He looked back down into the yard, at the black asphalt paving. He thought of jumping, of landing flat on the asphalt. He imagined his body sprawled there, blood oozing from the ears, the workmen crowding around.

He turned back to the office and looked at the chandelier. He imagined his body hanging from it, his belt around the neck, eyes bulging, tongue hanging out.

On his desk stood a six-inch paper spike. He imagined himself sprawled on the desk, impaled on the spike. He smiled. Spiked like a telegram from Arbitrazh. He laughed aloud and shook his head.

He sat at the desk. How would he behave as they played out their end game? Not suicide, he thought. No jumping from windows or falling on paper spikes or hanging by belts. And not flight, either. He would not take his savings from the bank and hop freight trains to Siberia.

To commit suicide, to run away: It lacked dignity. He would behave with dignity, because that was all that would be left. A little dignity.

There was also the question of protecting the innocent. Everybody who had ever had contact with him,

from Sonya to Dr. Fomina to his secretary, Svetlana
Igorievna, would come under the shadow of suspicion. As a prisoner he could testify to their ignorance
of his actions and his identity; as a corpse or a fugi-
tive he could not.

He put his hands over his eyes and groaned. He was
tired, exhausted.

"Chief?"

Kuznetsov lowered his hands, blinking wearily.
Svetlana peeked around the door.

"Chief, a message from Comrade Repin," she said.
"They want to see you at three o'clock."

"Fine, Sveta, thank you," he said, waving a hand
distractedly. Svetlana tiptoed into the office, closing
the door behind her.

"They want you at the...the Lyubianka!" she
whispered.

Kuznetsov stared vacantly. "Yes," he murmured.
"I see. Tell Evgeny Maximovich that I'll be there."

The Lyubianka. The place on Dzerzhinsky Square,
where people went in standing up and came out
chained in the back of a truck marked "Bread." The
Lyubianka. It was the place more feared than any
other. The ordinary-looking mustard-colored five-
story former office of an insurance company was the
headquarters of the Committee for State Security, the
KGB. A tall statue of Felix Dzerzhinsky stood in front
of it, the founder of the Cheka staring darkly at the
huge Detsky Mir children's department store on the
corner opposite the Lyubianka. Dzerzhinsky: the
benefactor of orphanages; the maker of orphans.

Kuznetsov smiled gently at the somber concern on Svetlana's face. He thought of a joke he once heard. He told it.

"What's the tallest building in Moscow?" he asked.

"What?"

"What's the tallest building in Moscow?"

Svetlana looked at him in consternation. "Well, I suppose it's the post office tower, but what . . ."

"Nope," he said, grinning. "The Lyubianka."

"What?"

"The Lyubianka, my dear," he said, chuckling. "From the windows of the Lyubianka you can see all the way to Siberia."

Kuznetsov burst out laughing at his own joke. He leaned back in his chair and guffawed. Tears came, and he pulled a handkerchief from his pocket and wiped his eyes.

Svetlana stared at him. "Alexander Nikolayevich," she said softly. "Under the circumstances I don't think that's very funny."

"Oh my dear, don't be so serious," Kuznetsov said, still chuckling and wiping his eyes. "This is just police routine. Just policemen going through their paces. Not to worry."

She smiled tentatively. "Well, I do hope so," she said. "But if there's anything you need, anything I can do . . ."

"No, not a thing that you can do, Sveta," he said. She started to leave. "Wait, there is one thing."

"Yes, Chief?"

"A nice hot glass of tea, two lumps."

"Sure, right away, Chief," she said, hurrying out of the office.

Three o'clock. It was only one-thirty. It would be so much easier if they would simply come and arrest him. But they wished to play him a little longer.

He smiled at the irony. He had been waiting for this moment for nearly thirty years. Now it was here, and an hour and a half seemed too long.

He took the papers from his "in" basket and sorted through them. Mechanically, he began writing notes in the margins, checking numbers; but his mind was not on the paperwork. The door opened; Svetlana Igorievna slipped in and put the glass of steaming tea on the desk. He glanced up and smiled.

"Thank you, Sveta," he said. "Thank you very much."

She started to leave, then stopped. "You know, Chief, the collective is fond of you," she said. "We respect you."

He nodded. How would the collective feel about him by this time tomorrow?

"Don't worry, my dear," he said. "Everything is in hand."

She left, pulling the door closed. Kuznetsov put the paperwork aside. He opened a drawer and pulled out a fresh sheet of paper. He smoothed the paper on his desktop and began to write:

My Dearest Sonya:
   It is with the bitterest regret that I bring myself to write to you. I do it partly because of selfishness; but I do it also because of love that failed to

die even after my betrayal of my homeland and of you.

I did not die in the war; I wish to God that I had. I betrayed the motherland, as you will know before you see this letter. I write not to torment you further, but to explain what happened, why I behaved as I did, not to justify myself but so you will know that it was never my intention to turn my back on you, to hide from you.

My life passed out of my control. The war, my captivity by the Nazis, the conditions here in the Soviet Union robbed me of choices. In desperation, I made a pact with the devil and I have paid dearly for it.

My hope was that I could live out the life I chose and remain dead to you until old age or careless habits made the hope a reality. But fate has not permitted that to happen. Perhaps it will be possible for me to remain dead in the eyes of our daughter. I will plead with the investigators to spare her the knowledge of her father's betrayal and to spare you endless interrogations.

I will not write now of the events that turned me to treason and which kept us apart. I can only say again that it came from desperation. My head was turned because youth and simplicity did not let me judge the consequences of what I was doing; I acted only because I wanted to be with you again. The investigators will tell you I sold myself to our enemies, but that is not true. They promised to get me into the Union in a way that would keep me out of the camps; they kept their promise.

I will do everything possible to protect you now; that is why I have not tried to end this misery by my own hand. I will be going to the Lyubianka in a few minutes; I will tell them the truth: that you know nothing, and knew nothing.

I should tell you that I saw you once after the war, though you did not suspect it. I went to Leningrad, to Number 58 Pestelya Street. You nearly caught me there. I was standing at the superintendent's door, and you told me she wasn't home; I ran away. You may remember it. I remember well that you said, "Maybe he's a criminal!"

Later on that same day I hid nearby. I saw you with your...

Here Kuznetsov paused and considered how to refer to Pobedontsov. At length, he sighed and continued writing.

... with your husband and our daughter. But I did not dare to try to speak to you. When I saw that you were happy, that you loved Pobedontsov, and that he loved you, I left Leningrad and did not return again. I followed your career in the newspapers and Party directories. I searched for the new name, Pobedontsova.

I must tell you that I at first felt great and painful jealousy of Pobedontsov. But in time I came to love the man who took my responsibili-

*ties and who brought light and happiness into
your life. He will despise me for what I have done
and am doing; yet I love him and I ask that you
thank him for me.*

*I weep, dear Sonya, for the pain and grief I
now bring you. I weep for what you must now
think of me. I weep for a lost and useless and unhappy life. You may hate me now; but please
don't hate the boy who loved you before fate
passed this bitter cup to me.*

*I love you, dearest Sonya; I kiss you, and our
dear child.*

Good-bye,

Kuznetsov stopped, the pen poised to sign his name.
He smiled, and for the first time since he left the DP
camp in Munich he signed the name his father gave
him:

Grisha

It was surprising how easily the name flowed from
his pen after all those years. It gave him a strong sense
of pleasure to see it written on paper. He read the letter; read it again; then he sealed it in an envelope. He
addressed the envelope in care of Sonya's office at the
Leningrad Party Committee, stamped it, and put it in
the inside pocket of his jacket. He looked at his watch.
It was half past two. Time to go to the Lyubianka.

He rose from the desk and arranged his papers in an
orderly stack on the left-hand corner, as was his cus-

tom. He picked up the glass of tea. He had not even
tasted it, and now it was cold.

He turned to the door, thinking that the cold, un-
wanted glass of tea was the last that Svetlana ever
would prepare for him. It had been a small but important pleasure when she brought him tea, and now
he was losing that pleasure. He looked at the office, at
the papers on the corner of his desk. His desk. No. His
no longer. They were leaving him—the desk, the papers, the office, the cold tea. Things were drifting
away from him, objects that had been his, pleasures
that had been his, small possessions to which he had
become accustomed—they no longer belonged to him.
Things fled from him like fleas from a dying dog; soon
he would have nothing left. Somebody else would sit
at his desk; somebody else would study his papers;
somebody else would drink the tea that Svetlana
brought. His world, meager and lonely as it was, had
begun to shrink. The boundaries of life were closing
in.

Already, before he even realized it, his apartment
was lost to him. He would never see it again. The
Volga River was beyond his reach; so was Leningrad.
He would never see the Black Sea, and he would never
learn to sail a boat. When he left the office, it would
pass beyond the boundary; then the factory; then the
Metro. Later, in the Lyubianka, his clothes would pass
through the boundary. His old, resoled brown shoes;
his penknife; his watch; all the familiar little things.

That is what happens when people die: They begin to lose things until only life remains, and it is the last to go. The world leaves them, slowly, then faster, and finally there is only life, and then not even that.

19.

Kuznetsov went into the outer office and handed the glass of cold tea to Svetlana, who stood beside her desk and looked at him somberly.

"Well, I'm going to my appointment now, Sveta," he said. "Please type the wastage figures. They're on the desk."

Svetlana smiled hesitantly. "Will you want them this afternoon, Chief?"

Kuznetsov had started toward the corridor. He paused. "No, dear Sveta, I won't be needing them this afternoon." He left the office.

Halfway down the corridor, Kuznetsov paused and took the envelope from his pocket and dropped it into a mail slot. The pickup would be in less than an hour. Even if they intercepted it, the important point was to mail it before going to the Lyubianka: Its existence would help Sonya even if she never received it.

He left the factory building through the main entrance. As he walked toward the gate he saw a gray

Volga sedan at the curb. From the rear seat emerged a man in a suit the same shade of gray as the sedan. The man lit a cigarette and leaned against the car, watching Kuznetsov through a cloud of smoke. When Kuznetsov walked through the gate, the man fell into place behind him, puffing on the cigarette as he walked.

In the Metro, Kuznetsov felt the man's presence behind him on the escalator but he did not look back. He stood at the edge of the platform waiting for the train, and he caught a glimpse of the man making his way through the crowd to stand a few feet away from him.

He heard the train coming. In the tunnel, the headlight shone and lights reflected off the shiny metal of the train's front structure. He tensed, and imagined the shiny metal smashing the bones of his chest and face, blood and flesh and cloth spewing from beneath the steel wheels. His head spun. The blast of air hit his face and the brakes screamed. The doors opened in front of him, and he let out his breath.

The man in the gray suit entered the car through the doors at the other end. He took a seat, glanced at Kuznetsov, unfolded a newspaper, and began to read. Kuznetsov could not see his face because of the newspaper.

He got off the Metro at Revolution Square, the man in the gray suit close behind him. They passed the Chinese Wall and the Metropol Hotel. At the corner of Karl Marx Prospekt, Kuznetsov paused and admired the facade of the Bolshoi, with its columns and flags. Clouds billowed in the blue sky. He had enjoyed a few nights at the Bolshoi, sitting high in an

upper balcony and looking down on the whirling figures of the dancers. Kuznetsov thought:

I'll never see the Bolshoi again.

The sun passed behind a cloud and Kuznetsov felt
chilled. The man in the gray suit stood at the curb in
front of the Metropol studying the grille of a foreign
car and smoking a cigarette. Kuznetsov looked at the
man, watching him draw on the cigarette and blow
smoke into the air. The man brought the cigarette to
his lips again and looked directly at Kuznetsov. They
held the gaze for a few seconds, until the man looked
away. Kuznetsov walked up Karl Marx Prospekt.

At the upper end of the prospekt loomed the four-
story facade of the Lyubianka, but Kuznetsov avoided
looking at it. He looked instead at the faces of the
people he met, busy women with shopping bags, men
smoking cigarettes, a portly Soviet Army colonel in a
brown uniform, carrying a net bag stuffed with
oranges.

The pedestrians rushed past Kuznetsov without
looking at him, but he examined each face with interest. A pretty girl in a green dress and wearing a green
ribbon in her hair glanced at Kuznetsov; their eyes met
and she looked away. Kuznetsov thought:

I'll never again catch a girl's glance.

He looked to where the girl's eyes had turned. A
sign advertising Aeroflot: "Fast, Safe, Efficient. The
best way to see the Soviet Union." It occurred to
Kuznetsov that the only time he'd ever flown in air-
planes was in jump training in 1946. He thought:

*I will never fly on a "fast, safe, efficient" passen-
ger airliner.*

He crossed Dzerzhinsky Square, waiting for the traffic lights to stop the busy swirl of cars rounding the tall statue of Felix Dzerzhinsky. Kuznetsov looked closely at the face of the brooding black figure. The eyes were cast down, their gaze aimed above the heads of the pedestrians in the square. Kuznetsov thought of his orphanage, named for Dzerzhinsky, the benefactor of orphans. He smiled at the statue.

Here is one of your sons, Comrade Dzerzhinsky.

He waved to the statue, and several people standing at the crosswalk looked curiously at him.

Kuznetsov crossed to the sidewalk in front of the Lyubianka and started up the steps to the tall, dark door at the entrance. A uniformed figure stood looking through the glass at him. Kuznetsov looked around; the man in the gray suit was gone.

He went inside and identified himself to the man in uniform. The guard made a telephone call. In a few minutes a young man in civilian clothes appeared.

"Kuznetsov?" the civilian asked. Kuznetsov and the uniformed guard were the only people there. Kuznetsov nodded.

"Follow me," the civilian said, turning.

Kuznetsov followed the young man up two flights of stairs and down a long corridor. They stopped in front of a door with the number 28. The young man tapped and entered, motioning Kuznetsov to wait. Kuznetsov stood alone in the quiet corridor until the door opened again.

"Go in," the young man said, standing aside.

Kuznetsov walked through the door. The inspector, Saltykov, sat behind a desk. To his right was Repin,

also sitting. Two men stood at Saltykov's left. The
young man who had accompanied Kuznetsov took a
seat at a table, opened a notebook, and took out a
pencil.

"Sit down, Kuznetsov," Saltykov said in his flat
voice. With a slight nod he indicated a straight-backed
chair in front of the desk.

Kuznetsov breathed deeply, went to the chair, and
sat uneasily on it, his back straight.

"We have some questions we'd like you to answer,
Kuznetsov," Saltykov said.

"If you please, comrade..." Kuznetsov checked
himself, and he began again. "If you please, Citizen
Inspector, I'm ready now to explain everything..." His
voice cracked and he licked his lips. "I'm ready to tell
you what you want to know; I'm happy to do it; I'm
very tired of hiding it...."

Kuznetsov cast his eyes down to the carpet between
his chair and Saltykov's desk; he concentrated on the
undulating design of red, blue, and yellow flowers. "I
have lived a long time with this, Citizen Inspector; now
I want to get rid of it, once and for all."

Kuznetsov's voice was becoming hoarse. He looked
up and saw that the inspector was smiling faintly and
exchanging a glance with Repin.

"You seem to have been right," Saltykov said.

Repin was bursting with suppressed excitement. He
nodded quickly. "Yes, yes, yes," he said. "I sensed it;
I sensed guilt."

The two men beside Saltykov's desk stared impassively into the middle distance. The young man at the
table sat with pencil poised, but he wrote nothing.

"Please continue, Kuznetsov," Saltykov said.

"I . . . I don't know how much you've learned," he said.

"Just tell everything," Saltkov said. "Tell if from the beginning. We'll want to hear everything from your own lips."

"Thank you, Citizen Inspector," he said. He breathed deeply and concentrated on the pattern in the carpet.

"I suppose the beginning would be in about June of 1945," he said.

"Did you say 1945?"

"Yes, that's right. I decided to do it because I was afraid of what would happen if I was repatriated with the others. We heard about the executions, the camps. . . ." He paused. "It must be said in my defense that the reports we heard were true, and that I was driven to . . ."

"What the hell are you talking about?" Saltykov snapped.

Kuznetsov looked up. Saltykov wore an expression of outraged consternation. Repin's nervous smile had vanished; he stared at Kuznetsov with his mouth half open. Kuznetsov leaned forward on the chair and looked from one to the other. He smiled as it dawned on him. Then he chuckled. He shook his head.

"What the hell is this?" Saltykov demanded, looking from Repin to Kuznetsov. "What do you think this is, a fucking music hall? What are you laughing at?"

Kuznetsov's chuckle turned to full laughter. He closed his eyes and shook his head, laughing aloud, laughing until he wept. Tears oozed from his eyes and streamed down his cheeks. Through the laughter he heard Saltykov:

"Shut up! Shut the fuck up!"

The laughter subsided and Kuznetsov opened his eyes. Saltykov stood at his desk, eyes flashing with anger. Repin sat dumbfounded, his mouth working. He found his voice.

"Alexander Nikolayevich, what are you talking about?"

Kuznetsov shook his head. "Of what am I accused?" he asked.

There was silence. Saltykov glared and Repin's mouth worked again.

"Of felonious theft, of course," Repin said. "You organized the stealing of copper wire...."

Kuznetsov interrupted him with another burst of laughter. He controlled himself and found his voice.

"You're a bloody fool, Genya," he said. "Citizen Inspector, our friend Citizen Repin didn't catch you a thief. He's caught you a spy. An American espionage agent. I'm not Kuznetsov. I'm Malmudov. My papers were forged. My name is false. I came by parachute in 1946...."

Saltykov's eyes bulged and he spluttered something unintelligible.

"Excuse me?" Kuznetsov said.

"You're what?" Saltykov's voice was a hoarse whisper.

"I made an agreement in Munich in 1945 to come to the Union on false documents and to report on Soviet military movements," he said amiably. "I was trained by the Americans to do this and I did it until

1948. I have not conducted espionage since that time, but of course I had to continue to live as Kuznetsov. I want to tell you from the outset, Citizen Inspector, that my former family from before the war knows nothing of me. I have made no contact with them. I have told nobody of this until this very moment. Nobody is guilty but me—"

Saltykov interrupted him. "Get him the fuck out of here!"

"Me?" Kuznetsov said.

"No, not you, God damn you!" Saltykov shouted. He turned on Repin. "Get him out of here! Take him and hold him!" He motioned to the men standing beside the desk; they stepped quickly to Repin's chair and pulled him to his feet. Repin stumbled out of the room between them, staring over his shoulder at Kuznetsov, eyes wide and uncomprehending.

"Now," Saltykov said, wheeling on Kuznetsov. "Explain yourself." He nodded to the man with the notebook. The man began writing.

Kuznetsov nodded and wiped at the tears, a smile lingering on his lips.

He felt light, airy, euphoric. A pool, a calm, spread through his body, beginning in his stomach; he felt as if he could float away.

He took a breath, and in a quiet voice he told his story, from the beginning. He told of Munich, the radio, the American lieutenant colonel, the Novgorod ex-corporal who cut his throat, the reports from the Kiev military command. He told it all, in all the detail he could remember.

It was growing dark outside when he finished talking. The room was quiet except for the scratching of the young man's pencil. The scratching stopped and Saltykov sat looking at Kuznetsov with an odd, puzzled expression.

"Yes," he said. "Yes . . . Malmudov." He pressed a button on his desk. "We'll see if what you say is true. We'll see."

The inspector frowned and peered at Kuznetsov. "Why are you smiling like that? What's to smile about?"

Kuznetsov sat for a moment in silence. The smile remained on his lips. The door opened behind him and he sensed the presence of the two men behind his chair. He rose and stood a moment, looking at Saltykov.

"Because I am Malmudov again, Citizen Inspector," he said, lifting his shoulders in a small, meek shrug. "I am my own self again."

From the Soviet News Agency TASS, Dec. 12, 1973:

MOSCOW, DEC. 12 (TASS)—THE TRAITOR MALMUDOV, G. N., WHO BETRAYED THE MOTHERLAND BY ENGAGING IN ESPIONAGE ACTIVITIES ON BEHALF OF THE UNITED STATES, TODAY WENT ON TRIAL FOR HIS CRIMES BEFORE THE MOSCOW REGIONAL CRIMINAL COURT. IN THE PRESENTATION OF EVIDENCE TO THE COURT, THE PROCURATOR, G. BESMERTNOVA, PROVED THAT MALMUDOV CARRIED OUT ASSIGNMENTS DIRECTED AGAINST THE STATE INTERESTS OF THE SOVIET UNION, INCLUDING THE SENDING OF SECRET RADIO MESSAGES CONCERNING THE LOCATIONS AND DISPOSITIONS OF ARMED FORCES OF THE USSR.

THE PROCURATOR ALSO DEMONSTRATED THAT MALMUDOV'S ACTIVITIES DURING THE PERIOD OF THE GREAT PATRIOTIC WAR LED TO THE DEATHS OF MEMBERS OF A UNIT OF THE RED ARMY AND TO THE CAPTURE OF OTHERS BY THE HITLERITES. MALMUDOV ALSO COLLABORATED WITH THE HITLERITES DURING THE TIME OF THE WAR.

BESMERTNOVA PROVIDED THE COURT WITH DETAILS OF SABOTAGE ACTIVITY CARRIED OUT BY MALMUDOV DURING HIS EMPLOYMENT AT AN ENTERPRISE ENGAGED IN THE MANUFACTURE OF GENERATORS. IT WAS PROVED THAT MALMUDOV, LIVING UNDER THE FALSE NAME OF KUZNETSOV, ORGANIZED THE THEFTS OF ESSENTIAL MATERIALS FROM THE FACTORY AND CAUSED SERIOUS FAILURES IN THE FACTORY'S FULFILLMENT OF THE TASKS ASSIGNED TO IT UNDER THE STATE PLAN.

THE PROCURATOR CHARACTERIZED MALMUDOV AS AN UNPRINCIPLED AND VICIOUS CREATURE OF THE FORCES OF CAPITALISM, WILLING EVEN TO SACRIFICE HIS OWN WIFE AND CHILD TO THE INTERESTS OF HIS BETRAYAL OF THE MOTHERLAND.

THE PROSECUTION INTRODUCED WITNESSES WHO CORROBORATED THE CHARGES AGAINST THE DEFENDANT. E. REPIN, WORKER OF THE FACTORY RED BANNER, DESCRIBED

MALMUDOV'S DESPERATE EFFORTS TO HIDE HIS
FALSE IDENTITY, AND SUBMITTED EVIDENCE OF
MALMUDOV'S PART IN THE DISRUPTION OF
LABOR PRODUCTIVITY IN THE RED BANNER
FACTORY.
THE TRIAL CONTINUES.
END/RHG

From the Soviet News Agency TASS, Dec. 13, 1973:

MOSCOW, DEC. 13 (TASS)—THE MOSCOW
REGIONAL COURT TODAY JUDGED MALMUDOV,
G. N., GUILTY OF CRIMES UNDER ARTICLES 64, 65,
AND 69 OF THE CRIMINAL CODE OF THE RSFSR,
DEALING WITH TREASON, ESPIONAGE, AND
WRECKING.
IN HIS FINAL STATEMENT TO THE COURT
MALMUDOV DID NOT DENY THE PROOFS OF HIS
SPYING ACTIVITIES AND HIS BETRAYAL OF THE
MOTHERLAND. AFTER CONSIDERATION OF THE
CIRCUMSTANCES OF HIS CRIMES, THE COURT
SENTENCED DEFENDANT MALMUDOV TO
DEATH, WITH CONFISCATION OF PROPERTY.
THE ATTORNEY REPRESENTING MALMUDOV
INFORMED THE COURT THAT THE DEFENDANT
WAIVED HIS RIGHT TO APPEAL AND THAT THE
DEFENDANT PETITIONED THE COURT TO ORDER
RAPID EXECUTION OF THE SENTENCE. THE
COURT DENIED THE PETITION, POINTING OUT
THAT SOVIET LAW PROVIDES A SEVEN-DAY
PERIOD FOR THE FILING OF APPEALS OR
PROTESTS BEFORE SENTENCE MAY BE ·
EXECUTED.
END/RHG

BUTYRKA PRISON
Moscow

REPORT OF EXECUTION OF DEATH SENTENCE
FORM NO. 288

NAME OF PRISONER   Malmudov, G. N.
No. 4886372

SENTENCING AUTHORITY   Moscow Regional
Criminal Court

TIME OF EXECUTION   0502 21 December, 1973

MEANS OF EXECUTION   Army Fire Team

REPORT OF EXECUTING OFFICER: The criminal
Malmudov, G. N., was duly and lawfully put to death by my
command at the above-stated date and time by a 12-man fire
team of the Moscow Regional Military Command in the
courtyard of the Butyrka Prison, in accordance with Soviet Army
Directive SA-1001 (Procedure for Execution by Fire Team). The
Criminal accepted the blindfold. The criminal fell under the
volley of the fire team, and immediately following the volley a
pistol round was fired into the criminal's head by my hand.

L. L. Gelets, CAPT, SA

REPORT OF MEDICAL OFFICER:
The above-named criminal was examined by me following
execution of death sentence at Butyrka Prison at the above-
mentioned date and time. I pronounced the criminal dead,
death being caused by general coronary and neural trauma
resulting from six bullet wounds in the facial area, five bullet
wounds in the chest area, and one bullet wound in the left
temple.

D. P. Ivanov, MAJ, MC SA

DISPOSITION OF REMAINS:
Remains of the criminal Malmudov, G. N., were buried on the
above-mentioned date in the burial yard at Butyrka Prison,
grave number 1159.

R. Linachev, Prison Quartermaster

DISPOSITION OF PERSONAL EFFECTS:
Confiscated.

L. P. Medvedev, Warden

20.

John Cabot spent more than two hours reading the
Russian woman's letter to her daughter, working
slowly with his disused Russian and referring frequently to an old, well-thumbed Russian-English
dictionary.

The letter told the story of her husband—as Malmudov before the war and as Kuznetsov afterward.
She wrote of visiting him in prison while he awaited
trial and execution, of hearing the details of the missing years. It was a dry and straightforward account.
She did not judge the actions he took, or failed to take.
She mentioned that he wept the first time she visited
him, and the last.

After he was shot, she said, she visited the prison
and asked the warden for her husband's personal effects. She was given a bundle containing a plain gray
suit, a shirt frayed at collar and cuffs, a dark necktie,
a pair of old brown shoes many times resoled and
without laces, a suit of underwear, an elegant little

ivory-handled penknife, and a wallet containing six rubles. She was told that his personal papers were taken as evidence against him in his trial. The meager belongings in his apartment and a savings account containing more than twelve thousand rubles were confiscated by the state.

The warden told her he died without last words, which she knew would be the case: He already had spoken his last words to her.

She was permitted to visit his grave in a remote, weed-choked corner of the prison grounds. The grave bore no name, only a numbered metal disk affixed to a steel rod. More than a thousand other similar metal disks stood in rows alongside his, silent testimony to the severity of justice in people's Russia.

Cabot came to the last page. The handwriting here was more labored, less flowing. The ink had been smeared in two places.

. . . And that is his story, darling Tatyana. I did not tell you then, because I was afraid that you would not understand. I myself had great difficulty understanding and forgiving. In truth, it has taken me this long. Out of pity and love for what he had been, I told him before his execution that I forgave. But I did not. I could not.

I was raised in the Party as an orphan is raised by a kind but stern foster parent. I served the Party, I lived by its rules. In the phrase that was popular when I was young, I knelt before the Party. I did it with pride and not humility, because I believed; I had faith. Not even the old women who bow at the altars of the orthodox churches have the faith that I had then. I believed.

But when I heard your father tell his story I began not to believe. I entered the dark and terrible wilderness of doubt and uncertainty. Only now have I come through to the other side to find, what? Not a new faith. I have found the opposite: cynicism, suspicion, despair. Disbelief.

I can no longer trust those whom we are obliged to trust. I cannot believe that what they are doing is right, or that they have a higher knowledge, or a better understanding.

Your father betrayed his motherland, that is true. But it was a small and justifiable betrayal. On the other hand, the motherland betrayed him, grossly and outrageously. We allowed Stalin and Kaganovich and Beria and Molotov—that whole damned, drunken, corrupt, ignorant lot—to beat and abuse poor, suffering Russia. We know now—and worse, we knew then—that Kaganovich killed a million people digging the White Sea Canal. Beria doped little girls and raped them. Molotov made dirty deals with the Nazis. And Stalin pulled all their strings. And we let them do it, all of us; especially all of us who knelt before the Party. It was Stalin's Party, the instrument of his corruption. And it is still Stalin's Party.

And the Americans? The Americans who boast of their freedom and their wealth and their morality? They are no better. They are worse, because they had a choice. When the NKVD was shooting our repatriated boys and sending them to work to death in Yakutia, the Americans could have done something to stop it; at least they could have refused to send them. But they sent them, except for a few they needed for their purposes. They chose those few not because they were cynical and corruptible; they chose them for the opposite reason: their love, their devotion. They chose those who would betray for love, and love alone.

Your father made the agreement with the Americans because he loved us and longed to return to us. But then he did not return to us for the same reason he made the agreement: He loved us, and could not harm us. The Americans saw that love in him and they knew they could use it.

Tatyana, darling, this disease that is growing in me will soon take me from this misery. I rejoice that it will be so, and that is why I refuse the treatments. Please do not despair for me. You may despair for our poor motherland; for your father; for good, decent Pobedontsov, who has borne all this with such kindness. But death will free me from a life that was wasted by the heartless, hateful cynicism of those we trusted. And death will take me to your father. I always belonged with him.

Forever loving,

Mama

Cabot sat for a few minutes with the final page in his hand. Then he gathered together the rest of it and retied it with the black ribbon. He carefully replaced all the documents in the Kholui box and closed it.

"Marian," he said, pressing the intercom button. "Any calls that need returning?"

"Yes, sir," came the voice from the box. "Mr. Evans would like to have a word with you."

He glanced at the clock on his desk. It was after six. "Yes," he said. "If he's still here, ask him to come on up."

Cabot picked up the Kholui box and leaned back in his chair, holding it so the lacquered surface glowed in the light. The gowned, jeweled, lovely figure of Princess Yaroslavna stood on the wall, the diamond of a tear on her cheek, weeping for her captive Prince Igor. He looked closely at the tear; its diamond perfection had been created by three strokes of a single-hair brush dipped in silver paint. It had taken a skilled Kholui artist perhaps ten seconds to create the tear, yet it would remain there on Yaroslavna's cheek for the ages. Painted grief. Permanent grief. Beautiful grief.

There was a tap at the door and it opened.

"Mr. Evans," Marian said.

"Yes, Bob, come in," Cabot said, gently placing the box back on his desk. Robert Evans, deputy director for operations, came into the office. He looked, as usual, spry and clean-shaven even though it was the end of a long working day.

"Well, Jack, you've had yourself holed up in here for the whole afternoon. I was getting worried," Evans said.

"Some interesting reading in that box of yours," Cabot replied, showing his deputy to the couch. "Drink?"

"Sun's well over the yardarm by now," Evans said. "A little whiskey if you have it."

"Have it," Cabot said. He opened the door of a bar disguised in the wall and poured two neat whiskeys from a cut-glass decanter. He handed one to Evans and took a seat.

"So what's up?"

"Well, it's that box, actually," Evans said.

"Oh?"

"Kellog, the fellow who brought it, has an idea that there's some mileage left in . . . what did you call the operation?"

"You mean Early Word?"

"Yes, Early Word," Evans said. "We did a little computer check. Believe it or not, two of the Early Word operatives popped out. And guess who they were?"

Cabot wrinkled his brow. "You mean two of the people we sent in?"

"Exactly," Evans said, grinning and leaning forward. "One is the chief German-language translator for the Ministry of Defense. The other is a senior communications specialist at the Central Committee. Hot stuff."

"Jesus," Cabot breathed. "Names?"

"A Vitaly Y. Lapin at the Defense Ministry; the communications guy at the Central Committee is named Viktor Vinogradov. Any recollection?"

Cabot frowned and took a sip of the whiskey. "I think I have some recollection of Vinogradov," he said. "Little unobtrusive blond fellow; wife in Odessa."

"Right on!" Evans said. "Wife in Odessa. What we have is that he's a bachelor, never went back to her."

"What about the other fellow?" Cabot asked. "I don't remember that name."

"Lapin is tall, rather elegant; he turns up at some public functions as a simultaneous interpreter. Known to like boys."

"Boys?" Cabot said.

"Poofter. Gay. Queer."

"Now I remember," Cabot said. "He was the one who wanted to get back to a cousin. A male cousin. I didn't like it at first. But I could see that he had a special attachment to this cousin. By God!"

"Should be a piece of cake to turn 'em on again," Evans said, rolling his whiskey glass back and forth in his hands. "Don't even have to get a boy for the queer."

Cabot looked into his glass for a long moment. "You know, this was not part of the deal we made with them, Bob," he said at length. "It was a fairly limited thing; frankly, we'd be violating a... an understanding."

"How firm, Jack?" Evans said. "We're lookin' at a gift horse here; this is the biggest break we've had since Shevchenko. Bigger. These guys are good!"

"Yes," Cabot said. "They could be damned good. But there was an understanding; not... firm, really, just a feeling."

Cabot fell silent and looked into his glass. He stood
and walked to the desk. The Kholui box lay under the
desk lamp, glowing in its lacquered perfection. The
tear on Yaroslavna's face sparkled.

Cabot touched the box, lightly. He put his finger on
the tear, then drew it away.

"Well, hell," he said. "Well, hell, it's a dirty job,
but somebody's gotta do it, Bob. So let's do like
General Patton. Let's let *them* do it, instead of us."

He grimaced and downed the whiskey.

"Turn those guys back on, Bobby, turn 'em back on
now."